ST. MARTIN'S

MINOTAUR
MYSTERIES

GET A CLUE!

Be the first to hear the latest mystery book news…

With the St. Martin's Minotaur monthly newsletter,
you'll learn about the hottest new Minotaur books,
receive advance excerpts from newly published works,
read exclusive original material from featured mystery
writers, and be able to enter to win free books!

Sign up on the Minotaur Web site at:
www.minotaurbooks.com

Also by Rhys Bowen

THE MOLLY MURPHY SERIES

THE CONSTABLE EVANS MYSTERIES

Murphy's Law

~A Molly Murphy Mystery~

Rhys Bowen

St. Martin's Paperbacks

MURPHY'S LAW

Copyright © 2001 by Rhys Bowen.
Excerpt from Death of Riley © 2002 by Rhys Bowen.

Cover photograph © Corbis.

ISBN: 0-312-98497-9
EAN: 80312-98497-7

Printed in the United States of America

St. Martin's Press hardcover edition / October 2001
St. Martin's Paperbacks edition / December 2002

St. Martin's Paperbacks are published by St. Martin's Press, 175 Fifth
Avenue, New York, NY 10010.

10 9 8 7 6 5

This book is dedicated to my favorite New Yorkers, Daphne Lincoff and Judy Gitenstein. Daphne—thank you for being a safe haven in the big city; and, Judy—thank you for being my eyes and ears on the spot, and for dragging me on adventures. Who else has been locked, inadvertently, in Gramercy Park?

My thanks also to my usual critics, John, Clare, and Jane, as well as to Trish Intemann for vetting all things Irish in the book.

Murphy's Law

❦ One ❦

T

hat mouth of yours will be getting you into big trouble one day."

My mother started saying that as soon as I could talk. It turns out she wasn't far wrong. By the time I was ten my refusal to hold my tongue had almost gotten us thrown out of our cottage. And a week before I turned twenty-three, I was on the run, wanted for murder.

The rhythmic puffing of the engine calmed me back to my senses. I had no clear memory of getting to the train station, but the pain in my ribs when I tried to breathe and the way I could feel my dress sticking to my back told me that I must have run every step of those five miles. About the state of the front of my dress I chose not to think. I pulled my shawl more tightly around me and glanced at the other people in my compartment. An old farm couple with weathered red cheeks already dozing in the far corner, a young mother with two lively little ones, plus another on the way, and a priest. He returned my glance and I looked away hastily, just in case priests could somehow read thoughts— or extract confessions. Wouldn't he be surprised to hear mine right now?

Every time the conductor walked through the train and glanced into my compartment, I was sure he was looking for me.

But then that was stupid, wasn't it? Justin Hartley was lying dead on my own kitchen floor but nobody would even know he was missing yet. My father and my little brothers weren't due home until evening and Justin was hardly likely to have told anybody at the big house where he was going. I couldn't picture him saying at breakfast, over the deviled kidneys or whatever disgusting dish the upper class had eaten this morning, "I'm just off down to the peasants' cottages to have my way with Molly Murphy."

So I had a few hours yet to make my escape. This train would take me all the way to Belfast. And then I probably had just enough money for a boat to England. After that, I couldn't say. Maybe I'd be able to lose myself in a big city like Liverpool. Maybe I wouldn't. Likely as not the police would catch up with me soon enough. It wouldn't be too hard to spot an Irish girl on the run, especially one with flame red hair like mine. Since I knew nobody in England, I had nowhere to hide. So it was only a matter of time, but I was going to go on running as long as I could. I've never been known to give up on anything without a good fight.

I stared out of the carriage window. It was a picture perfect day, sky like blue glass, sparkling clear, with just a hint of frost in the air—the sort of day that doesn't happen often in our Irish winters. The sort of day that would have made me rush through my chores, put the stew on the stove, and be off to walk along the cliff tops, with the wind at my back and the ocean at my feet. The sort of day when the gentry would be out, riding to hounds. A picture of Justin in his red coat flashed into my head. I'd always thought how handsome he looked in his red coat. I suppose I'd been a little in love with him when I was younger. Lord knows I never meant to kill him. I could almost feel that priest's eyes boring into the back of my head as I stared out of the window.

Green fields dotted with fine horses in them flashed past. The horses looked up in alarm as the fire-breathing monster approached, kicked up their heels, and ran off. How well they looked. If I could run that fast they'd not find it so easy to catch me.

When they did catch me, it would mean the rope around my neck—not much doubt about that. My hand went instinctively to my throat and I shuddered. Did you feel anything when they hanged you? Was it all over in an instant? Would it hurt? They certainly wouldn't listen to my side of the story. I'd killed an English landowner's son. That had to be a hanging offense, even if I was just trying to preserve my honor. But then peasant girls have no honor, do they? As Justin said, I belonged to him as much as any of his farm animals. I couldn't think of anyone who'd speak for me. Not my da—he'd be angry enough when he found I helped myself to the emergency fund in the teapot on the mantelpiece. It was supposed to be secret. We children all knew about it, of course, but the thought of my father's leather belt across our backsides had prevented us from dipping into it. Right now a leather belt across the backside seemed a good sort of punishment compared with what else might be waiting for me. My hand strayed to my neck again.

No, I wouldn't be counting on any sympathy from my da. He'd probably say I was leading Justin on with my loose ways. My loose ways had never stretched beyond going dancing on a Saturday night and maybe letting a boy walk me home, but that was enough for my father. In his day girls never talked back to their elders and never went out dancing without a chaperon. I did both. Frequently.

If my ma had still been alive, she'd have said I asked for it, too—always did have big ideas beyond my station and a mouth that was going to get me into trouble. It's a pity she hadn't lived long enough to say "I told you so." She'd have enjoyed that.

It suddenly came to me that I was completely on my own. Our relatives were either dead or emigrated to other lands. I had no real friends in the village of Ballykillin anymore. The other girls I'd played with when I was little were long married to local clodhopping louts without a thought in their head but food, beer, and bed. Myself, I was holding out for something better, al-

3

though I wasn't sure where I'd find it. The funny thing was that those girls pitied me—I was the spinster, too old for anyone to want me and hopelessly on the shelf. I'd drifted apart from them long ago, of course, when I was chosen for schooling at the big house with the landowner's two girls. Not that I could call Miss Vanessa and Miss Henrietta my friends, either. They'd always managed to make me feel like an interloper—in their well-bred, genteel way, of course. And now they'd gone off into English society and only managed a polite nod when their carriages passed me.

So I had no one on my side in the whole wide world. It was a frightening thought, but challenging, too. It meant I owed nothing to anyone. I was free of Ballykillin, free of all that cooking and cleaning for four ungrateful males, free to be who I pleased . . . if I could only get far enough away to start over. One thing was sure—I didn't intend to die yet.

It was late afternoon by the time we pulled into Belfast station. I covered my head in my shawl and blended in with all the women coming out of the linen factories, allowing myself to be swept along with the tide until I could make my way to the docks. Nobody stopped me as I got on the boat, but I kept my head covered and my face well hidden all the way across to England. I didn't sleep more than a wink all night, and by the time the coast of England appeared in the cold morning light I was hollow eyed and groggy.

Then I was there, in a strange city, a strange country, with fourpence in my pocket and no idea what to do next. As I came down the gangplank I looked across to see a big, beautiful ship with two fine funnels.

"Look, there's the *Majestic*. White Star Line," I heard a woman behind me saying. "You know—the one the O'Shea's boy is sailing on to America."

America, I thought with a wistful smile. That's where I'd be headed if I had more than fourpence in my pocket. Irish boys were always running off to America when they got themselves involved in the troubles with the English. I stepped out of the stream of passengers for a moment and stared up at that fine ship. My but she was huge. Standing there on the dock and looking up was like looking up the tallest cliffs I'd ever seen. You could put the whole of Ballykillin in her and then have room enough left for a couple of cathedrals.

The tide of people jostled around me, sweeping me onward and out of the docks. Then the crowd dispersed, as if by magic, and I found myself alone, facing a wide promenade lined with tall, elegant buildings, the likes of which I'd only seen in pictures before. One of them even had columns at the front, like a Roman temple. There were carriages outside them, and hansom cabs and ladies in big, beautiful hats and fur-trimmed capes strolling past. I forgot that I was penniless and on the run, and I stood there, savoring the moment. I was really in a city at last and it looked just how I had imagined it! The building with the columns had a sign on it saying Cunard Line. The other, even taller in red-and-white brick, White Star Line. Both their balconies were draped in black. It took me a moment to realize that England was still mourning the death of the old queen, now over a month in her grave. Yes, the flags were still flying at half-mast. I hadn't seen any such public displays over in Ireland, in fact I heard there had been dancing in the streets in Dublin. But then Victoria had never shown any particular love for the Irish, had she? Not that we hoped the new king Edward would be any better for us . . .

I was gazing up at those big buildings as I crossed the street. A blaring horn made me jump out of my skin as something low and sleek and powerful roared past me. So that was a motorcar! I stood watching it in admiration as it disappeared in a cloud of smoke. One day I'd have one of those, I decided, until I remembered that I was a criminal, on the run and not likely to be alive much longer if I didn't use my wits. At least I was in a big city now. I should be able to blend in with the thousands of Irish who lived here already. I'd get myself a job in a factory, find myself a room, and maybe I'd be just fine. Maybe.

I set off, wandering the back streets. I'd never even been in a city before—until yesterday in Belfast, of course, but Belfast wasn't half the size of this, and I'd been too frightened about getting caught to notice anything. I'd dreamed all my life of going to live in Dublin, or even London, in a fine house with my own carriage, and servants, lots of servants—always one for big dreams, I was, only they weren't exactly turning out the way I'd planned.

I soon decided that cities weren't all they were cracked up to be. Oh, to be sure, there were the grand houses along the waterfront, but a couple of streets back and it was a very different picture. Lots of gray, dirty streets with smoke hanging over them like a pall. It wasn't like the sweet, herby peat smoke of home. It turned the air brown, and the burned, bitter smell stuck in my nostrils.

I walked and walked. All those houses so close together—rows and rows of them crammed into the dark shadow behind the big wharf buildings. Tired, gray-looking women standing in doorways with babies on their hips. Hard-faced children playing in the streets. One of them threw a rock at me, then fled when I turned on him. I was suddenly feeling hungry but I had no money for food. First a job, then I eat, I told myself.

By the end of the day I was back in the dockside area, still hungry and still jobless. I'd found plenty of factories but they all had signs outside saying, No Workers Needed or, even worse, No Irish Need Apply.

The gray morning had turned into a rainy afternoon, not the gentle refreshing rain of my home in county Mayo, but a soot-laden drizzle that painted dirty streaks down my cheeks and spattered my white cuffs. A bitter wind was blowing off the ocean. My feet were hurting me. I was cold, tired, and hungry. The fear that I'd managed to keep at bay until now was seeping through. They'd surely be looking for me by now. If I didn't find a place to hide they'd find me soon enough and then it would be all over. Exotic smells came from the tall wharf buildings, spices and scents that conjured up distant ports. Maybe I'd be lucky enough to find an open door and a place to sleep for the night. Maybe something to eat, too.

6

I was making my way down a narrow alley, trying one door after another when I looked back and saw blue uniforms and helmets behind me. Two policemen were following me. I threw my shawl over my head and quickened my pace, but their heavy footsteps echoed from the high brick walls as they came after me. The alley turned a corner. So did they. Then I saw that I was trapped. It was a blind alley—high walls were all around me and the only way out was blocked by those two policemen. A door on my right was open a crack, although no light shone out. I had to take my chances. I pushed it open and stepped inside.

❧ TWO ❧

I found myself in a narrow front hall that smelled of boiled cabbage and drains. It seemed to be some kind of rooming house because there were notices all over the walls with house rules on them—no smoking, no drinking, no visitors, no animals, no cooking in the rooms. Next to that was a biblical text: Love thy Neighbor.

As I stood there, holding my breath and wondering what to do next, the front door opened and I found myself staring at the two policemen.

"One moment, miss," one of them said. "We'd like a word with you."

I decided to bluff it out. It wouldn't be the first time I got myself out of trouble by being brazen—of course, being brazen had also gotten me into trouble plenty of times too, but I didn't have time to think about that.

I tossed back my head and put my hands on my hips. "I noticed you following me all the way down the street. Have you nothing better to do than follow decent factory girls on their way home from the mill, or am I to thank you for guarding my honor?"

They were still staring at me with cold, suspicious eyes. "Do you live here, miss?"

I've never been very good at outright lies. I suppose the beatings my ma and pa gave us for lying really did make a lasting impression.

"Not exactly, sir. I'm just visiting my—"

"We've been told to be on the lookout for a young woman who resembles—"

At that moment the door nearest me opened and a woman's face looked out. "Is that you at last, Siobhan?" she demanded, frowning at me. "Get inside here right away, you lazy thing, and no excuses this time."

She grabbed my sleeve and jerked me in her direction.

"You know this young woman?" one of the policemen asked.

"You think I'm not knowing my own sister?" the woman said. "I sent her out over an hour ago to get me the powder for my headaches and where's she been all this time I'd like to know. No concern for her sister's poor head, have you, you ungrateful creature?"

Either she was crazy or her vision was poor, because she was clearly mistaking me for someone else. I decided to say nothing and hung my head, looking repentant.

"We're all sailing for America in the morning," the woman went on. "How was I going to stand all that time at sea without my headache powders?" She turned away, coughing.

The first policeman touched his helmet. "Sorry to have troubled you, missus. And you, too, miss. Good luck in America."

They went, leaving me staring at the woman. She was younger than I thought at first, but hollow eyed and very thin.

"I'm sorry," I said, "but you've made a mistake. I'm not your sister."

A smile crossed her tired face. "You think I don't have two good eyes in my head?" she demanded. "I was watching out of the window and I saw those two fellows following you and I decided no good was going to come of it. I've no love of the English police myself. I don't know what you've done but you don't look like a criminal to me." She opened her door wider. "Come on in with you. There's a kettle boiling on the grate."

She closed the door behind us. Two young children, a boy and a girl, were sitting by a poor excuse for a fire. They looked up at me with big, wary eyes.

"Hello," I said. "My name's Molly. What's yours?"

The woman put a hand on each of their heads. "This one is Seamus like his daddy and the little scrap of a person is my Bridie." Seamus continued to stare and managed a defiant half smile. Bridie hid her face under the quilt. "They've not been themselves since we left home and came here," she went on. "They don't know whether they're coming or going, poor little mites. I'm Kathleen O'Connor." She held out her hand.

"Molly Murphy," I said. "I'm very pleased to meet you, and very grateful to you, too. I know nobody in this whole town."

She poured boiling water into a teapot. "The landlady tells us not to cook in the rooms but the food she prepares isn't fit for man nor beast. And sit yourself down. You look ready to drop. Were those two policemen really after you?"

I glanced at the window, half expecting to see them still lurking nearby. "I'm afraid they were." I took a deep breath. "Look, you should know I'm on the run. It's possible those policemen were already onto me. So I ought not to stay here long. I don't want to get you involved. . . ."

"You think I'd turn a fellow Irishwoman over to the English police?" she demanded. Her accent was very different from mine, with all those harsh *arrrr* sounds of the north. "Whatever you've done, I'm sure it can't be that bad."

I glanced across at Kathleen's children. She seemed to pick up my meaning.

"You two will be wanting your tea soon, I'm thinking," Kathleen said to them. She fished in the purse that hung from her waist. "Here's twopence. How about taking your sister down to the fish shop on the corner and bringing us back twopence worth of chips?" She handed the money to the boy, who grabbed his sister's hand. "Come on, Bridie," he said. "And you better walk fast this time 'cos I'm not waiting for you."

The little one looked back fearfully at her mother. "Go on with you," Kathleen said, wrapping a scarf around the child's neck. "You need some fresh air or you'll not sleep tonight."

The door closed behind the children and Kathleen turned back to me.

"I killed a man," I said and watched it register on her face. "I didn't mean to."

"This man you killed?" she asked.

I stared into the fire. I had kept the whole thing blocked from my mind since it happened. Now I saw the details as if it was all happening in front of me—Justin bursting into my cottage, standing there with that insolent smile on his face, telling me there was no point in struggling because he owned me just as much as the beasts on his farm. For the first time in my life words had not been a good enough defense. What had kept the local boys at bay didn't work on Justin. He'd merely laughed and thrown me back across the kitchen table. Then there was the sound of my dress ripping as he got impatient and then my mighty kick that surprised even me, the surprised look on his face and the sickening sound of his head striking our stove . . . and all that blood.

"He was trying to . . . have his way with me, you know." I couldn't bring myself to say the word *rape*. "I pushed him away. He slipped and hit his head."

"Well then," she said, but I shook my head. "It won't make any difference with the jury, will it? He was the landowner's son. English gentry. You don't get away with killing the gentry, do you?" I kept staring into the fire. The hopelessness of the situation was catching up with me. "He tore my dress," I said and opened my shawl to show her. Suddenly I was very near to tears, but I don't cry in front of strangers.

"The beast," she said gently, in a way that brought me even closer to tears. "He deserved everything he got and more. Don't you worry. I'll not give you away. They're all beasts, these English. Why else would my Seamus have had to get away to America, leaving us to fend for ourselves these two years?"

She handed me a chipped enamel mug of tea. I took a big gulp and felt warmth returning to my body.

"First my brother and then my man," she went on. "They hanged our Liam, you know. Only nineteen, he was, and such a lovely boy. He and some of the boys tried to stop the landowner's agent from evicting a neighbor. The agent was killed in the struggle. It was in the dark of night in foul weather and I reckon they'd have got away with it, but someone betrayed them. One of their own, it had to be. They were all hanged." She turned away, coughing again.

"How terrible," I said. "And your man?"

"He tried to organize a trade union at the mill. They held a strike. The guard was called in and things got ugly. My Seamus had to flee for his life." She broke off with another coughing spell. "They managed to get him on a boat to America, but he can't come home again. There's a price on his head."

"But you're going to join him now, aren't you? That's wonderful."

A strange look came over her face. "Yes. Wonderful."

At that moment the two little ones burst back in with the bag of chips.

"Seamus ate some on the way home," Bridie exclaimed until she remembered there was a stranger in the room. Then she hung her head and slunk over to her mother.

"No doubt there's plenty for all," her mother said. "And we've meat pie left from yesterday. It's a feast we'll be having." She spread out the newspaper on the small round table. "Help yourself," she said to me.

"No, I couldn't."

"There's plenty. We'll not go hungry tonight and tomorrow we'll be dining in luxury on the boat."

"Will there be lots of food on the boat?" Seamus asked, in between cramming chips into his mouth. "Meat and sausages and everything?"

"Sure there will. As much as you can eat," his mother said.

We washed the food down with a cup of tea, then Kathleen

got the little ones tucked into the bed. She and I sat by the fire until the glow began to die down. We talked of home. She told me of her village in county Derry. I told her of my life in Ballykillin and swimming in the ocean with my brothers and running across the headlands with the wind at my back, making me feel as if I were flying. Already it seemed like a dream, or something I had read of in a book.

"So what will you do now?" Kathleen asked, leaning across to poke some life into the last of the fire.

I shrugged. "I have no idea. I had enough money to get me here but not farther. I was hoping to find a job in one of the factories, but it doesn't seem as if that's going to work, either."

"You've no kinfolk, nobody who'd take you in?"

"Nobody. My own family always said I'd come to a bad end. It looks like I'm going to prove them right. If only I could have come up with the money, maybe I'd have sailed with you on that lovely ship to America. You must be looking forward to seeing your man again, after so long."

She was still staring into the last of the fire. "Aye," she said quietly. She got up, went over to the bed, and pulled out one of the pillows. "You'll be warm enough in front of the fire," she said. "You can borrow my shawl."

"You really don't mind if I sleep on your floor tonight?" I asked. "I don't want to get you into trouble."

"You're not going anywhere else," she said. "And now that the little ones are sleeping, I've a favor to ask you in return." She sat down on the hearth rug beside me.

"Me?" I couldn't think what was coming next. Surely in my current state I was the last person on earth who could do anyone a favor.

"I want you to take the children to America for me tomorrow," she said.

I couldn't have been more caught off guard. "What?"

"When that ship sails tomorrow, I won't be going."

"Why not?"

"They won't let me," she said flatly, staring away from me

into the dying fire. "We had to have a medical exam before we could sail. The doctor says I've got consumption—the wasting disease. TB, he called it. He said they don't let you into America with TB."

I couldn't think what to say. We just sat there, staring at the coals.

"So I can't go there but their father can't come here to get them," she said. "I want them to have a chance at a good life. They say there's opportunity in America. That's where they should be. I want you to go in my place, Molly. Take them to their daddy."

"But what will happen to you?"

I looked up. Tears were welling in her eyes. "You don't normally recover from consumption, do you? But if the Blessed Mother worked a miracle and I did get over it, then I'd be on the next ship, believe me. Until then, I'll go back to my family in county Derry. I don't doubt they'll take care of me."

"What were you going to do if I hadn't come?" I asked.

"Take my chances. I'd be turned back, of course, but I hoped I could persuade them to hand over the little ones to their daddy. But now I know they'll get there safe and my mind's at rest." She looked up for the first time. "I think the Blessed Mother must have sent you here. You will do it, won't you?"

What could I say? The next morning I sailed for America with another woman's name.

❧ Three ❧

The first streaks of a red dawn were barely showing over the black silhouettes of chimney stacks when we made our way in silent procession to the docks.

Neither Kathleen nor I had slept much. We had sat there by the dying embers of the fire, talking in a way you can only talk to strangers you know you'll never meet again. When our conversation died, too, she went to lie down beside the little ones, her arms wrapped fiercely around them. I couldn't begin to imagine what she was going through right now. I pulled my shawl over me and tried to sleep, too, but my dozing was troubled by such terrible dreams that I chose the security of staying awake.

I must have nodded off just before dawn because I woke to find the little ones sitting up and Kathleen bustling around the room.

"There's the rest of that pie from last night if you're hungry." She pointed at the unappetizing remains on the table. "She'll have porridge going in the kitchen later but it's better maybe that she doesn't know you've been here."

I nodded and searched for my hairbrush in the bundle of possessions I'd hastily thrown together in my panic. Thank God I'd included it. I've always cared enough about my appearance that I wouldn't want to be seen with my hair like a rat's nest. The sin of vanity, my mother called it and made me confess it each week to the priest. I confessed it rightly enough, and said the three Hail Marys, but I couldn't say you'd notice any improvement. I was stuck with being vain.

"Come, Bridie," I said, showing the brush to her. "Let me make your hair pretty, too." The child had better get accustomed to my taking care of her. I hadn't really considered that aspect of it before. There had been too much to think of last night. But now it hit me—what if the children wouldn't go with me? I knew my own youngest brother and how he eyed strangers suspiciously. Would these two be willing to leave their own mother without a scene—and if they made a scene, we'd be found out pretty quickly.

Kathleen must have been thinking along similar lines. She took the child and led her over to me. "Let nice Miss Molly make your hair pretty for you, Bridie. She has a fine way with hair."

The little girl looked at me shyly, then let me run my brush through her straggly locks. I worked gently, careful not to tug. "My, but that's lovely hair you have," I told her. "They won't have seen a girl as pretty as you in America."

She giggled then, sensing that I was spinning the truth a little.

I glanced over her head at Kathleen, watching her with a look of hungry longing on her face. "Have you told them yet?" I asked. "Do they know what's happening today?"

"We're going on a ship," Seamus said confidently. "We're going to my daddy in America."

I continued to look at Kathleen. She kept silent.

"You have to tell them," I muttered as I leaned close to her on the pretense of helping myself to pie. "You can't spring it on them at the last minute."

"When the time is right," she muttered back. "I'm still thinking of the best way to tell them."

We dressed and packed up the remaining items, then we went out into the chill of the early morning. There was ice on the cobbles and our footsteps clattered, the sound echoing back, unnaturally loud, as we made our way along the alleyways. Our breath came out like dragon fire. You'd have thought the streets would be deserted that early in the morning, but there was hustle and bustle as we got closer to the docks. Workers were coming out of all those little houses, heading for the early shift at the factories. Women were already scrubbing steps. We passed into wider, grander streets and fine carriages and hansom cabs passed us, making for our ship, presumably.

Then there she was, the *Majestic*, with smoke coming out of both her funnels and people swarming around her like ants. A wave of excitement washed over me. In spite of all my worries and fears, this was, indeed, the kind of grand adventure I'd dreamed of during those long, silent days at the cottage in Ballykillin.

At the entrance to the docks a man was examining papers before letting people past. Kathleen pulled us aside, into the shadows, and rummaged in the bundle she was carrying. "Well, what do you know?" She managed a light laugh. "I've got tickets here for Seamus and Bridie, but I've gone and left my own ticket back home in Stabane. Isn't that just the stupidest thing you've ever heard of."

"Ma, how could you do that?" Seamus demanded. "Does that mean we'll not be going then?"

"I don't see why you two shouldn't go ahead," Kathleen said. "Miss Molly has her ticket. You can travel with her. She'll take care of you right enough and bring you safe to your daddy. And I'll just pop back home and catch up with you on the next boat."

I stared at her, but said nothing.

"But we want to be with you, Mama," Bridie said. "We'll come on the next boat with you."

"Indeed you won't," Kathleen said. "Not when your poor daddy's waiting for you, longing to put his arms around his little ones again. We'll not be unkind enough to make him wait any longer, will we now? And who knows—there might not be room for all three of us on the next boat, and we've a beautiful cabin ready and waiting on this fine ship. Miss Molly will take good care of you, won't you?"

"Of course I will," I said, playing along with her, although I wasn't very happy about the devious way she was doing it. Maybe she hadn't endured childhood beatings for not telling the truth as often as I had. "We'll have a grand time on the ship. Plenty of good food and games to play—and it's only a few days till we'll be in New York."

"There's only one thing," Kathleen said, beckoning the children close to her. "We have to play a little secret game."

The children were looking up with excited faces.

"Miss Molly's cabin is away at the other end of the ship," Kathleen said. "She wouldn't be able to take care of you, being so far away. So I've suggested that she move in with you two and take my place instead. Only one thing—they have the name Kathleen O'Connor down for that cabin, so they wouldn't let Miss Molly in, would they now?"

The two little ones were looking confused now.

"So what do you think we should do?" Kathleen asked.

"Ask them to change it?" Seamus asked.

Kathleen shook her head. "Too late for that. I think we should pretend that Miss Molly is me. That would be a fine game, wouldn't it? A secret for just the three of you. No need to tell another soul—right?"

The little ones giggled and glanced up at me. I forced a grin too. "Our little secret," I whispered, and touched my finger to my lips.

"Time to go on board now," Kathleen said. "Seamus, my love, are you big enough to carry the bundle?"

"I can do it." He took the bundle from her. It was half as big as he was, but he staggered along manfully with it.

Kathleen handed me the tickets. "How are you with the readin' and writin'?" she asked.

"I do both just fine."

"They'll ask you questions when you get to America," Kathleen said. "All the questions are on that sheet there—my maiden name and the village I came from and the date of my wedding. They might ask you any of those things, so make sure you learn them before you get there."

"Don't worry," I said. "Don't worry about a thing. Everything's going to be fine."

Bridie seemed to realize for the first time what was happening. She clung to her mother's legs. "I don't want to go without you," she wailed. "I want to stay here with you, Mammy."

"Hush now," Kathleen said, stroking the child's head. "You can't stay with me, little one. You have to go with Miss Molly. It won't be for long. I'll be with you very soon, I promise."

"You hurry up and catch the next boat, Ma," Seamus said. "Daddy will be wanting to know what has happened to you."

"I'll come as quickly as I can." There was a catch in her voice and I watched her press her lips together for a moment. "The days will just fly by and you'll have such fun." She put her arms around the children and buried her face in Bridie's scarf. "Be good children," she said. "Remember what I've told you. Remember to say your prayers and make sure you mind what Miss Molly tells you."

They nodded, looking at her solemnly as if they sensed what was going on.

"Go on then. Get going," she said. "I won't come any farther. I'll watch you from here."

"We'll wave to you when we get up on deck, Ma," Seamus said. "I've got my handkerchief. You watch and you'll see something white waving and it will be me."

"And I'll wave my handkerchief back." Kathleen tried to smile. "Go on. Away with you or you'll miss the boat!"

She gave Seamus, then Bridie, a quick kiss, then put her hands on my shoulders. "God go with you," she said. "May the Blessed Mother watch over the three of you."

"And you, too."

We looked at each other for a moment and then she turned and ran away. I took Bridie by the hand. "Come on, then. Let's go and find our cabin."

The dock was now bustling with activity. Carriages were arriving and disgorging passengers. Luggage was being put on a belt to be taken up into the boat. As we passed onto the waterfront a woman ran up and grabbed my arm. "You look like a kind person. My boy Sean. I haven't heard from him in three years. If you come across him, ask him to write his old mother, dying of a broken heart until she hears from him." She shoved a piece of paper into my hand. It had Sean O'Neil, formerly of Balymore, county Antrim, written on it in childish printing. I didn't like to tell her that my chances of meeting her Sean were very small. I nodded solemnly. "I'll do what I can."

"I'm here for every ship," she said. "I'm sure that in the end someone will find him for me." Then she ran and melted back into the crowd.

There was a broad gangway, draped with the White Star Line banners, going up to a deck festooned with flags where a band was playing. I led the little ones toward it. An arm reached out and stopped me.

"Where do you think you're going, then?" A seaman demanded.

"On board. We have tickets."

"Steerage passengers embark down there." He jerked his head to another gangway at the far end of the ship. It wasn't going up onto one of the decks this time, but straight into the bowels. And there were no banners. A long line of scrawny, ragged people were making their way up it, bundles and suitcases balanced on their shoulders, little ones in their arms. From behind closed gates came the sounds of wailing. A crowd pressed against those gates, reaching out arms, holding up babies. Every now and then a voice would rise over the communal wail. "God go with you, Eileen! *Conor*, my boy. My darlin' boy! May the Blessed Mother bring us together in the next life, if not in this one." A hand reached out and tried to grab me. "If you meet my man, my Mick O'Shae, tell him that his Mary wants to know he's all right. Mick O'Shae—have you got that?"

Bridie grasped my hand tighter. As I led her to join that line

22

up the gangway, I noticed two policemen, standing in the shadows, watching. I had almost forgotten that this wasn't an adventure—it was a desperate flight. Another few yards and I'd be safely on that ship. I lifted Bridie into my arms, so that her little body hid my face from the police.

Another man was checking names off a list at the bottom of the gangway. "Kathleen O'Connor, son Seamus, and daughter Bridie," I said, loudly. "Here are the tickets."

He checked me off and we went up the gangway, into the ship.

It was dark inside there and the line of people swept us along into a sort of staging area. It smelled unpleasant—the same kind of boiled cabbage and urine smell as the rooming house had, but with something added that I couldn't quite identify.

"Name?" A uniformed figure barked at me as we drew level with a desk.

"O'Connor. Kathleen, Seamus, Bridie."

"Just yourself and the two children, then?"

"That's right."

"And your husband? Where is he?"

I was tempted to tell him it was none of his business. After all, we'd paid for the tickets, hadn't we? "He's in New York. Waiting for us."

"He'd better be," the man said. "If he doesn't come to collect you from Ellis Island, they'll just send you straight home again. They don't want women and children who'll be a burden on the state."

"He'll be there," I said. "It was he who sent us the tickets. Now if you'd please direct us to our cabin, so that we can leave our belongings and then get up on deck to wave good-bye."

The man turned to another who was standing in the shadows behind him. "Hark at her," he chuckled. "Who do you think you are—lady muck? Women's quarters are down that way. Find yourself a bunk. You can take any one that's not occupied. And as for going up on deck—steerage means steerage. Next."

I had been dismissed. The crowd behind me shoved us forward. There was nothing for it but to lead the children down the dimly lit passage. Bridie had begun to get scared. "I want to go back to Mammy," she wailed.

"Remember our little secret?" I whispered. "You have to call me Mammy until we get to New York."

"I want my real mammy."

I looked around, hoping that nobody was listening. The passage was lined with cubicles, half shut off with slatted wooden doors. Inside each cubicle I could dimly make out six bunks—three on either side. Most of them seemed to be occupied by shadowy figures.

"Is there any space in here?" I demanded several times.

At last someone replied, ungraciously. "Top bunk and you're welcome to it."

"Where do we sleep, then?" Seamus asked.

A hollow eyed-woman poked her head out from the bottom bunk. "The children have to share with us, unless the boy is over twelve."

"I'm eight," Seamus said.

"Well, then, he belongs in here," the woman said. "Send him up the ladder and he can lift up your belongings."

"Go on up, Seamus," I said. "Stay up there with our things and I'll go check to see if there's anywhere better."

With Bridie still draped around my neck and holding on for dear life, I went up and down the hallway until I was convinced that there were no better quarters lurking around any corner. I helped Bridie up the ladder and examined the bunk. There was a thin mattress, nothing more. No sheets, blankets, nothing.

"Where do we get our bed linen?" I asked a neighbor.

"Bed linen?" Her chuckle ended in a rasping cough. "You're supposed to bring your own, dearie. Didn't they tell you that?"

I opened the bundle and found that there was a sheet in it, but no blanket. My shawl would have to do then. I was just trying to stow away our belongings on the little shelf at the end of our bunk when I became aware of a rhythmic thudding sound that echoed from the very walls. It was the ship's engines, now working up enough steam for us to sail.

"When can we go up and wave good-bye?" Seamus asked.

"I'm sorry, but they won't let us," I said, stroking back his hair the way I always did to my youngest brother. "It seems that we have to stay down here, because we haven't paid enough for one of the fancy cabins."

"But she'll be looking for us. I said I'd wave." He had been so brave until now—the man of the family, staggering across the dock with his big bundle. Now his lip quivered.

"She'd never have picked us out among all those people," I said. "She'll think she sees us waving with everyone else up there."

We had no idea when we left the dock but a gentle motion finally gave us the hint that we were at sea.

❧ Four ❧

Anyone who thinks that Atlantic crossings are glamorous should have traveled with us on that ship. It wasn't terrible—it was clean enough and they fed us, a big pile of bread and butter, tea and coffee, plus a hot meal once a day. When I say hot meal, it was actually a big pot of stew, dumped at one end of a table with the cry, "Come and get it while it's hot." Some people said it was better than they got at home. I don't know what their homes were like but it certainly wasn't as good as the meals I used to make for my da and the boys. But it was edible. I'll say that for it.

The worst thing for me was the darkness and lack of air. I was always in the open air. It was a two-mile walk from our cottage to the village and I did that most days. On fine days I was only inside when I had to be. My mother always said I was too wild for a girl, and I suppose I was—always clambering over rocks or even swimming in the ocean when nobody was looking.

We steerage passengers were allowed up on deck for an hour a day. The rest of the time we were locked away down in the hold, with the constant throb of the engine and the stale smell of unwashed bodies and worse. We were all herded together in a big open area with pipes running across the ceiling, lit by a couple of electric lightbulbs. There were benches around the walls and two long tables in the middle where we had our meals. The tables had sides to them, like trays—to stop the crockery from sliding off in bad weather, I supposed. There was nothing to do but to sit and hope that the time passed quickly and pray that the sea didn't get too rough. The children quickly found other little ones to play with. Seamus was off right away with the other boys. They'd huddle in the farthest corner, playing marbles, or disappear down the passages, trying to find ways out of our prison—only to be caught and sent back by the stewards. I didn't try to stop him. The children needed something to keep them occupied and it was good to see the boy playing.

Bridie, on the other hand, clung to my skirts and refused any suggestion that she join the other girls. She hid behind me when other children made friendly overtures and sat playing quietly with a sorry apology for a rag doll and a few scraps of fabric, which were her treasures.

We adults sat around with nothing to do, waiting for the next meal to break the monotony. The men smoked or played cards. Some of the women knitted and gossiped. I kept myself to myself. I didn't want to risk making any kind of slip of the tongue. So I soon got the reputation of being standoffish and snooty, but I didn't care. Just let me get as far as New York and I would be free.

By the end of the first day that gentle swell had grown to a real Atlantic roll that sent plates and cups sliding down the tables. People started to feel sick. Then I realized what the other smell had been—it was stale vomit. Myself, I believe that more people were made sick by the smell and lack of fresh air than by the rolling. I tried to tell the steward that, when he came to swab up the floor for the tenth time.

"If you'd only let some good fresh air into this place, or let us take a quick stroll on deck," I said.

"If I let you up on deck, you'd have the little'uns blown away in no time at all," he said, not unkindly.

It didn't affect me, but little Bridie took one look at the green faces around her and decided she didn't feel well, either. I was happy enough to tuck her in the bunk and stay with her. It gave me a good excuse to be away from the smell and the noise and the stale air of that room. If only I'd had a book to read and enough light to read by, the time would have sped by. But as it was, each day seemed like an eternity. That deep, dull *thud, thud* of the engine went through my whole body and pounded in my head until I wanted to scream.

I sat there in the dim light and made myself think about America. All my life I'd had big dreams—too big, according to my mother. Only lead to trouble in the end. It all came from educating me above my station. She'd been against it from the very beginning. She'd not even been grateful that I'd saved the family from being thrown out of our cottage. Because that was how it had all started. The landowner's agent had been around, trying to raise the rent again, bullying and threatening the way he always did. I was ten years old at the time. I'd stood there in the shadows, watching my parents bowing and cringing and pleading. Then I'd stepped out of the shadows and told that fat bully just what I thought of him.

It had almost got us thrown out, there and then. But somehow word of it got to the landowner's house—Broxwood Court, it was called—and my choice of descriptive words had made the Hartleys chuckle at their dinner party. The landowner's wife, Lady Hartley, was visiting from London, where she spent most of her winters. She expressed a wish to meet me and I was scrubbed up and brought up to the big house. I can remember my first sight of all that grandeur. I was too interested in taking it all in to be humble and mind my manners. Lady Hartley found me bright and refreshing, so she said. She thought it was a shame that a quick wit and a silver tongue like mine should go to waste, so next thing I knew, I was having lessons up at Broxwood with Miss Henrietta and Miss Vanessa.

I loved those lessons. There never could be enough books in the world for me. I devoured them all, geography and history and even Shakespeare and Latin. The governess said I was a joy to teach. Miss Henrietta and Miss Vanessa decided I was a teacher's pet and there was something really wrong with a girl who liked studying. Men don't like clever women, they told me.

I suppose they must have been right. They were both married by twenty and I was still an old maid at twenty-three.

Reading all those books had started to put big ideas in my head. I'd move to London or go to Trinity College in Dublin and be an educated lady and move in the highest circles. Unfortunately it had all come to an abrupt end when my ma died and I had to stay home to care for my brothers. That had pretty much snuffed out my big ideas. There was only one thing to do in Ballykillin—get married and raise a lot of babies of my own. I'd hoped maybe to take over from the schoolteacher one day, but she didn't look like she would be dying or retiring for a while.

And now suddenly I discovered that my dreams hadn't died at all. They had merely been sleeping in a far recess of my mind, ready to wake when opportunity knocked. And now it was knocking loud and clear. America—land of opportunity. I had heard the other women gossiping about it in the common room, how so and so's brother had gone there ten years before and now he had a fine house and carriage, or land of his own, or a business employing hundreds. Maybe I'd find my own way to prosperity in such a land! I lay on the bunk beside Bridie and let my fantasy roam—I'd start small, maybe working in a shop. And with the money I saved, I'd open my own shop—a bookshop maybe, and all the educated folk would gather there and we'd sit around talking, with me at the center of it all . . . if I could just get safely ashore and deliver these little ones to their father, then it would all be possible.

Then, on the third day out, I met O'Malley. I'd noticed him right away, of course, sitting with the card players at the table in the center of the room. He had the loudest laugh and I heard one of the men say, "You're a card yourself, O'Malley. I'll say that for you. A proper card."

There was something about him that made him different— the swagger, the way he showed all those big white teeth when he laughed and looked around to see if everyone had noticed how witty he was being. He was a big-boned man, almost handsome in a way, but he used too much brilliantine on his hair and he wore a bright red silk cravat around his neck. He talked too loudly. He laughed too loudly at his own jokes.

As I watched him, a young lad walked past the cardplayers' table.

"Well, look who we have here," he bellowed in that booming voice. " 'Tis the pretty boy himself, off to sing soprano in the church choir. Of course, he'll be singing soprano all his life, that one. If you handed him a naked girl, he wouldn't know how to rise to the occasion!"

The boy blushed, which made the men at the table laugh even harder. I took an instant dislike to that man O'Malley, even more than the teasing should have warranted.

Not having to hear his loud voice was another reason I was glad to stay out of the common room. On the fourth day out, however, Bridie was feeling a little better and declared she'd like a piece of bread and butter and a sip of tea. I went to find them and was coming back with the cup and plate in my hands when someone stepped out in front of me, blocking my entrance to the passage.

"Mrs. Kathleen O'Connor, so I understand." It was O'Malley and the way he was leering at me made me feel that my first opinion was entirely justified.

I nodded, politely. "That's right, sir. Now if you'd just let me pass to take the food to the little one in the cabin."

Instead he moved closer to me. His breath smelled of smoke and liquor. There was supposed to be no drinking on board, but I'd noticed him passing the flask around.

"Mrs. Kathleen O'Connor of county Derry? Of Stabane?" He was looking at me through hooded eyes, as if he was half asleep.

"That's right." I tried to push past him. He went on blocking the doorway.

"I've been speaking with your boy, Mrs. Kathleen O'Connor. He told me about you."

Surely Seamus hadn't given me away? I wasn't going to let this bloated toad frighten me. I'd just have to bluff it out.

"That's nice," I said. "I'm glad the boy has found someone to chat with. Tis a long, weary journey, cooped up down here."

"I'm finding one thing very interesting." O'Malley's reptilian eyes were fastened on me. "I used to know a Kathleen McCluskey in my hometown. I was friends with her brother and I heard that she'd married a Seamus O'Connor and gone to live in Stabane. Isn't that a coincidence?"

"I imagine the word is full of Kathleen O'Connors," I said. "Most parents are not too imaginative when it comes to naming their children and O'Connor isn't the most unusual name in the world."

"But in one small town?" O'Malley went on. "Stabane is a small town, wouldn't you say?"

"Small enough."

"So did you ever meet her—this other Kathleen O'Connor, married to Seamus?"

"I can't say that I did." I made an extra effort to push past him. "Now if you'll excuse me, I've no time to stand here gossiping, not with my little one in bed sick."

He let me go then. "I look forward to future chats with you, Kathleen O'Connor," he breathed into my ear as I walked past.

As soon as I was around the corner, I found that I was shaking. Just what did he know? And what did he want?

That evening I grabbed Seamus as soon as he climbed up to the bunk.

"That man O'Malley," I whispered. "He said he was talking to you. What did he want?"

"He just asked me some questions about home," Seamus said, staring at me innocently. "He asked me if I knew a village called Plumbridge and I said that my ma's kinfolk live there. He said he used to live there, too, long ago when he was a boy—wasn't that a coincidence."

"You didn't tell him, did you?" I whispered. "You didn't say I wasn't your mother?"

32

"I didn't tell him anything," Seamus said defensively. "I just said I'd been to the village where he grew up. That was all."

"If he tries to talk to you again, don't answer him," I said.

"Why not?"

"There's something about him that I don't like. And you shouldn't be talking to strangers."

Seamus shrugged and lay down to sleep. I lay awake beside him, wondering if O'Malley really knew the truth and what he could do about it.

The next day, our fifth at sea, I tried to avoid him, but he had an uncanny knack of popping up out of nowhere, just as if he were the devil himself. As I came into the common room, there he was, blocking my path again.

"My but that's a trim figure you have there, Mrs. Kathleen O'Connor," he said. His eyes were all over me. "A very trim figure for the mother of two children. Your husband must be very proud that you've kept such a figure. He'll no doubt be glad to get his hands around that neat little waist again."

"I find your conversation most offensive," I said, and tried to pass around him.

He laughed, showing those big white horse teeth. "Do you now? Or don't you secretly like it? How many years has your man been away? Isn't it nice to have a man looking at you with interest again—or maybe you've found a temporary replacement to keep the bed warm . . ."

I slapped his face. Hard. The sound of it echoed around the saloon and made everyone look up.

"One more insulting comment from you and next time it will be my fist," I said. I saw men grin and women nod approvingly.

"Come and sit you over here with us," one of the older women said, patting the bench beside her. "He's no gentleman, that O'Malley. That's for sure."

I was still so shocked, I went to sit beside her. "Who does he think he is, saying things like that?"

"One who likes to stir up trouble," she muttered. "I've been watching him. He's a man who likes a good fight. He'll bring trouble wherever he goes."

"He better not come anywhere near me again," I said loudly, "or he'll have Mr. Seamus O'Connor waiting for him when he gets to New York."

It was pure bluff. I hadn't even dared to think how I was going to approach an unknown Mr. Seamus O'Connor when I arrived in New York. What if he took one look at me and cried, "That's not my wife, it's an imposter!" Well, there was nothing I could do about it now. I'd just have to take my chances and play it by ear.

I looked up as young Seamus materialized beside me. He was crying and holding a handkerchief up to his face. Behind him was the youth whom O'Malley had teased. "The young lad got into a bit of a fight," the youth said, an apologetic smile on his sweet, boyish face. "He wound up with a bloody nose."

"They took my marbles," Seamus said, sniffing and wiping away the blood. "I won them fair and square and then they hit me when I tried to take them." He glanced up at the young man. "He helped get them back for me."

"Thank you." I smiled at the young man.

He smiled shyly. "I know what it's like to be bullied," he said. "I was youngest of seven. I had more than my share." He squatted on the floor beside me. "I saw what you did to that man O'Malley. Wouldn't I like to have done the very same thing. But if I'd tried it, I'd have probably wound up flat on my back with my teeth knocked out."

"That man is a troublemaker," I muttered. "My advice is to stay well away from him."

"I've been trying to. It's not easy."

"No, it's not. Sometimes I think he's just lying in wait, ready to pounce every time I come into the room."

He grinned. "He'll not be so ready next time to pounce on you. That slap must have been heard way up there in first class." He held out his hand. "The name is Michael. Michael Larkin. From Plumbridge."

"Another one?" I asked. "Is the whole of county Derry emptying out?"

"You have connections with the place, too?"

"Family connections," I said, not wanting to go into detail. "And I understand that O'Malley comes from there, too. Did you know him, then, before we sailed?"

He shook his head. "There's something about him seems familiar to me, but he must have moved away long ago. There were no O'Malleys in the town when I was growing up."

"Lucky for you," I said. "So what brings you to America?"

"There's nothing in Ireland for me."

"No family?"

He looked down at his feet. "My dad was killed when I was eight and my mother died right after of grief. An auntie raised me but she had sons of her own and couldn't wait to be rid of me. And there's no jobs. I hear they're building so many skyscrapers in New York that they can't get enough men to work on them."

"Skyscrapers?" I was unfamiliar with the word.

"Buildings so tall they reach to the clouds."

I laughed. "Get away with you!"

He smiled too. "Well, maybe not all the way to the clouds," he admitted. "But tall. Taller than church spires. Twenty floors high, that's what I hear."

"Twenty floors? Holy Mother, have you no fear of heights?"

"Me? No. Not after living where we do."

I realized that I had no idea where Plumbridge was—mountains or sea or bogs. What if they asked me questions when I landed in New York? It would be so easy to catch me out.

"So tell me about what it was like, growing up in Plumbridge," I said.

We spent the rest of the afternoon together. He played with Seamus and even got Bridie to smile. He was such a sweet innocent of a boy with the face of an angel—I could see he wasn't going to have an easy time in New York, especially not among the tough men who built skyscrapers.

We were getting close now. People murmured that sometimes the *Majestic* did the crossing in six days, if the seas were favorable. That might mean by tomorrow we'd be in New York Harbor. I felt the anxiety rising. Tomorrow I would have to bluff my way past the inspectors and meet a strange man I had claimed was my husband. There were so many things that could go wrong, so many ways for me to be discovered and sent back.

I tried not to think about it, but Michael Larkin, sensitive as he was, sensed that something was wrong. "Are you worried about facing the inspectors at Ellis Island?" he asked. "You've no need to be. As long as you're healthy and you've got the twenty-five dollars, they let you in."

"Twenty-five dollars?" I blurted out.

"You have to have twenty-five dollars in your pocket before they'll let you in," he said, his face full of concern. "Surely you knew about that?"

"No, I didn't." Had Kathleen known? I thought not. Maybe she had counted on Seamus meeting her with the money in his hand. I couldn't count on it. "Is it a fee you have to pay to get in?"

"Oh no, they don't take your money. It's just to show you've got enough to take care of bed and board until you get settled. They don't want a lot of beggars, do they?"

"What are we going to do?" I asked. "Will they send us back if we don't have the money?"

He looked concerned. "Maybe it's all right if your husband shows up to collect you, but I'm not sure about that." A big smile spread across his face. "I tell you what," he said. "I've got five pounds in my pocket, which is twenty-five of their dollars. Here. You take it."

"But then you wouldn't be able to get in."

"Of course I will. We'll both use it. You go ahead with the children. Then you find an excuse to come back and talk to me, and you can pass me the money. They've so many people to deal with that they won't even notice."

"But what if they won't let me find you? I can't risk that. No, you keep your own money, and if you can find a way of getting back to me, then I'll borrow it."

"Don't be silly." He thrust the money at me. "It will work. Other people are doing it—they say it's done all the time. Go on. I want you to take it. It will be much easier for a lady like you, with little children, to find a way back to me. Say the little one has left her doll behind. Her favorite doll. Her only doll."

I smiled. "For someone who looks like a choirboy, you have a devious mind."

"I'm not nearly as innocent as I look," he said. "In fact a man in a Liverpool pub suggested I'd make a fine confidence trickster. He said he was prepared to teach me the tricks of the trade."

"Did you take him up on it?"

"No, but I was tempted."

We laughed. It felt good to laugh again.

❧ Five ❧

Overnight the seas picked up again. We were thrown from side to side in our bunks until even I began to feel sick as a dog. It was all I could do to stagger my way down the corridor to get myself a cup of tea and a slice of bread in the morning. The common room was almost deserted, no sign of O'Malley—so even he had succumbed to seasickness. In which case, I thought, let it keep on rolling until we get to New York.

By the end of the day I'd regretted that remark. We rolled and heaved all day. The engines groaned and shuddered. All around were moans and sounds of vomiting. If only I had been allowed up on deck! I was determined not to vomit. After what seemed like an eternity, I noticed the rolling and pitching was becoming less violent. Maybe that meant that the coast of America was truly close.

When we woke in the morning the rumor was already spreading through steerage. The coast of America had been sighted. People were hurriedly repacking their bundles and piling them in the hallways. We started lining up by the door that led to freedom. The men stopped playing cards and stood dutifully beside their families. But nothing happened. We sat or stood, listening to the rhythmic thudding of the engines, waiting.

At last a door was opened and a steward appeared.

"Captain says you can go up on deck if you want," he says. "So that you can see the Lady."

The lady? Was this the start of the immigration process? I picked up Bridie, and Michael took Seamus by the hand, and up we went. The cold, stiff breeze in our faces felt wonderful. We blinked in the bright sunlight. Then we looked and gasped.

She was standing ahead of us, across the harbor, her crown glinting with gold and holding a light in her hand. Women around me were crying and I felt my own eyes misting up.

"See the pretty lady?" I whispered to Bridie. "That's Lady Liberty, waiting to welcome us to the New World."

When I turned to look away from the Statue of Liberty, I gaped at another spectacular sight—the isle of Manhattan. The sun was low in the winter sky and reflected back from thousands of windows in tall thin buildings, making New York glow and wink and sparkle like a magic city. I had never imagined buildings could be so tall.

Michael was standing beside me. "Would you look at that." He breathed. "Those buildings must be all of twenty stories high."

I laughed from the sheer delight of being in the fresh air and seeing my destination so close. "So you're having second thoughts now about working on one of those monsters?"

"Indeed I am not. Just think if I can tell my children one day that I helped build the tallest buildings in the world!" His face was glowing, too. "Will you be staying in New York, too?" he asked.

"I—I expect so." I wanted to tell him the truth, but I couldn't.

"Your husband has a job here, then? And a place for you?"

"I imagine he does. He'll be there to meet us and then we'll know."

"I hope we get a chance to meet again," he said shyly. "I mean, if you're in New York, I hope I'll be permitted to call on you and your husband. I've no family over here or anything. . . ."

"Of course we'll meet," I said. "We must arrange a time and place before we leave the ship."

He shrugged. "I don't know any places in New York."

"How about at that little park?" I pointed to the very tip of Manhattan that we were now passing. "Two days from now. Midday?"

A big grin spread across his choirboy's face. "All right. I'll be there. And you'll bring the little ones with you, I'm thinking. I'd like to see them again." He ruffled Seamus's hair and the boy grinned back at him.

I felt a warm glow of contentment. At least I'd have one friend in this new land. In two days from now I'd be safely ashore and I could tell him the truth—and maybe we could face the new land together.

We watched the tugs come alongside to tow us into port. The wind was bitter and the children began to complain of the cold, but I didn't want to go back below to that dark, smelly hold. There was ice floating in the harbor as we came into shore and the smoke hung in the frosty air.

"I'm thinking spring is a long way off in this place," Michael muttered.

We watched as the big liner inched into her berth. Crews stood ready with gangways. People rushed to go below and find their luggage.

"Hold on a tick." One of the stewards stopped the stampede. "Where do you think you're rushing to?"

"Getting our luggage," the woman said.

"You lot ain't going nowhere tonight," the sailor said. "Ellis Island don't process nobody after five o'clock, so you'll have to sleep on board and take the ferry in the morning."

"You mean we can't get off here?" a voice demanded belligerently. "What are the gangways for then?"

"Only the first- and second-class passengers are allowed to disembark," the seaman said grandly. "You lot have to clear Ellis Island before they'll let you land. Have to make sure you ain't bringing no filthy diseases into America, don't they?"

Dejected, we shuffled down below again. With the setting of the sun it had become too cold to stay on deck and too disheartening to watch the privileged classes go ashore, laughing and joking as porters staggered behind with their cabin trunks.

At least it was our last night on the ship, and there was no *thud, thud* of engine noise going through our skulls and nobody was being sick. They even served a passably good boiled beef and pease pudding for us and everyone was in high spirits as we went to our berths. I was coming back from the women's bathroom when a hand grabbed my wrist. I cried out in alarm as O'Malley pushed me into a dark recess.

"You've been avoiding me, Mrs. Kathleen O'Connor," he whispered, his big face close to mine. "What a shame. We could have become really good friends."

"Never in a million years, O'Malley. I'm rather choosy about my friends."

He laughed, flashing all those horse teeth at me. "I'm thinking you can't afford to be so choosy from now on, Mrs. Kathleen O'Connor. You might find that you owe a friend a favor—a really big favor."

"What kind of favor? What friend are you talking about?"

"Me," he said. "By the time we step ashore, you'll be owing me a favor, for not telling what I know to be true."

I felt physically sick but determined to call his bluff. "Which is?" I demanded.

"That you're no more Kathleen O'Connor than the man in the moon. I look at those children and I see Kathleen O'Connor's features in their faces. The real Kathleen—the one I knew when she was a young girl. I don't know what you've done with her, what trick you're playing. Maybe you and her husband plotted the whole thing between you. Maybe you're his fancy woman and you've done away with her. But whatever it is, you're trying to pull the wool over the eyes of the American authorities."

"You're talking rubbish," I said. "I never heard such rubbish in my life. You tell that to the American authorities and they'll send you home for being crazy."

"I imagine it would be easy enough to get the truth out of the children," he said.

That felt like a blow to the stomach. "You have no decency and no shame," I said.

He laughed again. "You're right. And you're not about to convert me now."

"All right. If you really want to know the truth," I said, moving closer to him so that we couldn't be overheard. "Kathleen is dying. This was the only way to get her children to their father. She begged me to do it for her. Now are you satisfied?"

For just a second his expression wavered, as if he might, after all, be human underneath. Then he smiled again. "Very commendable of you, whoever you are."

"The little ones know nothing of this," I said. "And they're not to know. It's Kathleen's wish. Do you understand?"

His grip on my wrist tightened. "So you'll be a free woman once you step ashore in New York? No little children like millstones around your neck? No man to fetch and carry for?"

I said nothing.

"Then I'm thinking we could come to a very nice deal that might suit both of us, Mrs. Kathleen O'Connor, or whatever your name is."

"A deal—why would I be wanting to do a deal with you?"

"Because you've no choice?" He was still smiling. I longed to slap his face again, but he had me pinned against the wall, my wrist firmly in his grasp. "If they find out who you really are, they'll send you back again, quick as a wink. Likely as not, they'll send the children back, too. What a sad thing that would be . . . and I'm the only one who knows the truth."

I looked at him with loathing. "So what are you trying to say?" I managed to get the words out evenly. I wasn't going to let him know I was afraid of him.

"I'm saying that you'll be earning good money in the city, a smart woman like you. Enough money to share with an old friend—an old friend who knew how to keep his mouth shut." He was grinning.

"You're despicable," I said. "If you're thinking that I'd pay you a penny—"

"But if you don't, you'll never be safe, will you? And I tell you what, if you play your cards right, you won't have to pay the cost of a room. Because I'm thinking that life could be terrible lonely for a man in a big new country. And terrible cold nights, too. A man needs a warm body at night beside him, and you've as fine a little warm body as I've ever laid eyes on."

That awful hooded leer again.

"Not if you were the last man in America," I said. I wrenched my wrist free of him. "So go ahead and do your worst, Mr. O'Malley. You might find it's you who gets sent back as a troublemaker and a liar!"

I shoved him away from me and ran down the hall to my bunk. Let him do his worst, I kept telling myself. Why should anyone believe him? But my heart was pounding. Somehow I had to get through tomorrow and deliver these children to their father. I'd come this far. I wasn't going to let myself be beaten by the likes of O'Malley.

❈ Six ❈

Next morning we were woken early, given mugs of coffee, and shepherded up to the deck, where they pinned labels to our clothes, like so many pieces of luggage. The tags bore our names and the name of the ship we'd arrived on. I suppose they had to do this for all the people who couldn't read or write, but it was all I could do to keep my mouth shut about the indignity. I had to remind myself that today was probably the most important day of my life. What happened to me today would change the outcome of my whole future. I couldn't afford to make any slips. I had studied all the details on Kathleen's form until I knew her family particulars by heart. Now I just had to make sure I was in the line ahead of O'Malley and safely through before he got near the inspectors. I had even toyed with various stories in my own defense—my favorite being the jilted lover who would say anything to make sure I didn't join my beloved husband again. Enough people had seen me slap his face on the ship to bring credibility to that story!

We were jostled across the deck, down a gangplank, and finally onto a ferry boat that had moored alongside. They kept on loading until we stood there like a lot of sardines, packed so tight that we couldn't turn around. Bridie started to cry.

"They're pushing me. I want to go home."

"But your daddy's waiting for us," I whispered. "In a little while we'll be going home with him, and you'll be warm and have good things to eat. . . ."

And what would I be doing? Would I just deliver the children and he'd say thanks and I'd be off on my own, trying to find a place to sleep in New York City? I'd lived on my wits so far and everything had worked out. I'd just have to pray that it kept on doing so!

When the ferry was as fully loaded as possible we set off across the harbor, away from the city. After yesterday's winter sunshine, today was filled with dense, dank fog and the captain sounded our foghorn every few minutes, to be answered by neighboring mournful toots. The damp cold was worse than the brisk wind of the day before. It seemed to get into our very bones and we huddled together, shivering. After a freezing half hour, grateful for the warmth of the other bodies around us, we saw a large red building looming out of the fog. A building in the middle of nowhere. It appeared to be floating on its own in the middle of the ocean.

"Ellis Island." The word went around the ferry and everyone jostled to try to get the first glimpse. It was imposing enough with its big brick arches and its shining copper turrets.

"It's brand-new," I heard one of the ferrymen say. "Only been open a couple of months. The old one burned down in 'ninety-seven. They've spent all this time and money building a new one."

It was then that I noticed we were not alone. A long line of ferries was waiting ahead of us, the first one docked and disgorging a steady stream of people.

"Four or five immigrant ships came in last night," the ferryman said. "We'll just have to wait our turn."

We waited and waited. It must have been past midday when we were allowed to dock. I tried to balance Bridie in one arm and my bundle in the other as we went ashore. Michael appeared at my side to take Seamus's hand and his bundle, too.

"Don't worry," he said, watching me glance over my shoulder

as we came down the gangplank. "I'll drop back in the line as soon as you're safely ashore, so that you can clear immigration first and get the money back to me."

"It wasn't that," I said. "I was trying to see where O'Malley had gotten to."

"O'Malley? Has he been bothering you again?"

"Last night," I said. "Making stupid threats."

"If that man comes near you again, I'll kill him," Michael said, then blushed when he saw my surprised face. "I could, you know. I might look young but I've done my share of fighting."

"We're near the front of the line," I said. "With any luck we'll be through and away before O'Malley gets off the boat."

We inched forward until we were standing under a big glass-and-steel canopy that led to the front entrance. Another line of people was brought to stand beside us. They looked very different and very foreign. There were women among them dressed head to toe in black, with scarves around their heads. There were men who looked like brigands, with wild beards and drooping mustaches. Then there were men in leather trousers, smart-looking women in fur coats, and a little girl who had a white fur muff around her neck, hanging from a chain that sparkled as if it was made from gems. What was a family like hers doing here? Someone said the ship had come from Germany. I suppose there must have been people from all over Europe on board. Anyway, there was a babble of outlandish tongues and a terrible smell, too. Even out here in the fresh air the smell of unwashed bodies wafted across to us.

It was cold and bleak on the dockside. The canopy did nothing to protect us from the swirling mist. The flannel petticoat and wool camisole that worked quite well against our own wintery winds did little to stop this kind of cold. I wrapped Bridie inside my shawl and we shivered together. We inched forward, one step at a time but that big brick entrance never seemed to get any closer. More ferries arrived. More people crowded onto the dock. More languages, different smells. If there were all these newcomers in one day, how could the city hold them all? Where would they sleep when they came ashore? How many more days before New York was full to bursting?

I kept my mind on such puzzles rather than on what might happen to me until we entered the building. Uniformed guards stood at the doors. "In you go, my fine cattle. We have nice pens for you inside," one of the guards called cheerfully, grinning to his fellow guard as he shoved the foreigners forward.

"Leave your baggage down there and look lively," he snapped to us. "Don't worry, it will be quite safe. That's what we have watchmen for," as some people protested being parted from their worldly goods. We were shown into a vast baggage room, where we piled our bags and bundles before we were sent up a long flight of steps. Men in white coats stood at the top of the steps, watching us. As immigrants passed them, they stepped forward and wrote letters in white chalk on the people's backs. When we drew level with them they looked at us but didn't write anything. I wasn't sure whether that was good or bad.

Then suddenly someone said, "Eye inspection." Before I could react, I was grabbed and yelled out in pain as a sharp instrument was dug into my eyelid, turning it backward. Bridie screamed as they came toward her and wriggled out of the way of the assault.

"Check needed on the child," one inspector said to his fellow and wrote a letter in chalk on Bridie's back.

"Do you speak English?" the man demanded.

"As well as you do," I replied.

"Oh yes." He examined my tag. "The *Majestic*, from Liverpool. Okay. Take the kid over to that room on your left. They'll want to check her eyes before you can go any further."

We joined the line at the door. A doctor in a white coat made me sit Bridie on the table, then his assistant held her while he turned back her eyelids.

"Both eyes are red," he commented to the assistant. "Possible trachoma. Need to keep her for observation."

"What do you mean, you need to keep her?" I demanded.

"In the hospital observation unit," the man said expression-lessly. "If it's trachoma, she'll be sent back where she came from."

"Of course her eyes are red," I exclaimed indignantly. "She's been kept standing outside in the bitter cold, hasn't she, and she's been crying. When she cries, she rubs her eyes and they get worse. There's nothing wrong with her eyes. They're as bright and clear as the light of day itself."

"You Irish could sweet-talk the hind leg off a donkey," the man said, but he managed a ghost of a smile. "Wait on the seats over there and bring her back in an hour."

It was the best I could hope for but it meant that my ship-mates would have gone ahead of me, both Michael and O'Malley. I sat the children down, instructing them not to move whatever happened and followed the crowd into the great hall they called the registry room. The entire room was full of wooden benches, and the benches were full of people. I could see now why the guard had made the joke about cattle. The benches were separated by iron railings, and so the whole effect was of the stock pens on market day.

"Where do you think you're going?" A guard grabbed my arm. "Back into the line and wait your turn."

"I just have to talk to a shipmate," I pleaded.

"That's what they all say." He frowned at me as if sizing me up, "Although I could be persuaded to get you through all this in a hurry. . . ."

"You could? That would be wonderful."

"For a small fee, of course. Shall we say twenty dollars?"

He wanted a bribe! I looked around to see who might have overheard. Other guards were standing nearby. Now I started to wonder—was this whole place corrupt? If I had to bribe some-body before they'd release me, then we'd be here forever. Unless they had listened to O'Malley. Then I'd be sent straight back to Ireland. I tried to spot his bright red cravat among the throng, but it was impossible. There must have been close to a thousand people in that room and more streaming in all the time.

I hurried back to the children, who hadn't moved an inch,

and I watched the clock on the wall until the hour was up. Then I took Bridie back to the doctor.

"You see," I said triumphantly. "Take a look at her eyes now. Not a speck of red in them, is there? Tell me when you've seen brighter eyes?"

He laughed as he looked at them. "Bright as the light of day, like you said," he said. "Off you go and good luck to you. You're lucky to have a very persistent mother, little one."

"Oh, but she's not my . . ." The last of Bridie's sentence was lost as I whisked her away. That was close. I'd have to make the children understand that I had to play the part of their mother for just a while longer.

We joined the line to enter the registry room.

"Name and ship?" An inspector turned over my label as if he was delivering a package. "O'Connor, *Majestic*, huh? The bench for names beginning with O is full at the moment. Sit over there until we tell you to move forward."

I perched on the end of a bench with the children. As we sat there, watching people move past us, I had time to take in the very size of it. I'd never seen a church even half as big as that room—or as high, either. If you looked upward toward the vaulted ceiling, it was like being in a great cathedral. A huge American flag was draped from the balcony, which ran all the way around the hall. A babble of languages surrounded me and rose to echo back from that high ceiling.

Every so often a name was called and someone ahead of us got up, looking around anxiously before shuffling away down the aisle, but the hall never seemed to empty out. Then, by mid-afternoon, when the children were complaining about being hungry and I could feel the pangs of hunger myself, a buzz of excitement went around the great hall. Figures appeared on the balcony above—men in top hats and finely dressed ladies. They stood there, peering down at us. Was this the afternoon amusement for the New York upper classes—to take the boat to Ellis Island and see what riffraff had landed today? Looking around me, I had to admit that we did rather resemble a zoo. Mothers had babies at their breasts and little ones climbing over them. Men were to be seen scratching themselves. The *Majestic* crossing had not been pleasant, but at least we had come through with no vermin on us. We could give a prayer of thanks for that.

When quite a large crowd had gathered on the balcony, a voice addressed us through a megaphone. "To all of you newly arrived in our great country, welcome. *Willkommen. Benvenuto.* I am Edward McSweeney, administrator of Ellis Island, and today we are honored to host our neighbors from New York City. His Honor, the mayor of New York, and other dignitaries from the city, have come across the chilly harbor to perform the official ceremony of dedication of these new buildings. As you may know, the old Ellis Island burned down three years ago. We have now built it up again, bigger, better, and fireproof!"

He waited for applause, not seeming to realize that most of his audience didn't understand a word he was saying. There was polite clapping from the ladies and gentlemen on the balcony.

"I now call upon Mr. Robert Van Wyck, his Honor, the mayor of New York City—now the second largest city in the world—to say a few words."

The mayor took over the megaphone. "My dear new Americans," he said. "You have come to a land where all things are possible, all dreams can become reality for those who dare. To those of you who are Irish I say a special Irish welcome. You'll find that many of our most distinguished citizens are Irish like yourselves. Many of our aldermen here in New York City are Irish to the core. They rose from humble circumstances like your own through hard work and through the power of politics. The message I give to you—never underestimate the power of the Irish vote. If we stick together and work for the good of the whole, we can accomplish great things.

"To all you new immigrants I say this—work for the good of the whole. Get involved. Exercise your right to vote. This is a wonderful country. A free country. For the first time in your lives, you have the right to choose. You have the right to direct your own future. Make the most of it!"

Some of the foreigners seemed to get the gist of this. They nodded to each other, smiling, then they clapped, although they glanced around nervously in case the police might be watching.

"This is a special day," the mayor continued. "Today I unveil a plaque, officially dedicating this magnificent new building. A special cake has been baked by our wonderful New York Italian community and I understand that you'll all get a slice once I've cut it."

Even the foreigners understood this one. They smiled and nodded to each other.

"And since Ellis Island is geographically part of our great city, and you'll all be stepping ashore there in a little while, I've brought some of our finest entertainers to make this a festive occasion."

I don't know about anyone else sitting on those hard benches, but I didn't want to be entertained. My nerves were as taut as violin strings. The sooner I faced those uniformed inspectors and got through this ordeal, the better. Still, I didn't have much choice. A Signora Torchelli, whom they announced as a famous opera singer from Italy, now performing in New York, sang us a song in Italian. She certainly had a big voice to match a big body. It echoed around that hall and bounced back from the newly tiled walls. Then the mayor introduced the toast of vaudeville, that famous monologuist and comedian, the darling of the Irish, Billy Brady.

I'd never heard of him. Neither had anyone around me. Obviously not the darling of the Irish in Ireland. He came to the front of the balcony—a big, jovial man with a round moon face and curly hair. "For my first monologue, I'm going to remind those Irish among you of home," he said. He turned away, and when he turned back he was wearing a gray wig and a head scarf. Then he launched into a monologue about an Irish grandmother coming to New York. My, but he was funny. He had that Irish grandmother to a tee. All the Irish in the audience shrieked with laughter. The non-English-speakers stared blankly, trying to catch what might be making us laugh. When the monologue had ended, he took off the scarf, put on a monocle, and did an impersonation of the president, Mr. McKinley. This didn't go down so well. None of us knew a thing about Mr. McKinley. We didn't even know what he looked like or whether Billy Brady was doing a good impersonation of him. But the dignitaries up in the balcony were laughing away, so he must have been good. We clapped politely.

The afternoon concluded with the famous Irish tenor, Edward Monagan. He sang "Tis the Last Rose of Summer," and there wasn't a dry eye in the house. Irish mothers and fathers sobbing into each other's arms, children crying because their parents were. Me? I just wished he'd get on with it and leave. I've never been much of a one for sentimental songs.

After the song had ended the mayor's party began to move away. I thought they were leaving and breathed a sigh of relief.

"When do we get the cake?" Seamus whispered in my ear.

"Any time now, I should think," I started to say when there was a commotion on the stairs and I saw that the mayor and some of his party were coming down, into the registry room. A couple of men with cameras ran ahead of him. He stopped to pose on the steps and flashes went off, filling the air with a bitter, burning smell. Then the mayor came down the aisle toward us, shaking hands and patting babies.

"He's acting more Irish than the Irish," I overhead a guard behind us mutter.

"Yes, well he's only here because of Tammany. He knows he's in Tammany's pocket," his fellow guard responded. I didn't know what that meant at the time.

The mayor came closer. More handshakes. More pictures. We happened to be so close to the aisle and the mayor's eyes fell upon Bridie, snuggled sleepily upon my lap.

"Here's a little Irish miss if ever I saw one," he said, attempting to pick her up. "And what's your name, darling?"

"Tell the gentleman it's Bridie O'Connor," I prompted, but of course she hung her head shyly and tried to squirm away from him.

"Bridie Connor—what a lovely name for a lovely child," he said. He tried to set her on his knee and motioned to the photographers to take his picture with her. "Welcome to America, Bridie," he said.

Bridie started to cry again, but before I could do anything, the Irish comedian, Billy Brady popped up behind the mayor and made such funny faces that the child actually started laughing. It was the first time I'd heard her laugh. People around us joined in, and soon half of Ellis Island was laughing.

The mayor patted her head and handed her back to me. "Lovely child. Take good care of her," he said. "Gee, but I could do with a whiskey and soda," I heard him mutter to Billy Brady as they made their way out of the hall.

❧ Seven ❧

After they had gone, little paper boxes of cake, like you get for weddings, were passed around among us. They had "Souvenir of the official dedication of Ellis Island, February 27, 1901" printed on them and a picture of the mayor. Most of us were hungry enough to eat the cake without noticing the picture. We'd just finished when Mr. McSweeney, the administrator, addressed us through the megaphone again.

"I'm sorry but the mayor's visit has made it too late to be able to process everyone tonight. Those of you in the back rows of the room, you'll be served supper and then you'll spend the night in the new dormitories, here on the island. But don't worry, we'll try and get you through as quickly as possible in the morning." This message was repeated in other languages. I saw people on other benches turning to mutter to each other, but they didn't make a fuss about the news, like the Irish and English people around me were doing. I suppose in their countries they were used to things going wrong and not being able to do a thing about it.

"Right, come on. Get a move on. Off to chow," the guard barked as soon as the dignitaries had disappeared. I gathered up the children, staggering after the official in a daze. I had managed so well this far but asking me to wait and worry another whole night was just too much. I felt as if I might cry at any moment.

I pressed my lips tightly together and shuffled behind the other immigrants as we were led into a dining room full of long tables. Stewed meat and potatoes were served, along with white bread and milk. Some of the foreigners fell upon the white bread as if they'd never tasted such a delicacy before.

After we had eaten, the women were told to follow one guard while the men followed another. We were led through to another building and then upstairs to a dormitory full of iron beds.

"If there's not enough beds, you'll have to make do with the floor," the guard said, looking unconcerned. "There's extra blankets you can sleep on."

Luckily we got a bed. Bridie had held up so well until now, but the sight of this large room, full of strange women, was too much for her. She burst out crying. "I want to go home. I don't like it here." I pressed her to me before she wailed out, "I want my mammy" for the whole world to hear. I rocked her, I held her, I sang to her until at last she fell into an exhausted sleep. Seamus curled up and went to sleep, too. I lay beside them, staring at the ceiling, willing sleep to come. The place was full of strange and uncomfortable noises—the hiss and knocking of the pipes in the central heating system kept jarring me awake. I'd never been in a place with heating before and found it uncomfortably hot. Then there was the sigh of the wind, the mournful bleating of foghorns and the slap of waves, mingled with the snores and coughs of a hundred other women.

One more day and I'd be free. If I could just keep going one more day . . . if O'Malley didn't betray me . . . if the children didn't give me away . . . if the English police hadn't put out a bulletin on me. I very seldom prayed but I prayed now. Holy Mother, let it soon be over. Get me out of here safely and I'll say Hail Marys every day for the rest of my life.

I drifted into uneasy sleep, then woke with a start in the middle of the night. One dim light cast long shadows across the sleeping room. Sounds of sleep whispered around me. I reached out my arm and touched the coolness of the sheet. Bridie was not in the bed beside me. I leaped up and looked around. Seamus still lay curled up like a small animal, sound asleep. Nothing moved on the neighboring cots. There was no sign of Bridie.

I felt my heart hammering in panic as I moved between the rows of beds, whispering her name, bending to search under each bed, carefully stepping over each sleeping body, until I had covered the entire dormitory. She wasn't there. I ran out into hallway. One dim light glowed at the far end. Where could she have gone? What would have made a child like her, frightened of her own shadow, go off into the terrifying unknown shadows of a strange building?

There were a couple of lavatories just down the hall from the dormitory. I tried them both but she wasn't there, either. I must wake someone, I decided. I must get help. I started to run, blindly, my footsteps echoing back from newly painted walls and stone floors. Someone must be awake in the eerie silence of this sleeping building. I came around a corner and there she was, heading for an open doorway.

"Bridie," I called. She didn't respond. I ran up to her and went to grab her before she entered the room. "Bridie, what on earth were you thinking to . . ." Then I saw that her eyes were wide open and staring, like a person possessed. It took me a moment to realize that she was sleepwalking. Poor little mite, after all the shocks of that day, no wonder her sleep was unsettled. I remembered that it can be harmful to wake sleepwalkers too abruptly. I moved ahead of her and was about to kneel to wake her as gently as possible when a figure loomed out of the dark room ahead of us.

"Where the hell do you think you're going?" a big voice bellowed.

I swept up the terrified child and looked up to see a big man in the peaked cap and braided uniform of a guard.

"This is the men's dormitory," he said, coming up to us in such a threatening way that I backed hastily. "What are you doing hanging around here?"

"I'm sorry, but the little girl was sleepwalking," I said. "There's no need to shout at us. We're going back to the women's dormitory this minute."

"And make sure you stay there," he thundered, "Or you'll be sent back where you came from."

I could feel him watching us as I carried the sobbing child back to the safety of the women's dormitory. When I went to sleep again, it was with my arm tightly around Bridie. I wasn't taking any chances.

Women were stirring around me. It was hardly light and the room was distinctly chilly. Surely there was no need to get us up before dawn, was there? But there were lights on in the hallway outside and I could hear alarmed voices shouting and running feet. Something was wrong. A fire? Maybe this grand new building wasn't as fireproof as they thought. But I couldn't smell smoke, and it certainly wasn't what you could describe as warm.

At that moment the electric light was turned on in our room and a guard stood in the doorway. "Everybody up and downstairs to the dining room now," the guard commanded. "There's coffee down there. Wait until you're told what to do next."

He hurried us out and down the stairs to the dining hall. Men from our ship were already sitting at one of the long tables. Wives went to join husbands. I could hear the whisper running from table to table like wildfire. "Yes, in our very room. I saw it myself. Horrible, it was . . . poor man . . ."

I glimpsed Michael Larkin sitting among the men. He usually looked pale but today he looked positively ashen. I hurried up to him. "I'm so glad to see you're still here," I said. "Do you know what happened?"

A woman leaned across him. "A man was killed," she said in a hoarse whisper.

"An accident?" I asked.

A man farther down the table leaned toward us. "No accident. The fellow had his throat slit from ear to ear."

"A fight?"

58

The man shook his head. "In his sleep, it must have been. Someone who knew what he was doing, that's for sure—and a powerful sharp knife. I was only three beds away and I heard nothing. None of us heard a thing."

"The poor man," the woman beside me said, crossing herself. "To come all this way and then that. Still, he did ask for trouble, didn't he?"

"Who was it?" I asked. "Someone we knew?" Before Michael could answer, the woman spoke again. "Why, it was that man O'Malley," she said. "The one you slapped across the face."

I have to admit that my first reaction was one of relief. O'Malley was dead. He wouldn't be stirring up any trouble for me with the immigration inspectors. He wouldn't be waiting to make things hard for me in New York. He wouldn't be making trouble for anyone. He was gone. I knew that any good Catholic would be praying for his immortal soul at this moment, but I had never been a good Catholic. I was glad he was gone. Now I was one step closer to being home free.

I squeezed myself and the children onto the bench beside Michael.

"In your dormitory, was it?" I asked. He still looked shocked and ashen.

"I was the first person to discover him," Michael said. "His throat . . . he was wearing that red neck scarf . . . bright red . . . and all that blood . . ." He closed his eyes and shuddered. "I wished him ill, but not like that. No human should be butchered like that. . . ."

I put my hand on his arm. "Here, drink a cup of coffee. You'll feel better."

After about an hour of sitting, waiting, and speculating we were led through into the great hall they call the registry room. There were only enough of us to fill the front few benches and the hall echoed to the clatter of our feet. They obviously hadn't allowed any more ships to land. The big room was cold and drafty without the benefit of all those bodies. I found myself shivering and wrapped my shawl close around me.

Bridie, completely unaware of the horrors of the night, was full of beans and wanted to run around. She squirmed and fussed on my lap until I let Seamus take her off into a corner where the other children were playing. It was then I noticed that men were guarding the doorways—they weren't dressed in the braid and peaked caps of the island guards, but in blue uniforms and tall helmets. Instantly recognizable as policemen. They stood, motionless, watching us.

A group of men came into the room. Some of them were uniformed, too, but the administrator who addressed us yesterday was with them, deep in conversation with a young man wearing a derby and the sort of tweed jacket you might see in Ireland. I wondered if they had already detained a suspect, but then the young man looked up, nodded, and laughed. Clearly not a suspect, then.

Mr. McSweeney stepped out in front of us and held up his hand for silence, although we had been sitting in close to silence since we got there. "As some of you have heard, there has been a terrible tragedy. A man has been killed. You will all be asked to make a statement to the police. Interpreters will be provided for those who don't speak English. Please remain in your seats until you are called."

Then the young man in the tweed jacket stepped out in front of us. "We'd like to thank you all for your patience. I'm Captain Daniel Sullivan of the New York City Police. I'm running this investigation." He was brawny, well built, and looked far too young to be a captain of anything. "If any of you have anything at all that might help us solve this vicious crime, anything you know about the man who was killed, anything you saw or heard last night, then please come and tell me or one of my men. Even if you think it's something very small or unimportant, tell us. The last boat left the island at six o'clock last night, which means, as I'm sure you can figure out, that the crime was committed by someone who was among us last night and is still among us. None of you will be leaving this island until we've got this matter solved."

Interpreters got up and presumably translated what had been said. There were moans of anguish as the foreigners understood. One by one we were directed to stations where policemen and inspectors checked off lists. I went up when it was my turn. They asked my name and a clerk checked me against a master list.

"Traveling alone?" the policeman asked.

"With my children, Seamus and Bridie. My husband will be meeting us when you let me out of this place." I was surprised how easily the words came out.

The policeman leaned over the desk and glanced at the master list. "You came on the *Majestic*. I see you're from the same part of Ireland as the man who died. Did you know him?"

"I'd never set eyes on him before I got on that ship." At least I didn't have to lie.

"But you did talk to him on the ship?"

"I talked to a lot of people. We were cooped up together there for seven days. Someone pointed him out to me and told me his name. That's how I knew who he was. He was a loud kind of individual. You couldn't help but notice him."

"When you say loud, do you mean aggressive? Did he pick fights? Did you notice him having an argument with anyone in particular?"

I could hardly say, yes, with me.

"No, I just meant that he laughed loudly when the men played cards. He had a loud voice."

The men exchanged a glance, then the policeman nodded. "Thank you, Mrs. O'Connor. That will be all."

❧ Eight ❧

I t was over. As easy as that. I went back to my seat. The children were still playing in the corner. I sat down and smiled at my neighbor. Suddenly I felt very hungry. Porridge with real cream, the way I used to make it at home, would have gone down a treat. But nobody brought around refreshments. The questioning must have taken an hour or more. Then the young man in the tweed jacket stepped out in front of us again.

"Sorry to have to detain you like this, when I know you're all itching to get ashore." He had an Irish name but the accent was very different from the brogue I was used to. "Some of you are now free to go. Interpreters, would you please tell those people who came on the *Graf Bismark* that they may now proceed to the usual immigration clearance. The following passengers from the *Majestic* are also free to leave." He read out a list of names. Mine was not among them. "Some of you have been asked to remain for further questioning. You may have information which can be of help to us. I don't anticipate you should be kept much longer—most of you."

The addition of those innocent words made alarm shoot through me. The more I was questioned, and maybe the children, too, the easier a slip would be. I had been so strong, so alert all this time. Now I just wanted it to be over and done with. We sat on the benches and waited. I looked around, trying to spot Michael, but I couldn't see him. I couldn't remember hearing his name called, but then I'd been listening so intently to hear my own name that I might have missed it. But he couldn't have gone, could he? Not when I had his five pounds in my pocket.

I jumped when someone prodded me in the back. "They're calling for you, Mrs. O'Connor." A policeman was beckoning me into a side room.

"Can you watch the children for me?" I asked one of the Irish women who was sitting beside me. The last thing I wanted was the children questioned.

"Don't worry, my dear, they'll be safe with me." She patted me on the hand, as if she was sorry for me.

I was led through to a little room with a desk and chair in it. The young New York detective was sitting at the desk, scribbling notes on a pad. He looked up when I came in.

"Mrs. O'Connor? Mrs. Kathleen O'Connor?"

There was something in the way he was looking at me—I could sense the heightened interest. He knows, I thought. He's been in touch with the English police and he recognizes me.

"That's right, sir." I sat on the chair indicated.

"From Stabane, county Derry. Sailed here on the *Majestic* to join husband, Seamus O'Connor, of Twenty-eight Cherry Street, New York City?"

"That's right, sir." I was determined to keep my answers as short as possible. If he was Irish-born, or even if he mixed in Irish circles, he'd spot instantly that my accent was not from county Derry.

"You say in your statement to my officer that you didn't know Mr. O'Malley, that you had never met him, even though you both came from the same small town of Plumbridge. Is that correct?"

"I have no idea where Mr. O'Malley came from. I had never met him before."

He looked up and there was a glint in his eyes. I noticed his eyes for the first time. He was what we call Black Irish—supposedly descended from those Spanish sailors who were able to swim ashore from the wreck of the *Armada* in Queen Elizabeth's time. He had unruly black curls that he had attempted, unsuccessfully, to slick down with a center part, a roguish cleft in his chin, and eyes that were an alarming blue. A very attractive man. I stared for a second before I remembered where I was, who I was supposed to be, and what was happening to me. Then I looked down at my hands again.

"Mrs. O'Connor," the policeman went on, "it has been reported to me by several of your fellow passengers on the *Majestic* that you were seen striking Mr. O'Malley. Do you make a practice of going around striking men you don't know?"

"He made an indecent proposal to me," I muttered, still looking down at my hands. "He was trying to take advantage of a woman traveling without her husband."

"Was he now?"

I glanced up. For a fraction of a second I had seen what seemed to be amusement flash across his face. "So you hit him. Do you normally react so violently, Mrs. O'Connor?"

"I slapped his face," I said. "A woman is allowed to defend her honor when she has no man to protect her, isn't she?" I only realized as I was saying it that I seemed to be making a practice of defending my honor with violence recently. The two cases would tie together very nicely in police eyes.

I looked down again.

"And did Mr. O'Malley take the hint?" Captain Sullivan continued. "Did he bother you again?"

"No, sir. He took the hint."

"So you never had contact with him again?"

"No."

There was a long pause. I just kept staring at my hands. A clock ticked loudly on the wall above us. I could hear the lapping of waves outside the window.

"Now here's another interesting thing, Mrs. O'Connor," Sullivan continued. "Your name came up in another context."

I tried to keep breathing evenly so that he wouldn't notice my rising panic.

"You were seen leaving your dormitory in the middle of the

night. You were also seen, by two separate witnesses, running away from the men's dormitory, looking scared."

I looked up now, staring at him defiantly. "Did the two witnesses happen to mention that I had a child in my arms?" I demanded. "The little one had been sleepwalking. I caught her just before she went into the men's dormitory. Do you think I'd have brought her along for company if I'd gone in there to kill a man?"

Again the flash of interest before the frown returned.

"And I understand that the poor man had his throat cut from ear to ear," I went on. "I don't know where I'd be finding such a knife. I've witnessed the cutting of a pig's throat before now. There's a lot of blood. I don't think I'd have managed it without getting blood on my dress. So take a good look at me. I haven't had access to any change of clothing. Do you see any blood?"

I stood up and turned around. He was watching me with that same half-concealed amusement. "Sit down, Mrs. O'Connor," he said. "Nobody is suggesting that you killed Mr. O'Malley. For one thing I don't think you'd have had the strength. He was a big man. Whoever did it was taking an enormous risk. The first cut had to sever the windpipe so that he couldn't cry out. That would take a very sharp knife and a lot of muscle power—as well as experience in killing."

"And you've not found anyone with blood on his clothing yet?" I asked. "That would seem the most obvious thing to look for. None of us can get downstairs to our baggage."

"Are you telling me how to do my job, Mrs. O'Connor?" He asked it without malice, and smiled. He had rather a wicked smile.

"Sorry, sir. I just want to get out of this place and see my husband again."

"Oh yes, of course you do." Did his face fall? "But we have to get to the bottom of this while we have the opportunity. It's not often we detectives have the chance to tie up a case so easily—the suspects all in one place with no way to leave. And such a daring, outrageous crime. Somebody must have seen something. It's just a question of waiting until somebody talks."

He leaned back in his chair and examined me carefully. "I don't know why, but I get the feeling that there's more you could tell us. You're holding back on something, Mrs. O'Connor. Wouldn't you like to get this murder solved so you could leave the island and go home?"

"Of course I would, but there's nothing I can tell you. I didn't know O'Malley. And you yourself said I wouldn't possess the strength to kill him."

"But you could have been an accomplice. You could have brought your child along as an excuse and kept watch outside the men's dormitory while your accomplice was committing the crime inside."

"That's ridiculous," I said. "And anyway, the guard was there. He can tell you. He came out of the men's dormitory and yelled at us. That's when I ran away."

"The guard?" He sat up straight again making his chair clatter upright. "You're saying you saw a guard in the men's dormitory? In the middle of the night?"

I nodded. "I grabbed Bridie just as she was about to walk into the room. He appeared and yelled at us. From the way he was yelling, he obviously thought I was coming to visit one of the men. And he stood there watching until I picked up the child and ran away."

"This guard—you'd recognize him again?"

"I think so. He was a big man, a lot of whiskers, a paunch, and a big voice."

He stood. "Harris!" A young policeman poked his head around the door. "Have all the guards assembled and tell me when you're ready."

He sat down again and smiled. "Thank you, Mrs. O'Connor. That is most helpful. If you can identify him, at least we'll be further along." He paused, tapping his pencil on the table. He was a very energetic man, never still, I noticed. "I'm wondering why he didn't volunteer the information himself that he saw you hanging around the men's dormitory. Surely that counts as suspicious behavior."

"Unless he had something to hide himself," I suggested.

He stared at me.

"He could have committed the crime," I went on.

"And why would an island watchman want to kill an immigrant?" he asked.

I shrugged. "Robbery? He had a fine gold watch, money in his pocket?"

"You're traveling steerage, Mrs. O'Connor," Captain Sullivan said. "If any of you had anything worth stealing, you'd have paid for a cabin."

This, of course, was true. I got up. "So you'll not be needing me anymore until I have to identify the guard for you?"

Again he looked at me long and hard as if there were questions he was considering. "Well, I think you can wait outside for now. I'll know where to find you if I have more questions," he said. "You can't swim away." And he smiled that cheeky smile again. In any other circumstances I'd have enjoyed flirting with a man like him. But I was a married woman, looking forward to joining her long lost husband. I was also, it seemed, under suspicion.

Just as I was leaving the room, a young uniformed policeman came in. "Sorry to interrupt, sir," he said. He had a definite Irish brogue. Was the whole of New York from Ireland?

"Yes, what is it, Lynch?"

"About his boots, sir. O'Malley's boots." Sullivan looked up with interest. "Well, sir, we took them off, and they're very good quality, sir. They've name of a bootmaker in London inside them and they're very well made—lined with kid and all."

"Are they, now?" Sullivan glanced at me. I had been the one who had just suggested that O'Malley might have had something worth stealing.

"So I thought, sir," Lynch went on excitedly, "that either this man O'Malley isn't what he seemed, or he stole the boots. In which case maybe Scotland Yard has a file on him."

"I've already telegraphed Scotland Yard with a description of the man," Sullivan said. "And I'm waiting to hear back from Dublin, too, with anything they can give us on his background. Have you located any luggage he might have stored down in the baggage room?"

"Two of the lads are down there right now, sir. We'll bring it up to you when we find it."

"Thanks, Lynch. Good work," Sullivan said.

"I was thinking, sir, about the boots," Lynch went on hesitantly. "If he was wearing fine boots like that, then maybe the motive was robbery."

Sullivan noticed me standing in the door. "You can go now, Mrs. O'Connor," he said, curtly. I tried not to smile.

More sitting and waiting in the big, drafty room. Then a line of uniformed guards filed in, looking surly and escorted by a couple of policemen. Daniel Sullivan beckoned me. "Take a good look and tell us which man you saw," he said. "Don't be nervous."

I walked down the line of navy blue uniforms. Then I shook my head. "I don't see him here," I whispered to the captain.

"Is this all the guards?" Sullivan asked. "Everyone who was on duty last night?"

"Some of the night shift would have gone home on the first boat this morning," one of the guards answered.

"I thought nobody left the island!" Daniel Sullivan's face flushed red with anger.

"No immigrants." The administrator stepped out of the shadows. "But some of the night shift boys went home on the boat that brought the day shift, as usual. They'd gone before we realized . . . We only discovered the crime when the shifts were changing."

"So you're saying that any number of people could have sneaked away from the island?"

McSweeney laughed uncomfortably. "Oh no, that's not possible. Only men working on the night shift. It's a government launch. They wouldn't let anybody who wasn't an employee aboard."

"Damn," Sullivan muttered, then glanced up at me apologetically. "Sorry, ma'am."

"I've heard worse," I said.

He took a deep breath. "Okay. I want all the off-duty guards brought here as soon as possible. Everybody on the roster. I want them back here this afternoon. Got it?"

"They won't take kindly to being woken in the middle of . . . ," McSweeney began.

"I don't care a d—, a fig about their feelings. A man has been murdered. One of them might well have vital information. Get the list to my men and we'll bring them in right away."

"You've no authority to do this!" McSweeney called after him. "This is federal property. We've called in the U.S. Marshals and they're on their way."

"This island falls within the boundaries of New York City, Mr. McSweeney," Daniel Sullivan said. "And any crime committed in New York City is handled by the NYPD. Besides, we're not dealing with cattle rustling here. This is murder, McSweeney. I doubt your federal marshals have handled a murder inquiry in their lives."

He strode away from the line of guards with me following him. Then seemed to remember me and turned back. "Sorry to detain you even longer, Mrs. O'Connor. Are your children all right? Go and get them something to eat. Say that Captain Sullivan says you should be fed."

We went through to the dining room. Other detainees were sitting around with cups of coffee. Still no sign of Michael Larkin. I asked several people. Some thought he had been released and gone. Nobody had seen him recently. Only I knew that he wouldn't have gotten past the authorities without that five pounds.

The day seemed to go on forever. It was dark and gloomy, with fog swirling past the windows and mournful tooting from ships going up the river. The two children were unusually quiet and good.

"Will they keep us in prison here forever?" Seamus whispered to me.

I ruffled his hair. "It's not prison and we'll be out by the end of the day. Not long now, I promise."

"You said that when the ship was going up and down, but it was two more days," he said accusingly.

I smiled. "This time I really promise."

The afternoon went on. I kept glancing at the clock on the wall. If they didn't get here soon, I'd be detained for another night. I wondered about Seamus O'Connor. Had he come to the island hoping to meet us yesterday? Was he pacing the shore today, waiting for word that he could come and take us home? And after all that waiting and hoping, to find that his wife hadn't joined him, after all. It hadn't really struck me until now that I was the bringer of the very worst news possible. It was possible that Seamus would be so distressed or angry that he'd give me away. When I was a child we used to lay old planks across the fast-flowing brook and dare each other to walk across. We would do it, never knowing when the rotten old wood would give way and tumble us into the icy water and rocks. That was how my life felt at this moment—never knowing at which moment the rickety boards would give way.

❧ Nine ❧

The radiators made the small waiting room uncomfortably warm and stuffy. I was dozing when Bridie climbed onto my lap. "The men have come back for you," she said. I had been dreaming of home.

It took me a couple of seconds to regain my senses and to see that two policemen were waiting for me.

"Captain Sullivan is ready for you now, Mrs. O'Connor. They've brought all the guards in. If you'd come this way."

"I'll be back in a minute. Watch your sister," I said to Seamus as I followed the men from the room.

This time there was a long line of uniformed men. Some of the uniforms had obviously been put on hastily and some of the men clearly hadn't shaved. They all looked disgruntled at being dragged here during their time off.

"You know what to do, don't you?" Daniel Sullivan asked me. "Let me know if you recognize the man you saw last night."

I fell into step beside him and we walked slowly down the line. So many faces, but none of them I recognized until . . . there he was! It had been dark last night and he was standing in the shadows, but surely that had to be him. Big, brawny, lots of whiskers . . . I leaned close to Daniel Sullivan. "That's the one," I said. "That man there with all the whiskers."

We continued to the end of the line. Daniel went to speak

to the administrator. "Boyle!" he called. "Would you step this way please?"

The big man followed him and was escorted by Captain Sullivan into a side room. I found that I was shaking. If that man had been a murderer and I'd just identified him, wasn't it possible that I was now in danger? What if he escaped or was released and came looking for me? Why had I opened my big mouth again and gotten myself involved when I could so easily have said nothing?

Nobody told me what to do, so I went back to the children in the dining hall. There was coffee and bread available, but I wasn't hungry. It wasn't long before Daniel Sullivan himself came looking for me.

"Can I have a word with you, Mrs. O'Connor?" He led me outside of the room into the deserted hallway.

"You're sure that was the man?"

"Not completely sure. He was in the shadows and the lights were very dim, but he's the only big one, with a paunch and lots of whiskers. That's what I saw."

"Only he wasn't here last night, Mrs. O'Connor. He was on the day shift yesterday and he left on the six o'clock boat."

"He can prove that, can he?"

"We'll check it out, of course, but why would he have any reason to lie?"

"If he had something to hide?"

He glared at me. "You're back to this something to hide rubbish again. If he wanted to rob immigrants, he could get himself stationed in the baggage room and help himself when no one was looking. He wouldn't be the first. But you don't carry a big, sharp knife around with you unless you're intending to kill. And why would he pick out one sleeping man over another?"

"He recognized O'Malley as someone he had a feud with long ago?"

"Rather far fetched, wouldn't you say? Boyle was born in upstate New York and he's never been out of the country."

"How do we know O'Malley was never here before?"

A brief frown crossed his face. "We don't," he said. "We've requested information about his past. Then we'll know more. But there was a guard on duty last night who covered the men's dormitories. He's a thin little Russian immigrant with a black beard. And he said no other guard was assigned to that area."

"They could be in on it together."

He stepped forward and grabbed me by the shoulders. "You know what I'm thinking, Mrs. O'Connor. I think you might be spinning me a good yarn to get yourself off the hook." Suddenly he seemed to realize that he was holding me. Myself, I was all too aware of those big strong hands on my shoulders. We stood there, just for a moment, like that, then he dropped his arms awkwardly and cleared his throat. "Now I have two courses open to me, Mrs. O'Connor. I can't hold you here any longer—this is federal property, but the idiots here aren't equipped to handle crimes of this magnitude. So I could take you straight to the city jail and hold you there for questioning. I don't recommend the city jail. The inmates call the cells there the Tombs—" he waited for the alarm to register on my face—"or I can release you to your husband, for now, on the understanding that you don't go anywhere and you are available to come to police headquarters whenever you are summoned."

"But you are going to check out that guard's alibi, and try to find the knife?" I suggested.

"You seem determined to teach me my job, Mrs. O'Connor. The knife, I'd imagine, is already lying at the bottom of New York Harbor. And it will be easy enough to check out Mr. Boyle's movements." He paused. "There is, of course, a third option."

Dramatic pause. I swear I could hear my heartbeat echoing in that tiled hallway.

"You could tell me everything you know about this man O'Malley right now. Save us both a lot of trouble. I don't think you killed him, but I still get the feeling that you're hiding something from me. If you're shielding somebody, remember this. The man who killed O'Malley is a violent, dangerous, opportunistic murderer. Do you want that kind of person out on our streets?"

I took a deep breath. How I wished I could tell him the truth and get this nightmare over with. "Look, Captain Sullivan, I wish I could help you, but I really, truly can't. I swear by the Blessed Mother that I never saw O'Malley before in my life until I boarded that ship. I had an unpleasant encounter with him during which he made bawdy remarks and I slapped his face. But that's all. Now please—I've got two little ones and a husband I haven't seen for over two years waiting and worrying about me."

Again he looked at me long and hard, then he nodded. "Off you go, then. But don't think about running away. The Irish network is strong in this country. We'd catch you again before you could blink."

"I have no reason to run away," I said.

Sullivan beckoned to a young officer standing nearby. "Escort Mrs. O'Connor and her children to the inspectors and let them know that she may be handed over to her husband."

We followed the young policeman through the registry room and up to one of the inspection stations. "Mrs. O'Connor is free to leave," the young policeman said. The inspector glanced at my papers, then at me and the children.

"You're traveling alone? Is someone here to meet you?"

"My husband is waiting for me, unless he got discouraged after two days and went home."

He waved my papers at me. "And everything that's written on this paper is true? Can you read or write?"

He was a young man with a high stiff collar and a big hooked nose. I sensed him looking down this nose at me. "Read Shakespeare, write Latin," I answered.

I saw his eyebrow raised. "In which case what are you doing at the bottom of the heap?" There was sarcasm in his voice.

"I married the man I loved. I didn't say I wasn't foolish."

That caused him to smile. "Now I have to ask you the following questions: have you ever been convicted of a crime?"

"No, sir," I replied, dropping my eyes. I was glad that he hadn't asked me if I had ever committed a crime. I was sure my face would have given me away.

"And I have to ask also—are you an anarchist?"

"No to that also."

He handed the papers back to me. "Here you are, Mrs. O'Connor. You have your twenty-five dollars, do you? I'll have you escorted down to the baggage room. If your husband is outside, you can go."

Then I was passed and a free woman, almost. And he hadn't even looked at the five-pound note I had in my pocket. I glanced back to see if Michael was anywhere in sight but a young official motioned me to follow him.

"You'll change your money here," he said. "I'll wait."

It wasn't a query, it was an order, and he stood there, leaning against the wall, watching me. I decided it wouldn't hurt Michael to have his pounds changed into dollars for him. I went up to the barred counter and handed through my five-pound note. The man behind the bars gave me an encouraging smile. "For you," he said, "For the lovely lady, nice shiny new coins. Here you go."

He handed me a pile of silver and copper coins. I took them, five pennies and some small silver coins. Less than a dollar in all. The man must take me for an idiot!

"Very nice," I said, "And now I'd like the rest of it, please. Dollar coins will do very nicely for the other twenty-four that you owe me."

"I'm getting it. I'm getting it," he snapped and slammed the coins down on the counter. I took my time to count them. I was angry enough to explode. It was perfectly obvious the fellow had been trying to cheat me. He hadn't reckoned on my reading English so well and having a quick brain. How many poor devils were cheated out of their savings here, and out on the street with no money for the train fare or a room? I glanced around. I could go back and find Captain Sullivan. He might be interested to hear that wholesale trickery was going on at Ellis Island. But on the other hand, he might not. And if I made a fuss, these people might change their minds and come up with an excuse to send me straight back to Ireland.

"Thank you so much, sir," I said with a smile that let him know that I knew. "Twenty-four silver dollars it is. How lucky my old father taught me to count, wasn't it? Come children." I went to take Bridie's hand, then I exclaimed, "Don't tell me she's left her favorite doll back in there. I'll have to go back for it or she'll not sleep tonight. Watch the little ones please. I won't be a tick."

Then I ran back past the astonished inspector, past the inspection station before anyone could stop me. I was in luck. Michael was just coming out of a side room. He stood looking around in a rather dazed manner. I rushed up to him and shoved the pile of coins into his hands. "Michael! Am I glad to see you— I've been looking everywhere. Here. Twenty-five dollars. I had them changed for you," I closed his hands around the coins. "There's rather a lot. Don't drop them. I have to go. Meet you at that park. Noon tomorrow."

"Kathleen, wait," he called after me. "I can't . . . you don't understand . . ."

"Noon tomorrow," I mouthed, and ran back to the waiting children.

We retrieved our bundles and came out onto the dock. A fierce, bitter breeze was blowing, splashing up waves over the side and dotting the harbor with white caps. We stood, blinking in the light of the setting sun. Seagulls were screaming and the American flag was flapping like crazy. Suddenly we were thrust into a world of noise and motion and color. It was hard to adjust.

"Is your husband here, missus?" our escort asked.

I bent down to Seamus. "Do you see your daddy?" I whispered.

A short, stocky man was eyeing us with interest, half taking a step forward from the crowd that stood on the dock.

"I—I think that's him," Seamus whispered.

"Go and run ahead to him. See if he recognizes you."

Seamus took a couple of hesitant steps. "Daddy?" he asked.

"Seamus? My boy?" The man's face broke into a delighted

grin and he also started to trot forward. "I'd not have recognized you. You're all grown up. Come and give your old daddy a hug."

Seamus flung himself into his father's arms. Bridie and I followed.

"And where's my little girl?" Seamus the elder looked up. I pushed Bridie forward but she clung to my skirts. "And where's Kathleen?"

The inspector was still hovering. I took the plunge. I rushed up to him and flung my arms around his neck. "Pretend you know me or they'll be taking the little ones back to Ireland again," I whispered. "Pretend that I'm Kathleen. I'll explain all when we're alone."

His arms came awkwardly around my waist. We stayed like that until the inspector had gone back into the building.

"I'm sorry to do this to you," I said, releasing him and re-wrapping my shawl around me, "but Kathleen couldn't travel with us. She sent me with the children so that they'd get to you safe and sound."

"She couldn't travel?" He looked confused. He looked the typical Irish country boy—round, innocent-looking face, short and stocky, probably not too quick on the uptake. I'd danced with enough clodhopping boys at home who looked just like him. "But I sent her the ticket. She must have got it."

"She left it at home in Ireland, by mistake," Young Seamus said. "She had to go back for it and she'll be coming on another boat."

"She did what?" The father looked at me, completely confused now.

I took his arm. "It's freezing out here. Let's get the children onto the ferry and I'll explain."

"Come on, young Bridie. It's time you hugged your father," he said, and swept her up into his arms. She allowed herself to be hugged and kissed, then he held her in one arm and took the bundle in the other as we walked toward the waiting ferry boat. We must have looked just like a family.

79

❧ Ten ❧

As soon as the ship was under way, we found ourselves a corner of the cabin, out of the icy blast of wind. I tapped the children on the shoulder. "If you go and look out of that window over there, you'll get your first real view of New York City where we're going to live. See if you can count how many floors there are to those skyscrapers."

Seamus was looking at me questioningly as the two children pushed their way through the crowd. I took a deep breath. This wasn't going to be easy. How do you break such news to a person?

"About Kathleen," I began. "That wasn't true—she didn't leave her ticket behind. She just told the children that to explain why she wasn't traveling with us. She gave her ticket to me so that I could come in her place."

"Why would she do that?" He still looked completely bewildered, and now a little suspicious.

"They wouldn't let her travel, Seamus. She had to have a medical exam and they found out that she had TB—consumption. They don't let anyone with consumption into America."

Now he looked really shocked. "Consumption? But—but most people die from that, don't they?"

I nodded. "She's gone home to her family in county Derry, Seamus. That's why she wanted to make sure that the children got to you safely."

A tear had squeezed itself out of the side of his eye. He wiped at it with his sleeve. "I'd have gone back to her if she'd told me. I'll still go back to be with her. I don't mind taking the risk. She shouldn't have to suffer and die alone."

"Don't be silly. What good would that be? What would happen to the children if their mother dies and their father is hanged?" I touched his arm. Even though he was a stranger I'd just met, I felt that I knew him. "Miracles do happen, Seamus. Maybe the Blessed Mother or one of the saints will cure Kathleen and she'll be able to come and join you."

"I'm thinking you're one of the saints yourself," he said. "Coming all this way to bring my children to me."

I had to smile at this. My old mother in heaven would be having a good laugh too, no doubt. "Nowhere near a saint, I'm afraid. My journey here suited the both of us. I was on the run from the police, just like you were. I had to leave Ireland in a hurry. Meeting Kathleen was a godsend for me."

"So those English bastards were onto you, too?" he snapped. "Pardon my language, miss, but just thinking of them brings out the worst in me."

"My name's Molly," I said. "Molly Murphy."

He held out his hand. "Pleased to make your acquaintance, Molly Murphy. And I'm most grateful for what you've done for my family."

I started laughing. "Anyone watching us will wonder what's going on. A married couple with two children and we're shaking hands like two strangers."

He laughed, too, then the smile faded. "My poor Kathleen. If only there was some way . . . if only we could think of some way."

"Maybe a way will present itself," I said, although I couldn't see how. "Maybe Ireland will get home rule. Maybe we'll chase out the English once and for all."

"Amen to that," he said. "If I thought there was any chance of that, I'd be on the boat tomorrow, raring to fight!"

"Your young ones need you now," I reminded him. "You'll have to be mother and father to them."

A worried look crossed his face. "I've no experience of raising children. What will I do? You'll come back with us for tonight, will you? It's nothing fancy. I've been living with my cousin and his family until Kathleen got here. I'd been saving for a place of our own but I wanted her to help choose it. It's very important to a woman to choose her own home."

I looked at him kindly. Kathleen certainly hadn't married for looks, but there was no denying that her man had a good heart.

"Of course I'll come back with you. I've nowhere else to go," I said.

"Thank you. That's grand. I'm feeling it's not going to be easy for the children. I'll have to tell them the truth, won't I?"

"Eventually," I said. "Let them go on hoping for now, until they're settled in at least."

He nodded, still fighting back tears. "She didn't say a thing when she wrote to me," he said and he stared out across the bleak waters. "Why didn't she tell me?"

"She only just found out when she had the medical exam. She didn't know herself before that."

"Oh, so she's not suffering very much yet, then?"

"She seems just fine," I lied, remembering the hollow eyes and the cough. "Who knows, maybe she'll get better yet."

Young Seamus pushed his way through the crowd, followed by a disheveled Bridie. "We saw it—New York City and there was a building with hundreds and hundreds of floors."

"It went right up to the clouds," Bridie added.

"It did not!" Seamus said scornfully. "But it was taller than the church spire at home. Are we going to live in a building like that, Daddy?"

"Almost like that," Seamus the elder said. "We are up on the fourth floor. I hope you've got good strong legs because there's a lot of stairs."

"They must have very good legs to walk up to the top of those buildings," young Seamus commented.

His father reached out and ruffled his son's hair. "They

have things called elevators in those grand buildings. I saw one for myself the other day. You'll not believe it. You step in this little box and it takes you up, like by magic. You don't even feel it, but when you get out, you're at the top of the building."

"By magic?" Bridie looked excited. "Is this a magic city, Daddy?"

"Absolutely. Any dream can come true here, so they say. You just have to work at it for a while . . . sometimes for quite a while," he added under his breath.

The ferry boat was coming in to its dock. We jostled our way up the gangplank and then we were on shore. I was standing in America, a free woman with a whole new life ahead of me.

Seamus took his son's hand. "Come on, young'un," he said with a crack in his voice. "Let's go home, shall we?"

The sun had set while we had crossed on the ferry and the city was plunged into twilight. As we left the dock and went among those tall buildings we were in nighttime gloom. Gas lamps cast anemic pools of light, but between them lurked frightening shadows. A clock on a church tower chimed five.

"Daddy, how soon do we get to your house?" Seamus's little voice echoed my own uneasiness.

"We have to cross to the other side of town," Seamus the father said. "This is the West Side and we live on the East Side. It's a fair walk but you can do it, I know. And it starts getting brighter, too, as we get toward the middle—electric lights they've got now on the Bowery. 'Tis a sight to behold all right."

One dark street led into another. If Seamus hadn't been guiding us, we'd have been hopelessly lost, and probably at the mercy of criminals, too. I noticed several unsavory types eyeing us from the shadows. Sometimes there were saloons on street corners with men coming in and out of them. Then there began to be more lights—open shop fronts with kerosene lanterns hissing away. And then, mercy of mercies—we came to the broadest street of all, and here all was full of life. The stores were all open, and there were bright electric lamps in the streets that made it look almost like day. Cabs and carriages clattered past, and then, with a clang clanging of its bell, a streetcar came toward us, gliding on silvery tracks. We just stood and stared—those of us who had never seen an electric streetcar before, that is. I've no doubt that Seamus was used to it by now.

"How does it go, Daddy—there are no horses," little Seamus gasped.

"Electricity," Big Seamus said grandly. "See, it runs on those tracks, like a small train. New York City is full of marvels, my boy. Full of marvels. Tomorrow, if you're good, I'll show you a big hole in the ground and do you know what they're doing there? They're building a railway to run under the city. Imagine that. Oh yes, this is the place to be all right."

I was still staring like a delighted child at the shops full of merchandise, the streetcars, the electric lights, taverns, eating rooms, and even theaters. There was everything you might need or dream about right there on that one street. I decided I was going to like living in a city.

We crossed that wide street, staying close to Seamus as we dodged through the traffic. Then we walked by a brightly lit theater. Flannagan's Irish Delight was the sign in winking lights. On a billboard outside was plastered " 'When Irish Eyes Are Smiling!' An all-new review starring the best and brightest of Ireland's stars—straight from their phenomenal success in Dublin and Belfast: Taffy and Rosie, the Shannon twins will clog dance their way into your hearts; Ireland's own darlin' boy, Billy Brady will tickle your fancy with his wicked recitations, and the pride of old Ireland, Edward Monagan, with the golden voice will bring tears to your eyes."

We passed on. I said a silent prayer of thanks they hadn't also sent Taffy and Rosie to entertain us that afternoon. Now we left the main streets and plunged into another maze of smaller streets, but these weren't dark and threatening. They were dark because there was no electric light, but they were full of life and noise. Everywhere there were men with barrows and handcarts, and these handcarts were piled with every sort of merchandise you could imagine—fruit, vegetables, fish, pots, pans, fabric—why, it was better than the Westport fair that we went to once a year when I was a child.

"Is it some kind of market day here?" I asked.

"No, it's like this every day," Seamus answered. "Most new immigrants can't get a job straightaway, especially if they can't speak English. So they go and get themselves a pushcart and they sell things. They start off small and get bigger."

"What about you? Do you have a job or a cart like this?"

"Well, I'm Irish, aren't I? We're the lucky ones. They know we've got good strong muscles and we know how to vote, too."

"What does that mean?"

"It means that the power that runs this city is Irish, and if they want to count on our votes to stay in power, then they make sure we're employed and happy. That new subway train I told you about—I'm digging that tunnel. They have plans to dig tunnels all over the city, so I reckon that should keep me nicely employed for quite a while—God willing and the roof don't collapse, like the saying goes here."

We worked our way down the narrow cobbled streets between the pushcarts. It was quite dark by now and I just hoped that what I was treading on was squashed fruit and not something worse. The smell was none too savory, I can tell you that.

The other thing I wasn't used to was the noise level. Those pushcart men were calling out their wares, mostly in languages I didn't know, but sometimes in broken English, too. People were standing in doorways or out on balconies, yelling across at other people, and children ran squealing, dodging in and out in street games. And to top it all there were barrel organs or hurdy-gurdies stationed on street corners, playing competing tunes. It was lively enough, that was for sure, but overwhelming to newcomers like ourselves. Some dark, ragged children ran up to young Seamus and gave him a push before his father boomed, "Go on, clear off before I belt you one."

Then they dodged away laughing and shouting out in a language that was probably Italian.

"Daddy, I'm tired," Bridie complained, and Seamus hoisted her to his shoulder again. "Not too long now. Hear that foghorn? That's coming from the East River. That's where we're going. Number Twenty-eight Cherry Street—right in the middle of the Irish quarter. The Fourth Ward. Safe and sound."

We turned at last onto a street that was longer and straighter than most we had been through. Not so many pushcarts, either. There was noise spilling out of a saloon and someone started singing "Where the mountains of Morne come down to the sea."

A window above our heads opened and a woman's voice shrieked, "You get in here this minute, Kevin O'Keefe, or you'll get such a walloping, you'll not be able to sit down for a month."

Suddenly I wanted to laugh. I'd come halfway around the world and here I was, back at home!

Seamus came to a halt outside one of the tall brown buildings. "This is home, children. Now we just have to walk up the four flights of stairs and we'll be there." He pushed open the front door and stepped aside with a chivalrous bow. "After you, Miss Molly."

I nodded, thanked him, and stepped inside. The stairway was in pitch darkness and stank as if half the dogs in the world had peed on it. I was only halfway up the first flight when my foot touched something soft and warm. There was a scream and the object beneath my foot wriggled. I think I screamed, too, and only just stopped myself from plunging down the stairs.

"I think I stepped on a baby!" I shouted into the darkness.

"That will be the Donovans' brat again. She's got so many kids she can't keep track of them. Now there's a new baby and the one above it has learned to crawl, so it's off and away with no one keeping an eye on it."

I reached around in the dark and picked up the squirming, bawling bundle.

"Do they live on this floor?" I made it to the landing.

"Door on the right," Seamus said. He banged on it. It was opened a crack and several pairs of suspicious eyes peeked out.

"Ma, I think it's the health inspector, got Ginny," a child's voice screamed.

I held out the child. "I'm not the health inspector. The little one was lying on the cold stairs in the dark. I stepped on her."

"Ma, Ginny was out on the stairs again. See I told you Freddy wasn't watching her."

"Well bring her in and shut the bleedin' door! Yer lettin the cold air in."

The door opened more than a crack to reveal flickering candle light and a room that seemed to be full of moving shadows. A middle-sized girl, skinny and filthy, snatched the baby from my arms. "Thank you," she said, and closed the door.

I followed Seamus and the children up the dark stairwell, stunned. One more flight, then another. On this landing—it must have been the third floor by now—there was a big stone sink, full and spilling over onto the floor. I picked up my skirts and hurried past. One last flight and there we were. By the time I reached the landing the door was already open, but most of the light from it was blocked by an enormous form, almost filling the door frame.

"Where are they? Where are those precious little ones?" a voice boomed out.

"Children, this is Auntie Nuala," Seamus said. "Give your auntie a kiss."

Bridie was swept up, protesting, into a very large bosom.

"Well, don't just stand there," the voice boomed again. "Come along inside with you. I've made a good warming stew. No doubt you'll be starving after what you've been through and . . . ," her voice broke off. Seamus and the children had gone into the room. I hesitated in the doorway. The large woman's gaze had fastened on me.

"Holy Mother of God!" she exclaimed. "Where is Kathleen and who, in God's name, is this?"

❦ Eleven ❦

My later impressions of Nuala O'Connor were no great improvement on the first one. Seamus had taken Nuala aside and filled her in on the situation, while she eyed me critically all the time he was talking. "But she could be anybody," I heard her say. "She could have murdered Kathleen in her bed, thrown her over the side of the ship. Who knows?"

"Hush. Don't let the children hear you." Seamus covered his mouth with his hand and gave us a sideways glance. "They seem very fond of her. And young Seamus himself told me how his mother came to the docks with them and how he wanted to wave to her."

"But she's not thinking of staying here?" If she thought her voice didn't carry, she was misjudging the volume of her whisper. And even though I heard every word, those suspicious looks were expressive enough.

"I asked her to, at least until the children were used to me," Seamus said.

"And where's she going to sleep, I'd like to know."

I was longing to tell her what she could do with her apartment and her beds, too, but I didn't want to walk out and leave the two little ones tonight. That would be one shock too many for them. Besides, I reminded myself, I had nowhere else to go. So I bit my tongue and stood there, pretending I hadn't heard. I had time to take in my surroundings and I wasn't too thrilled with what I saw. Our chickens at home had a better-kept place to roost than this. There was one old armchair losing its stuffing, a rickety table, and the rest of the furniture looked as if it was made from old boxes and packing cases. Pots and pans were stacked on a shelf along with bread, sugar, and other supplies. There had been rose-patterned wallpaper on the wall but it had peeled away in great strips, revealing holes in the lath and plaster beneath it. The whole thing was lit with one anemic oil lamp. I tried not to shudder.

"Well, it's catch as catch can around here," Nuala said, in a louder voice, now seeing my dismayed look. "You have to take us as you find us."

"Don't worry, Nuala. I'll be looking for my own place now that the children are here," Seamus said. "It won't be for long that you're packed in like sardines."

"When Mother comes, eh, Daddy? We'll get a place of our own then?" Young Seamus said, giving the room the same critical appraisal as I had.

"When your mother comes, that's right." Seamus found it hard to get the words out.

"You should tell them," Nuala said.

"When the time is right. Not now." I stepped between her and the two children.

The large woman came across the room to face me. "And what might your name be, miss?"

I held out my hand and forced a smile. "It's Molly Murphy, from Ballykillin, near Westport."

"Seaumus has no doubt told you, I'm Nuala O'Connor. I'm married to that useless body of a cousin of his. Finbar! Wake up! We've got company."

A figure roused itself from the darkness in the far corner and staggered to its feet. Finbar was in direct contrast to his wife—Jack Sprat and his wife from the nursery rhyme books. He was small and thin and bony, with a drooping mustache that seemed too big for his face and a worried look. Mind you, I'd have been worried at the thought of coming home to that dragon every day. He embraced Seamus, patted the children, and then looked at me enquiringly.

"This is Miss Murphy, who kindly escorted the children over on the boat," Seamus said before Nuala could say anything. "Kathleen was unavoidably detained."

Finbar smoothed down his rumpled clothes. "Excuse the way I look, miss. Just taking a little nap before work, you know."

"Little nap before work!" Nuala sniffed. "You drink more than you earn at that godforsaken saloon. And those children of yours are growing up idle and useless just like their father."

"Where are the children, Nuala?" Seamus asked.

"God only knows. Out to all hours they are. Running around like heathen savages. Now young Malachy is talking nonsense about joining a gang. A gang, I ask you."

Almost on cue there was a clatter of feet on the stairs and the door burst open.

"And what sort of a time do you call this?" Nuala demanded, facing three scruffy boys with her hands on her hips. "Did I or did I not tell you that I want you home before it's dark?"

"Yes, but—"

"I'm not hearing any excuses. Malachy, go and get the wooden spoon."

"But Ma, there was a fight."

"Holy Mother—you weren't in another fight after what I told you?"

"Not us, Ma. Guys. Grown-up guys bashing away at each other!" the smallest boy exclaimed, his face alight with excitement. "Down on the dock—that icehouse near the bridge."

Nuala turned to her husband. "See, I told you he was asking for it, didn't I? Trying to get the ice contract with the fish market from under the noses of Tammany."

"You reckon it was the Tammany thugs teaching him a little lesson?" Seamus asked.

"Sure as hell it was." Finbar nodded. "Everyone knows Tammany has the monopoly on ice. You don't go against Tammany, not if you want to live long."

"Who is Tammany?" I asked. There was that name again.

"Not who, what," Nuala said. "Tammany Hall. They run the city. When there are elections, the Tammany ward bosses come around and tell you who to vote for."

"But that's terrible," I exclaimed.

"Not if you're Irish, it's not," Nuala said confidently. "Tammany is Irish to the core and if they put someone in power, then he better be good to the Irish, or Tammany will choose another candidate next time."

"Anyway, Ma, that guy won't be going against Tammany for a while," the oldest boy said. "You should have seen his head—all bloody and his eye hanging out and—"

"Were the police not called?" Seamus asked.

The boys grinned. "The police were there, all right. They were watching and cheering. I think one of them even used his nightstick!"

"The police wouldn't go against Tammany," Finbar muttered. "They know which side their bread is buttered on."

"That's enough of that," Nuala said. "Where are your manners? Say hello to your cousins, just arrived from the old country."

Seamus put his hands on his children's shoulders. "Boys—this is young Seamus and this is Bridie. These are your cousins, children. Malachy, Thomas, and James. Go on. Shake hands."

Seamus held out his hand but Bridie hung back, not eager to say hello to three tough, scruffy boys.

"And who's that?" the oldest was staring at me.

"I came over on the boat with them. Your auntie Kathleen wasn't able to travel at the last minute," I said. "My name's Molly. You're Malachy, are you? I've a little brother called Malachy myself."

He gave me a half grin.

"Right. Let's get down to eating now we're all here. James, set the table."

"What are we having?" James asked as he cleaned off a table surface of various objects.

"Fish stew."

"Not fish again!" Malachy complained.

"If you're lucky enough to have a mother that works at the fish market, you take what the good God provides," Nuala said. "And if he provides fish heads, you get fish stew."

I'd been wondering about the pervading smell in the apartment. Now I realized—it was fish.

But as it turned out, the stew wasn't too bad, and the long walk had certainly given me an appetite.

"So you'll be trying to find yourself a job in New York will you?" Nuala asked me, her gaze hinting that I'd be an added expense to feed. "Or will you be heading out of town to your relatives?"

"I've no relatives over here," I said. "I'll be looking for a job right away."

"Because food isn't cheap, you know. Neither is gas. Which reminds me . . . ," she looked up at Seamus. "You've not got a dime on you for the meter, have you, Seamus? The gas ran out before I'd finished cooking and there's no sense in asking this good-for-nothing—"

"Don't worry, Nuala. I've got a dime." Seamus reached into his pocket.

I squeezed myself onto a bench made of a wooden board across two packing cases, feeling distinctly uncomfortable. Bridie sat close beside me, her little hand clutching at my skirt.

"I'll help you wash up," I said as soon as dinner was over.

"Right you are." Nuala jerked her head. "The sink's down one flight. Mind you don't trip in the darkness and fall and break your neck."

Surely that overflowing cesspit wasn't the only sink in the place? I gritted my teeth and went down to wash the dishes in the cold, dirty water. Afterward Nuala dried them on a towel so caked with grime that they ended up dirtier than they started.

By this time the children were ready for bed. Those same planks and packing cases were now lain on the floor with blankets on them.

"Do you want to sleep on there with your cousins?" Nuala asked young Seamus, "or will you be sharing your Daddy's bed tonight?"

Seamus looked unsure as to which was the safer choice.

"They can both share my bed, if you like," I said. "They're used to sleeping like that from the ship."

"There's no bed in the house for you," Nuala said. "You can choose between that chair or the floor." She turned to her sons who were now settling themselves on the makeshift bed of planks. "You three move over and make room for your cousins. You can sleep head to toe, like sardines, for tonight. Tomorrow we'll have to work something out."

"No, I think I'll take the little ones in with me," Seamus said. "It's mighty cold in here tonight. I don't want them catching a chill on their first evening in New York."

I ended up in the chair. At least it was out of the draft that now swept in under the door. There was one kerosene stove, placed between the bedroom and the living room, but it did little to keep out the bitter cold. I wrapped myself in my shawl and hugged my knees to my chest, trying to stay warm. The sooner I got out of this place, the better, I decided. In the morning I'd look for a job and then . . .

Then, just as I was dozing off to sleep, I felt a small hand brush against me.

"I'm scared," Bridie whispered. "I want to sleep with you." And she climbed up onto my lap. I held her close to me, and stroked her hair. Obviously I wouldn't be going anywhere for a while.

I was awakened by the clatter of pots and pans. I opened my eyes but it wasn't yet light. I could just make out the large shape of Nuala, bustling around in the darkness. Finally I had to answer the call of nature. I had avoided the bucket in the corner that everyone else had used during the night and I asked, tactfully, where the lavatory might be.

"Down in the yard at the back. But there's still the bucket in the corner. Fin hasn't thrown it out yet."

"Thanks, but I'll go down."

I held onto the wall as I went down. It felt damp and icy to the touch. Behind the stairs a back door swung open to the narrowest courtyard you could imagine. It was actually a well in the middle of a tall building. If you stood in the middle, you could almost touch both walls. I looked up and saw line after line of laundry, all stiff with frost, hanging in the dark like so many ghosts. I shivered. This was a terrible place. I just hoped that Seamus would get the children out of here in a hurry.

There were two outhouses on one side, both filthy and smelly. We had an outhouse at home, but my father always made sure it stayed clean. I used it, and hurried back inside. I paused at the sink in the hallway to wash my face and hands. By the time I reached the apartment again, the children were up and Nuala had put doorstops of bread and mugs of tea on the table. Seamus appeared with his son in tow, both looking bleary eyed and tousle haired.

"Sorry I have to leave you today, son," Seamus said, "but I can't take another day off or the foreman will fire me. Your auntie Nuala has to be at the fish market at six but Miss Molly and your cousins will keep an eye on you, I expect."

"Shouldn't we enroll Seamus at a school?" I asked. "You boys go to school, don't you?"

"They're supposed to," Nuala said, glaring at them, "At least until Malachy can get a job as a delivery boy at the fish market next year."

"Oh, Ma, school is for sissies," Malachy said. He turned to me. "The only school around here is full of Jews."

"And what's wrong with that?" I asked. "Do they beat you up?"

"Jewish kids beat us up?" Malachy grinned at Thomas. "Nah, they don't go in for fighting, but they don't like us. They don't want us there. The teacher is Jewish, too—she's always saying we make trouble."

"Well, I expect she's not wrong," Nuala said.

"And they're always speaking Yiddish to each other so we can't understand them," Thomas said. "Even the teacher speaks Yiddish sometimes. And you know what? They like reading and writing. They take books home with them and all."

"They're a lot of sissies," James agreed. "We can lick 'em easy. Can't we, Mal?"

"Well, I want you going to school, young man," Seamus said. "Your mother would want you going to school." He paused, looking down at his son with tenderness. "But I suppose you can take a few days to settle in first. Better to wait until we see where we'll be living."

Nuala and Seamus left soon after, Finbar slept undisturbed in the corner, and the boys wanted to take young Seamus out to show him the neighborhood. Seamus insisted on taking Bridie with him, although she wanted to stay with me.

"You need to learn your way around, Bridie," he said. "Come on, you can't be a baby all your life."

I had to agree with that. She had come to a tough world. The sooner she adapted to it the better. So they went. I was left alone in the cold, dark apartment with Finbar snoring in the corner. A few more days and then I would find myself a job and a place to live. I looked around the place and wondered if I should attempt to clean it up. It could certainly use it, but would Nuala take it as an insult? Leave well alone, I told myself.

By mid-morning the children weren't back, but Finbar had awakened. I decided to go out. It might take me a while to find my way down to the gardens at the southern tip of Manhattan where I had planned to meet Michael at noon. The sky was leaden and a light snow was falling as I came out onto Cherry Street. There was a layer of slush underfoot, mixing with the debris that littered all the streets. People hurried past, bundled against the cold. A few mangy dogs scrounged in the gutters. A horse's breath came out like steam from an engine as he trotted past pulling a large cart piled high with barrels. I tried to follow the river down to the tip of New York City and came upon a great bridge, so high and wide that it took my breath away. My, but they knew how to build things in this place. It was a strange contrast to see the towering sweep of the bridge above the dingy, dirty, squalid alleyways beneath it. I pressed on. My hands were icy now inside my cotton gloves and my face felt raw with the bleak wind. It was never as cold as this in my part of Ireland. I was already wearing my spare camisole and two pairs of drawers and they definitely weren't enough. When I earned money, I'd have to invest in warmer clothes. I glanced at the storefronts as I went past. What sort of job would I be likely to find? I knew how to keep a house clean and feed hungry males, but that was all—apart from reading Shakespeare and writing Latin, as I'd told the inspector. But a lot of use Shakespeare was. Education was only a benefit to ladies of leisure, and it didn't look as if I'd be one of those for a while.

I heard a clock striking twelve just as I came to the little park at the tip of Manhattan. Ahead of me was an expanse of gray water with a clear view of Ellis Island and Lady Liberty. I quickened my pace, scanning the pathways eagerly to see if Michael had arrived ahead of me. But he wasn't anywhere to be seen. The area of dying grass and skeleton trees was deserted, apart from a couple of seagulls, perched on a low wall. I hadn't realized how very anxious I was to see him again. He was my one lifeline in a city of strangers. Maybe we could make plans together. I wished there was some way we could find a place to share. I'd have welcomed his company. Of course, it wouldn't be seemly to share a room . . . unless we pretended to be brother and sister, of course. Maybe I'd suggest it to him and see how he took it.

It was bitter cold out there, with the winds coming straight across the wild gray waters of the harbor. Every time I turned into the wind, it took my breath away. I stamped my feet to keep the life going in them. Hurry up, Michael, I commanded silently. Twelve fifteen. Twelve twenty. He wasn't going to come. I felt a wave of disappointment flood through me. I had been relying so much on seeing him again. Perhaps seeing me again didn't mean as much to him. Perhaps he'd found himself a job right away this morning and was already up there, hammering away on one of the new skyscrapers. My chances of meeting him again in this city of a million people were very slim.

Cold and dejected, I turned away. All the way along South Street I kept looking back, just in case he'd come late. But the park remained deserted until it was lost from view. The cold was cutting through me like a knife. I decided to move away from the river and out of the wind. When I finally reached Cherry Street I was dreaming of a hot cup of tea and warming my hands over that kerosene stove. As I approached the building a dark form stepped out of the shadows.

"Mrs. O'Connor?"

I turned to see two men in blue uniforms standing behind me.

"Mrs. Kathleen O'Connor?" His face was expressionless. "We were on our way to find you. We must ask you to accompany us to police headquarters. Captain Sullivan would like to speak to you."

I noticed then that there was a black paddy wagon, pulled by two horses, waiting a little way down the street. As they led me to it, I was conscious of lace curtains moving, eyes watching me.

❧ Twelve ❧

One good thing to be said of police headquarters—it was warm. The warm air enveloped me as the police officer opened the door and ushered me inside. I was glad because I was one big shiver by now. I couldn't tell whether it was from being out in the cold so long or because I was scared. A little of both, I suppose.

"This way, please."

One of the policemen led me up a flight of linoleum-covered stairs and along a hallway lined with glass-fronted cubicles. At least he had said please to me, which must mean I wasn't under arrest yet.

"In here." A door was opened and I was ushered inside. "Mrs. O'Connor for you, sir."

Did those alarming blue eyes light up as I went in? Or was it the delight of a spider when a fly blunders into its den?

"Ah, Mrs. O'Connor. I'm so glad we found you with no trouble. Do sit down." Daniel Sullivan was in his shirtsleeves. He wasn't wearing a tie and his collar was open. Definitely a striking man.

"Mrs. O'Connor. Remember when we spoke yesterday, I suggested how much simpler it would be if you told us everything you knew?" A very long pause. "We've been in touch with Scotland Yard and with Dublin and some interesting facts have come to light. Very interesting facts . . . You weren't quite straight with us before, were you, Mrs. O'Connor?"

My heart was racing. They had discovered my true identity. Would they be obliged to ship me home to be hanged in England or would they try me here? Did they hang people in America, or hadn't I heard something about an electric chair? I had no alternative but to keep up the bluff as long as I could.

"But I did tell you everything. I told you I had never met O'Malley before we sailed from Liverpool. I told you that we had an unpleasant encounter on the boat. After we left the boat I never saw him again and that is God's truth. I'm prepared to swear to it on the Bible if you like."

I stared defiantly, right at those blue eyes. Sullivan reached for a sheaf of papers and studied them for a moment. The warrant for my arrest. It had to be.

"Several things have come to light, Mrs. O'Connor," he said. He was enjoying this. The spider closing in for the kill, then. "We went through O'Malley's baggage. Very interesting—there was nothing on his person, nothing in his trunk to identify him. No photos of loved ones, no letters, nothing personal in any way. Another mystery—you remember the boots. Good quality, London shoemaker? The clothing in his trunk was good quality, too. Some of it bore a laundry mark which we are now checking. And there was a bag containing gold sovereigns. O'Malley was not a poor man, which makes me wonder why he chose to travel steerage among the poor. Any ideas, Mrs. O'Connor?"

"None at all, sir. As I said, I didn't know him."

"Ah. Well, something else came to light in his trunk. It was hidden in the lining. A couple of newspaper articles. You can read, can't you?"

This time I had no desire to give him the same sarcastic reply. I took them when he handed them to me. The first was from the *Times*, London, Oct 1889. PLUMBRIDGE NINE HANGED AT BELFAST GOAL. "The nine young Irishmen responsible for the savage murder of land agent Henry Parkinson were hanged at six o'clock yesterday morning in the courtyard of Belfast Jail.

They were found guilty at the Belfast assizes last month of will-fully beating Mr. Parkinson with such force that he later died from his wounds. Mr. Parkinson was attempting to carry out his duty and evict the tenants of a cottage on the land of Major James Astburn, squire of county Derry . . ."

I could sense Daniel Sullivan looking at me. I wasn't sure what I was supposed to say. I turned to the second newspaper article. It was from the *Flaming Brand*, Unofficial Voice of the Fenians. "Today nine patriots died, murdered by the English for trying to protect one of their own. When Major Astburn of Strat-ford Hall, county Derry decided to raise the rents on his prop-erty, many of his tenants were unable to pay. This was followed by a spate of evictions. Nine young men of the village of Plum-bridge took it upon themselves to prevent Major Astburn's agent, a hired bully brought in from England, by the name of Henry Parkinson, from carrying out his orders. On his way to a cottage occupied for generations by the O'Meara family, Parkinson was waylaid under cover of darkness. When he attempted resistance and drew his gun on the young men, they set upon him, beat him and left him on the roadside.

"There were no witnesses to this scene, the weather being inclement and the hour late. Mr. Parkinson did not live to tell his tale and his assailants belonged to a secret society, sworn to silence. They would have remained anonymous had they not been betrayed by one of their own. A tenth man was there that night, a man who claimed to have no part in the killings. He melted away into the darkness, made his escape over the sea, and turned in the names of his friends. Whereupon they were immediately arrested, tried, and sentenced to death. They died not knowing that they had been betrayed by one of their own."

Sullivan was looking at me inquiringly again. "Was the man O'Malley?" I asked.

"You tell me, Mrs. O'Connor."

"But I told you, I never met—"

He produced another sheet of paper. "This message just came by telegraph from London. The names of the Plumbridge Nine.

Shall I read them to you, Mrs. O'Connor? Brendan Sheehey, Thomas Larkin, Liam McCluskey—"

Then, of course, it hit me. I felt the blood rush into my face. I had heard this story before, told to me by Kathleen O'Connor as we sat beside her dying fire. 'My brother Liam, only eighteen years old.' Kathleen O'Connor's brother had been one of the Plumbridge Nine.

"Your maiden name was McCluskey, was it not?"

Tell him now, a voice inside me was yelling. Tell him the truth. It can't be any worse than what will face you here.

"Yes, sir."

"And your family did come from the town of Plumbridge, in county Derry?"

"Yes, they did."

"And I'd be right in guessing that Liam McCluskey was your brother, then?"

Kathleen's brother, not mine! I stared down at my hands. A chillblain was beginning on one of my red and raw fingers.

"Interesting fellow, O'Malley," Captain Sullivan said. "It's obviously an assumed name, of course. Scotland Yard had never heard of him. Nobody in Dublin could place him. So who was Mr. O'Malley really? Can you supply me with his real name? Save us all a lot of work. Of course, we'll find out soon enough. That bootmaker will be tracked down, the laundry marks will be identified, and then we'll know. But it would help if you told us now, wouldn't it?"

"I really don't know, Captain. I swear I do not know Mr. O'Malley. I had no reason to kill him. Besides, you yourself said that I wouldn't have the strength to cut his throat as violently as it had been cut."

"As I told you before, Mrs. O'Connor, I don't see you as the murderer, but the accomplice and maybe the brains behind it?" I glanced up to see him watching me closely. "Shall I tell you what I think happened that night on Ellis Island? I'm not sure if this whole thing was planned on Irish soil. Maybe you had been following O'Malley for years, seeking vengeance, waiting to strike. Maybe it was just a lucky coincidence. You boarded the *Majestic* and couldn't believe your eyes when you recognized your fellow passenger, now calling himself O'Malley."

"In which case, why didn't I get rid of him on board? We were allowed up on deck for an hour most days. One well-placed shove and he'd be overboard. Why wait until we got to America, to a place that was heavily guarded, with people around us everywhere?"

"Maybe he was on his guard all the time on the ship. You never had a chance to find him alone and unprotected. I think you realized it would be your last chance to kill O'Malley before he got away onto a vast continent and vanished. It was a huge risk, but you had to take it. One of you slipped into the kitchens and stole a large meat cutting knife—one is missing, by the way. Then you kept watch outside the men's dormitory while your accomplice slipped inside and with one daring stroke killed O'Malley in his sleep. Can you tell me anything to make me change my story, Mrs. O'Connor?"

"Only that it's a pack of lies," I said. I was tired of being meek and mild. If I had to go, I'd go fighting. "And who is this accomplice supposed to be, I'd like to know? The guard I saw in the men's dormitory?"

Captain Sullivan nodded to the policeman who was standing outside the door. I looked up as footsteps came down the hall and then I gasped. Michael Larkin was being escorted in between two burly policemen, his face as white as the shirt he was wearing, his innocent eyes as large as saucers. He looked at me and recoiled in horror.

"Are you going to claim that you didn't know this young man, either, Mrs. O'Connor?"

"We met on the boat," I said. "Michael was very helpful with the children."

"And you never met in your hometown? Never once saw each other in church?"

"I moved away, years ago, to live with an aunt." The words just came out. Lie upon lie. I was surely destined for hell the way I was going.

"And you never saw this lady before you got on the boat?" He turned to Michael.

"No, sir, I never did."

"And you never worked out that your next of kin were involved in the same famous trial? You never sat on the same court benches, waiting for the verdict? Never stood outside Belfast Jail, waiting for the final, terrible moment together? I find that hard to believe."

"I was not present at any of the events you speak of." I stared back, challenging him.

He leaned back in his chair and looked at me. "I'm curious. You don't sound the same. I'm no expert on Irish dialects, but you don't speak in the same way. Why is that?"

"I told you, I lived with an aunt over on the west coast when I was young."

"One of you is going to crack in the end," Sullivan said. "I wouldn't like to guess which of you, at this stage. It's not very pleasant in the Tombs, is it, Larkin? Perhaps when Mrs. O'Connor has had a taste of what it's like down there, with the prostitutes and the pickpockets and the scum of New York City—when her little children are starting to cry for their mother . . ."

"Stop it," Michael shouted. "She had nothing to do with it. I swear she had nothing to do with it at all."

"And I'm sure Michael had nothing to do with it, either," I said. "He's not a violent type. He's a kind, gentle person. And where was the blood on his clothing, if he'd just slit a man's throat?"

The alarming eyes fastened on me. "But there was blood on his clothing, Mrs. O'Connor. There were spatters of blood on his jacket and his handkerchief was soaked in blood." He swiveled his chair to look at Michael. "I've got the right man, trust me. What better motive than vengeance for the death of a father? Isn't that what all the great tragedies are about? I'll take it to court and I'll make it stick. My only dilemma is you, Mrs. O'Connor. Were you in on this or not?"

"I told you, she wasn't," Michael shouted. "Now let her go."

Sullivan got to his feet. "The man says to let you go," he said. "You're a woman with small children, so I'm going to give you the benefit of the doubt, for now. But I've got more evidence coming in from Britain all the time. And I'll be watching you. So don't think you're off the hook, Mrs. O'Connor. You're not."

I got to my feet, too. "You're making a big mistake, Captain Sullivan. When you find out O'Malley's true name, and his background, then you'll know that neither of us had any reason to kill him."

"I hope, for your sakes, that will be true, Mrs. O'Connor."

"And in the meantime you've got a violent killer running around loose in New York City and you're doing nothing to find him."

As I swept down the hall with all the dignity I could muster, Michael reached out to grab my arm. "Kathleen, you will help me, won't you? You're the only person who believes in me. You're all I've got."

"I'll help you, Michael. I promise."

"You're the only one who can save us both. If they ship us back to Ireland, we'll hang."

The policemen pushed him past me and down another stairway. His voice echoed up the tiled stairwell long after he had vanished from my sight. I stumbled down the front stairs and out onto the street. I had just promised a man that I would do the impossible.

❧ Thirteen ❧

I came out into the late afternoon hubbub that was New York. People everywhere, all of them in a hurry, all wrapped and bundled like mummies against the snow that was still falling. I struck out in what I thought was the direction of the East River.

What have you done? I asked myself. How could I have volunteered to take responsibility for a man's life? How could I possibly prove he was innocent? The answer came immediately: by finding the one who is guilty. I would have to produce someone who had a better reason for wanting O'Malley dead—and I had no idea how I could do that. The English police might be able to find the details on O'Malley's background, but I never could. I'd just have to start with what I knew.

And what did I know? I knew that someone on Ellis Island killed O'Malley and that person was someone who spent the night on the island and had no method of leaving until the government boat early next morning. So that meant it was either an employee on night shift or a fellow immigrant.

The only fact that I knew for sure was that a guard had appeared from the men's dormitory and the only guard who resembled him claimed he had not been on duty that night. Surely that was an important point. Either the man was lying, or someone had been impersonating a guard to gain access to the men's dormitory. Maybe the guards on duty hung up their jackets and caps during the long night shift and it wasn't too hard to borrow one for a while.

So the first thing to look into would be the guard Boyle's alibi. Did he really leave the island on the last boat of the evening? Was he at home that night? I'd go down to the docks first thing tomorrow and question the boatman myself.

I felt charged with energy and excitement. I would do this, and when I had found the truth, I would take great delight in turning the facts over to that self-satisfied Daniel Sullivan!

Of course, there was one small point I had overlooked. I paused at the edge of a busy street, then jumped back as a cab clattered past me, spattering slushy mud in my direction. The point I had overlooked was whether or not Michael was truly innocent. He's a sweet, gentle boy, I reminded myself. Look how good he was with the children, how kind he was to me. And he planned that clever scheme with the money while we were heading for the island. Surely he wouldn't have been carefree enough to do that if his mind was full of murder. But something was nagging at the back of my own mind. It was that conversation we had as we waited to enter Ellis Island. "If he bothers you again, I'll kill him," Michael had said. "I could, you know. I'm not as innocent as I look."

I hurried across the busy street, dodging traffic and feeling the icy slush engulfing my feet. I had to trust him. He was trusting me. Not that I would have blamed him for killing O'Malley. Hadn't I wanted to kill the man myself? I just couldn't see young Michael Larkin sneaking to the kitchens, taking a butcher knife, and calmly slitting a man's throat. That would require a different personality altogether.

The wind off the East River was like a knife cutting through me. I leaned into it and ducked my face into my shawl. Another small point I had overlooked . . . Daniel Sullivan had obviously asked for background details on both Michael and myself. Any good policeman would do that, wouldn't he? And when the details came back about Kathleen O'Connor and her brother Liam then he might smell a rat. What if they sent a description, or worse still, a picture? If he found out I wasn't Kathleen O'Connor, then it would only be a matter of time before he found out who I really was. I had been so intent on saving Michael that I hadn't realized that I might still be in mortal danger myself.

It was a pity that Daniel Sullivan and I had to be enemies, I thought. In other circumstances I might have enjoyed flirting with him, instead of having to match wits with him to save my own skin.

The dismal buildings of Cherry Street loomed up out of the snow. I climbed the dark stairway without treading on any babies and knocked at the door on the fourth floor. Nuala opened it and stood staring at me, hands on hips.

"Well, would you look at that? Turning up like a bad penny! We never expected to see you again."

"See, I told you she hadn't gone away, Bridie," young Seamus said as the little girl ran to hug my knees. "She was fretting for you all day, Molly. She thought you'd gone away without saying good-bye."

"I'd never do that, Bridie darling." I picked her up and she snuggled to my cold cheek.

"Didn't Mrs. O'Keefe see her being shoved into a paddy wagon with her own two eyes?" Nuala demanded, looking for affirmation to Finbar who sat slouched at the table, a large mug of tea in his hands. "Shoved into a paddy wagon, that's what she said. I had a feeling from the very first time I set eyes on her. That one's no better than she should be. I said it to you last night, didn't I, Fin?"

I'm better than you, I wanted to say. But I really couldn't risk being thrown out into the snow on a night like this. I'd freeze before morning.

"If you really want to know," I said, "the police needed my help. A man was killed on Ellis Island and I was the only one who saw the man who might have done it."

"I told you, it was in the papers this morning," Finbar said, showing, what was for him, considerable enthusiasm. "A man called O'Malley. His throat was slit from ear to ear."

"Holy Angels protect us," Nuala said, crossing her vast bosom. "Do they not have watchmen on duty at that place anymore?"

I didn't think it wise to inform her that it might have been one of the watchmen.

"Why would anyone want to do a terrible thing like that?" Nuala demanded.

"To stop him from getting into America, I would have thought," Finbar muttered.

This was an angle that had never struck me before. Of course, it made sense. O'Malley had made it as far as Ellis Island. Somebody had to make sure he didn't go any farther. Why? I had no way of finding that out, until the police uncovered O'Malley's true identity. I didn't suppose that Captain Sullivan would be willing to share details with me. But it was worth suggesting to him. For one thing, it might show him that neither Michael nor I were his prime suspects. I had a lot of work to do tomorrow.

"And I suppose your grand helping out at the police station meant that you had no time at all to be finding a job for yourself?" Nuala demanded. "If you're going to be here any longer, you'll be expected to pay your share of the upkeep of this place."

"My share? There's no way I could possibly earn enough to—," I blurted out, in my usual way. I was about to say "to pay for the fleet of maids it would take to clean up this pigsty," but little Bridie was clinging to me as if I was a lifeline. I swallowed back the rest of the sentence at the last moment. "To repay you for taking me in," I finished lamely, hating myself.

Nuala smirked. I wasn't sure whether she was easily flattered or sensed my insincerity.

"Don't worry. I'll be out looking for a job first thing in the morning," I said.

"They're in need of fish gutters at the market," Nuala stated.

"It's not the most pleasant work in the world but it's money, and beggars can't be choosers."

I tried not to shudder as I imagined standing out in the cold, gutting raw fish until my hands were as raw as the fish themselves. "Thank you for the suggestion," I said. "But I do have an education. I'm hoping for something better."

"Hoping for something better!" Nuala sniffed. "Hark at Miss High and Mighty!" She turned to Fin. "Maybe she's thinking of applying to be mayor of the city? Or a professor at the university? I expect she'll move up to Fifth Avenue next to the Vanderbilts when she leaves us."

Finbar chuckled as he slurped his tea.

"Lord, get me out of this place in a hurry," I prayed.

I passed another uneasy night curled awkwardly in the armchair. Bridie insisted on sleeping beside me again, which made it even more cramped. I was wound up like a watch spring and sleep wouldn't come. So many things to plan. I had to find a job, but I also had to find enough facts to save Michael before the federal marshals insisted on having him shipped back to Ireland, or Daniel Sullivan sent him for trial here. The more I considered it, the surer I was that Michael didn't do it. I remembered his face that morning after the murder. He had looked white and shaken when he told me how he had discovered the body. And I still couldn't picture him slitting a throat. An ordinary person, not a trained assassin, would take a knife and plunge it desperately into a body, hoping that the stroke had killed. It took skill and know-how to slit a throat. Someone who was trained to kill then. That's who I was looking for.

I'd start with the boatman and see if he could back up Boyle's alibi, then I'd work from there. It shouldn't be too hard to trace down a fellow Irishman. It seemed everyone knew everyone else in this community. And if his alibi was true, what then?

As I lay there, listening to the snores coming from the next room—hard to tell if they were Nuala's, Finbar's, or Seamus's, although my bet was on Nuala—I went through the whole journey on the *Majestic*, trying to remember everything I could about

O'Malley—who had talked to him, laughed with him, or argued with him. He'd gotten into some heated arguments, but they were only after the men had been drinking and were soon forgotten. The only people with a real bone to pick were myself and Michael. Unless there was someone else who was following O'Malley, biding his time and waiting for the perfect moment to strike. When I saw Daniel Sullivan again, I'd ask to see the passenger list. It was possible that some other names were linked in some way to the case of the Plumbridge Nine. Of course, Daniel Sullivan would probably have checked that already, but it was worth a try.

I remembered O'Malley teasing Michael well enough. Michael had turned red and walked away. He hadn't said a word back. Did that mean he was keeping his anger bottled up inside? My thoughts moved on to my encounters with O'Malley. In a way I was lucky that the killer had chosen that method to dispatch O'Malley. If it had been poison or any more feminine method, I'd have been locked up in the Tombs by now for sure. Half the ship had seen me slap his face and tell him to stay away from me. I remembered how kind Michael had been, how he'd come up to me that first time with Seamus after the lad had gotten into a fight and . . . Wait! I sat up, making Bridie stir and moan in her sleep. That was when he got the blood on his jacket and his handkerchief! Why hadn't I thought of it before? The child's nose had been pouring blood. He had loaned the boy his handkerchief and then shoved it back in his pocket. Obviously he had forgotten to wash it out. I'd go to Daniel Sullivan first thing in the morning. Or maybe I'd do some snooping first and then go to him with an impressive bag full of information that would prove Michael (and me) innocent.

I lay back, closed my eyes, and soon fell into an uneasy asleep.

In the morning when I heard Nuala bustling around, clanking pots and pans, I got up right away. I accepted a cup of tea and a slice of bread, then washed at the sink on the landing, put on my clean blouse, and tidied my hair ready to go out. "I'm off to find a job, then," I said.

She nodded approvingly. "If it's the fish market you're heading for, ask for old Kilty. He's the one that will set you right."

It would be a cold day in hell before I'd be asking for old Kilty, I thought grimly. After making Seamus promise that he'd look after his little sister until I came back, I kissed Bridie and told her that I'd return before it got dark. Then I made my way cautiously down those stairs and out into the chill of morning. No snow today but what had fallen yesterday had turned to sheets of ice, making walking treacherous. I was beginning to get an idea of the layout of the town by now. Luckily the city seemed to be built on a thin strip of land, with water on both sides, so that if you walked long enough in any direction, you'd come to the shoreline. That was a comforting thought when it came to getting lost.

Of course at that time I was so naive that I didn't realize there were parts of the city where a woman just didn't go alone. As I cut inland and walked through the neighborhood back-streets, workers were hurrying to early-morning shifts. I saw a group of young girls, arm in arm, dancing down the street and into a square brick building. They were laughing and joking with each other—they obviously worked somewhere that didn't fill them with dread, I decided and ran to catch up with them.

"Excuse me." I tapped the nearest girl on the shoulder.

They turned around in surprise. They had darker skins than mine, impressive amounts of dark hair piled high under their hats and scarves and liquid brown eyes.

"Are you going to work?"

Most of them looked at me blankly, but one nodded. "Sí. Work."

"What kind of work do you do?"

She indicated the brick building ahead of us. "Shirt—we make shirt." Then she mimed working at a sewing machine. I had never used one, but I picked things up quickly and I might be able to bluff my way through for a while. And it would certainly beat gutting fish. "Do you think there are any jobs going? Could I come with you to meet your manager?"

She didn't quite understand this, but pointed up the stairs. I went up ahead of them. A large balding man with his shirtsleeves rolled up and a pencil stuck behind his ear was coming out of a glass cubicle at the top of the stairs. He looked at me in surprise.

"Hello," I said. "I was wondering if you needed any more workers? I'm hardworking and honest."

He was still staring at me in surprise. "You no Italiano," he said. "This Italiano place. *Se non parla Italiano . . . ,*" And he spread his hands expressively. "Italiano girl work 'ere," he finished as the girls arrived at the top of the stairs and walked past me, giving me curious stares.

"You're saying you only take Italian girls?"

He nodded. "Italiano girl make shirt 'ere."

"So what do the Irish make, then?" I demanded, feeling annoyed that I wasn't even going to be given a chance.

"Trouble," he countered.

He turned his back on me and walked away down the passage.

I walked around some more and tried several other factories and shops. It didn't take long to realize one thing. New York was not an American city. It was a collection of small Italian, Jewish, German, and God knows what else villages, all slapped down next to each other. And Germans only hired other Germans, Jews other Jews. So the sensible thing would be to find out what the Irish did and get them to hire me. I already knew about the fish market, but the idea was not appealing. I passed the vaudeville theater with its banner proclaiming, " 'When Irish Eyes Are Smiling'—straight from their phenomenal success in the Old Country." But the theater was shut tight at this hour of the morning and I couldn't think of anything I could do there, anyway. I neither sang, danced, nor told jokes well enough to do so in public. There were saloons and eating houses around the theater, but they, too, were closed tight at this hour. So I'd do my investigating first and look into a job there later.

I made my way, with more than one wrong turn and dead end and even a close call when a drunk lunged at me from a gutter, to the docks and the pier where we had landed from Ellis Island. I could see the island now, its redbrick towers floating improbably across the harbor, not too far from that other improbable sight, the Statue of Liberty. A group of longshoremen told me where the government launch departed from, along with some crude suggestions about how I could entertain myself and them until it arrived from the island. I told them what they could do with their suggestions, making them roar with laughter, and walked past, my nose in the air.

A little while later the launch pulled into the dock. It was almost empty, apart from a couple of young men in neat uniforms—inspectors probably. No use in asking them if they knew anything about an island guard. I waited around until the crew came ashore—a surly-looking captain and a young boy whose cheeks were red from the bitter wind.

They looked at me warily as I asked my question. Were they the crew on the night the man was murdered on the island?

"What do you mean, were we the crew?" the older man almost spat at me. "We're the only damned crew they've got. I'm the master of the ship."

"Wonderful." I gave what I hoped was an impressed smile, although the ship was nothing to shout about—a small cabin behind the wheelhouse and a strip of open deck all around. "Then you might remember which of the guards you ferried across the night before. I'm asking about the guard called Boyle—a big man, lots of whiskers. Did he ride across with you either the night before or the first boat next morning?"

"How in blazes do you think I know or care who rides across with me?" he snapped. "It's hard enough work piloting my ship past all the traffic in this harbor. I don't notice who gets on and who gets off."

"But you'd notice if someone wasn't wearing his uniform?"

He nodded. "The boy probably would. He's the one who casts off."

I looked at the boy. "Do you know the guard called Boyle? Would you remember whether he took the last boat from Ellis Island the night before the man was murdered?"

The boy stared at me blankly. "There's a lot of people works on the island, ma'am. They comes and they goes. And when it's cold weather like this, they makes straight for the cabin and stays there. So I couldn't rightly say—"

"And I couldn't rightly care," the old man finished for him. "We gets paid to sail this thing across to the island and back, not to remember who sails in it." He dug the boy in the side. "Come on, young'un. Let's go get some breakfast."

And they walked away from me without another word. So much for my first attempt at interrogation. My respect for Daniel Sullivan rose a little. He seemed to be able to get answers out of people. Of course, he could threaten them with the Tombs, which certainly helped. . . .

I wasn't sure what to do now. I hung around the dock area a while longer, wondering who else might have noticed whether Boyle did or did not take that last boat back to the city. All we knew was that he had signed out on the island. That didn't mean he had left with the other members of his shift. So that would be the next thing to find out. I'd have to be back here when the last boat of the day docked and ask his fellow guards if they remembered. Of course, if Boyle was among them, it would make it not only difficult but dangerous. I had been regarding this as an academic exercise and it suddenly struck me—if Boyle was the killer and he found me poking my nose where it wasn't wanted, I'd be in a lot of danger. So maybe I'd better start with a more subtle approach. I would need to find out where he lived. Daniel Sullivan would know, but I wasn't about to go asking him.

Just as I was chilled to the marrow and about to head away from the waterfront I noticed two men in Ellis Island watchman uniforms making for the moored government launch. I ran up to them.

"Excuse me, but you work on the island, don't you?"

"Yes, ma'am," one of them said. They were young, fresh-faced men and they were looking at me suspiciously as if they weren't sure of my motives.

"I wonder if you know a guard called Boyle. Big man, lots of whiskers."

"Bully Boyle? Yes, I know who he is," one of them said.

"Bully?"

"Just a nickname. I think his real name is Bernard, isn't it, Dan?"

Dan nodded.

"You wouldn't have been on the same shift as him the night before that murder on the island, would you?"

"What's this all about?" the other man asked.

"I'm trying to help a friend of mine. The police have him locked up in the Tombs at the moment. I just wondered if either of you took the same boat as Mr. Boyle the evening before the murder."

"I might have," the first, friendlier, one said. "I think we were on the same shift, but I really can't tell you whether he was on the boat with us. It's been so cold lately, we all make for the cabin and stay there. It's a tight squeeze so I really only noticed the men right next to me. Why are you interested in Mr. Boyle?"

"Because the police think that someone might have borrowed his uniform to commit the crime." This was an outright lie, but I didn't want Boyle to think he was suspected.

The men looked at each other, then the first one shook his head. "Sorry, but I really can't be of help. At the end of the shift I'm so tired, all I can think of is getting home and putting my feet up."

"Would either of you happen to know where Mr. Boyle lives? Maybe I could go and talk to him myself."

"I have a feeling he lives in Hell's Kitchen," one said, looking at the other for confirmation.

"Somewhere around that area," the other confirmed. "A lot of the Irish guys seem to live there."

"And where would I find Hell's Kitchen?" I wondered for a moment whether they were pulling my leg. Surely there wasn't really a place called that?

"You just follow West Street along the docks until you get to Twenty-third. It starts around there. Between the Hudson and Eighth Avenue. It's quite a way from here. I'd take the El if I were you."

"The L?"

"The elevated railway. See the steam coming up over there? That's the train stopping at the Hudson Street Station. And I wouldn't go there alone, miss. It's not the sort of neighborhood a young girl like yourself should be wandering around in."

I couldn't say I had no money for the elevated railway and nobody to call upon to go with me. Seamus would probably come with me if I asked him, but he was working from sunup to sundown. And I wasn't about to wait for Sunday. I'd have to take my chances now.

"Thank you for your concern, sir," I said. "I won't do anything foolish."

Then they went on their way down to the harbor, and I started up West Street, along the edge of the Hudson River.

❧ Fourteen ❧

I walked to the place they call Hell's Kitchen. It was a long way, but without money for any kind of fare, walking was my only option. The soles of my boots, none too new to start with, were starting to let in icy water and my toes felt bruised and numb. I'd have to find a job soon. I wouldn't get through the winter. I followed the waterfront, dodging around piles of merchandise, drays loading and unloading, and more than one improper suggestion.

It seemed to go on forever, block after endless block. I had never realized before how big a city could be. And all those tall buildings rising before me. And I could see that Michael had been right—wherever I looked, there were new skyscrapers being built—great steel frames towering into the sky like giant spiderwebs, sometimes with just the upper floors filled in, so that at first glance the masonry appeared to be hanging in midair, suspended by magic. At least it wasn't snowing, I told myself to keep my spirits up. Because, to tell you the truth, I was a little alarmed about what I might find in Hell's Kitchen. I had read Dickens. I knew all about the London of Fagin and that was what I was picturing now—cutthroats, pickpockets, and worse. After all, Ballykillin had been a sheltered life. A few men got drunk and beat their wives on Saturday night, but apart from that it was a peaceful kind of place. If you don't count Justin Hartley, that is.

* * *

There had been few signs of life during the last mile or so. Buildings had few windows on the ground level and many of those were closed tight with bars or shutters. No friendly, open storefronts as there were in the Lower East Side neighborhoods I had come from. When I finally saw an open saloon on a street corner, I plucked up my courage and went inside. It was dark and dingy, with a row of stools lined up at a high bar all along one side. It stank of stale beer and smoke, but at this hour it was, mercifully, almost empty.

"Hi, there, sweetie-pie," a man sitting at the bar called as he spotted me. "Come on in and let me buy you a drink, girlie." His words were slurred and he was eyeing me with blurry hope.

"Thank you but I'm not here to drink," I said. "I'm just asking for directions and nowhere else seems open around here." I looked around at the other men. "I'm looking for a district called Hell's Kitchen. Have you any idea how I get there?"

The men looked at each other, grinning.

"Hell's Kitchen you're wanting?" the barman asked. "And what would a young lady like yourself be wanting there?"

"I'm looking for a man who is a guard on Ellis Island. His name is Boyle. I'm told he lives in Hell's Kitchen."

"And what's this Mr. Boyle to you?" a man sitting at a table in the far corner asked aggressively "Did he do you wrong, sweetie?"

"I am most certainly not your sweetie," I replied, making them all grin even harder. "And I think it's highly unlikely that I'll ever be your sweetie. I need to speak to Mr. Boyle about a crime he might have witnessed on Ellis Island."

"A crime?" Their eyes were wary now. "Are you working with the police or something?"

"Don't tell me they have female 'tecs now!" The man in the corner said, nudging his companion.

"Yes, I'm helping the police," I said, trying to sound convincing. "So if you could just give me directions, I'll be on my way."

"You're in it, doll," the man at the bar said, grinning at the bartender.

The bartender nodded. "That's right, miss. This is the part of the city they call Hell's Kitchen. It used to be—well—wilder than it is now. Nowadays it's quite respectable, isn't it, boys?"

"Oh, sure. Very refined," the man at the table said. "Almost like being in church, isn't it, Paddy?"

They sniggered again. I wanted to get out of there in a hurry, but I had to keep on asking questions.

"So would it be too much to ask if any of you know Mr. Boyle?"

"Bully Boyle, you mean? Big man. Works as a watchman?" the barman asked. "Yes, he comes in here sometimes."

"Does he live around here?" I asked excitedly.

"Paddy would know. He's another of them damned Irish. Where does he live, Paddy?"

"Over on West Twenty-ninth, I think."

"Does Mr. Boyle come in here often?" Maybe he had been there on the night of the murder, which would have definitely established his alibi.

"Not often. He just pops in from time to time," the barman said, looking at the others for confirmation. "I reckon he pretty much does the rounds."

"He does when he's flush," Paddy said. "One saloon after another, free drinks all around when he's flush."

"So—has he been flush recently?"

"And why should we be telling you how much money he has?" Paddy demanded. "What's the betting she's his wife, come to check up on him?"

"Or she could be his fancy lady, wondering why he hasn't paid her a visit lately?" another of them suggested.

"Or his landlady, wondering why he hasn't paid the rent!"

"He's a good guy, salt of the earth, and I won't say anything against him," the man at the bar declared into his almost empty pint mug.

"I'm not connected to Mr. Boyle in any way, except that I was on Ellis Island when a friend of mine got mixed up in a crime," I said. "Mr. Boyle might be able to set things straight for us, that's all."

"Then you best go ask him yourself," Paddy said. "West Twenty-ninth. It's only a few blocks from here."

I was glad to be outside again in the cold, crisp air. I set off again in the direction of Boyle's street, but I was getting cold and tired and hungry by now. I wished I'd been able to slip away an extra slice of Nuala's bread from under her eagle eye. It was awful knowing that I had no money and no way of earning any. Those thoughts were going through my mind at the very moment that a man approached me.

"Pardon me, miss." I turned to look at him. He was smartly dressed, wearing a derby hat and white spats, and he was carrying a silver-tipped cane. "Are you looking for work by any chance?"

I stared at him, wondering if he was an angel in disguise, been sent to rescue me. "Yes, I am, actually. Do you know someone who's hiring?"

"Me," he said. "I'm looking for a smart, pretty young lady like yourself. In fact you'd do very nicely, I think. You're Irish, aren't you?"

"Yes, I am."

"Just arrived off the boat?"

"A couple of days ago."

"Living with your family here, are you?"

"No, sir. Living with acquaintances at the moment. As soon as I find a job, I'll be getting a place of my own."

"Perfect." He smiled, revealing an impressive gold tooth. "If you'd be so good as to follow me then."

He led me down one backstreet after another. I wondered what kind of work he was offering. None of these buildings looked big enough to be factories. At last he knocked on a dark green door. It was opened a few inches and he muttered something, looking back once at me, then beckoned me inside.

I was unprepared for what was inside the door—thick carpet, plush sofas, and chairs, a crystal chandelier hanging from a painted ceiling. These were the sort of furnishings they had at the Hartley's mansion, not behind a plain door in a poor part of the city.

"Holy Mother of God," I exclaimed. "Whose house is this?"

He smiled. "Nice, isn't it? Madame Angelique likes to live well. Wait there and I'll fetch her to meet you."

A maid? I wondered. Being a maid wouldn't be all bad. I might get room and board, and I'd certainly get enough to eat. I looked up as a door opened and a large woman came in. The first thing I noticed was that she was wearing makeup. Her lips were bright red and her cheeks had circles of rouge on them, too. She paused in the doorway and looked at me through a lorgnette. "Ah, yes. Nice cheekbones. A little too skinny for my taste, but she might do quite nicely."

She glided into the room. I noticed the tiny feet. It was amazing how her fat body disappeared into tiny silk slippers. I smiled at her shyly. "I'm a good worker," I said. "I'm used to hard work. I'm not sure what you're wanting, but I'm a fair cook, too. Would there be room and board with the job?"

Her small, piggy eyes sparkled with amusement. "Oh yes. Room and board would definitely be provided." She came very close to me, took my chin in her pudgy hand, and peered into my face. "You have just left your home, child? You are all alone here now?"

"I have some acquaintances, that's all."

"But you need a job and a place to stay? Then I think this might suit you very well." Her accent was slightly foreign— French, maybe?

"What sort of work would I be expected to do?"

"The work isn't hard," she said. "You would be instructed in your duties by some of my other girls."

"When could I start?" This was indeed a miracle. I couldn't

wait to see Nuala's face when I told her I was moving to a place that had real crystal chandeliers.

"Why not now?" She looked at the man who had brought me. "Then I should go and get my things right away."

"Your things?" She looked amused again. "After today I do not think you will be needing your things. I am sure that you own nothing worth retrieving when I am going to supply you with a whole new wardrobe of the finest fabrics." Another glance at the man, who wasn't looking entirely happy. "The dressmaker was coming this afternoon, anyway, wasn't she? We could have her measured up."

"If you say so. You really think she'll do?"

The hand grasped my chin again, squeezing it almost until it hurt. "She has the air of freshness, of innocence, don't you think? It could be most appealing."

"Yes, but—"

"No buts, Jimmy. I make the decisions around here, and don't you forget it. Do I or do I not have a feel for selecting girls?"

There was a strange undercurrent going on. I felt a jolt of uneasiness. "Excuse me, but exactly what are you hiring me for? Is it a maid you're wanting?"

"Oh no, my dear. Nothing so awful as a maid. Your duties will be much more pleasant. We run a little club here. Very exclusive. We only allow in the most cultured of gentlemen, I can assure you. You will sit and chat with the gentlemen, you will persuade them to buy you champagne—"

"But I don't drink champagne."

"—which you will not drink, of course. And then, you will entertain them for the evening."

"Entertain? But I'm afraid I neither sing nor dance."

The woman shot a glance at the man. "You will not be required to either sing or dance. Now please. No more questions. You are quite fatiguing me."

I might have been brought up in sheltered Ballykillin, but I wasn't completely stupid. I had heard of things like this, whispers about Colleen Duhig who ran away to Dublin and came to a bad end.

"Wait a minute," I said. "I think there may have been some mistake. I'm not . . . I mean, the kind of work I think you're offering . . ."

"But you already accepted the job, didn't she, Jimmy?"

I noticed that Jimmy had moved to stand in front of the door. For the first time I began to feel truly alarmed.

"Look, thank you for your kind offer, but I've changed my mind. I'll be going now." I took a bold step toward the door. Jimmy didn't move. His arms were folded. He looked amused, too.

"Let me tell you something about myself," I said, "The last man that tried to rape me, I killed him."

"Splendid. Then you'll want to lie low for a while. You see, it was fate brought you to us today." Madame whatever her name was moved around me, examining me from all angles. "Peach, I think, to highlight the hair. Red hair is so striking when done properly. Or green, do you think, Jimmy? Irish green for a sweet colleen?"

I wasn't sure what to do next. I looked around the room, wondering if there was something I could use as a weapon, but Jimmy looked like the sort of man who was not to be trifled with. If I broke down and cried, begged, told them I had planned to become a nun, would anything touch that woman's heart enough to let me go?

While we stood there, with time and reality suspended, there was a knock at the front door, a special knock, four short raps followed by one long. Jimmy opened it a sliver, not taking his eyes off me. A man squeezed past him into the room.

"Whaddya got there, Jimmy? New recruit?" he asked, then his eyes narrowed. "What the hell ya doin' with her? She was in the Harp Saloon half an hour ago, asking questions. She's working with the cops."

A hand flew out and struck me across the face. "You think you make a fool of me, girl?" the large woman demanded. "Who sent you here? That scum at the police department? If they think they can spy on Angelique and close us down, they can think again. They'll never get a thing on me."

My cheek was stinging and my heart hammering. "Wait a second, you don't understand," I shouted. "I'm not here spying on you. I am helping the police solve a murder that has nothing to do with any of you. I'm working with Detective Sullivan."

"Danny Boy Sullivan? The pretty boy himself?" Madame laughed. "He couldn't detect a pig in the middle of its sty."

I picked up on this straightaway. "You're right," I said. "He's useless, which is why I'm having to do the work. He's got my friend"—no, make it more tragic—"he's got my fiancé, the man I love, locked up in the Tombs. He's all for sending him back to Ireland to hang for a crime he didn't commit. I'm just trying to find out the truth, so that I can convince this Captain Sullivan to let my dear Michael go."

Madame turned to Jimmy. "And so you blunder into Hell's Kitchen alone, asking questions? You're right, Jimmy. She really is too naive." She looked back to me. "My dear, sweet little one. Your life may be counted in hours or minutes if you persist in poking your nose where you are not wanted. If you take my advice you will go back where you came from and stay there."

My heart leaped. She was going to let me go.

"But I have to help Michael," I said. "I was just trying to find one of the Ellis Island guards who might be able to help me. They said he lived around here."

"She was asking about Boyle," the newly arrived man said.

"Boyle? Do we know him?"

"Bully Boyle. He's been here before."

"Oh yes, Bully Boyle. The good tipper." She smiled, then looked hard at me. "This man Boyle—why do you seek him out?"

I felt as if I was walking on eggs. One false step and I was dead. "I thought he might have been on duty and unknowingly spotted the real killer." Careful not to implicate him. Careful not to seem too eager. "I know I'm grasping at straws, but the police are sure my Michael did it and they're not even looking any further."

"The police are idiots." Madame spat onto her plush carpet. She turned to Jimmy. "Take this girl to Boyle's. And you," she gripped my cheek, squeezing it none too gently, "you watch your step. You are not in your Irish village now." She snapped her fingers in demonstration. "Go on. Get out. And don't come back."

I didn't wait to be told twice.

❦ Fifteen ❧

I stood alone outside the tenement where Bernard "Bully" Boyle lived. Jimmy had escorted me by way of back alleys, then left me to my own devices when we reached this broader, safer-looking street. "It doesn't do for me to be seen here," he said, after his sharp eyes picked up a policeman patrolling the block. "But you keep your eyes open from now on. You're lucky that Angelique took a shine to you or you'd be dead meat by now."

I did consider myself lucky. I had tried to keep a cool head all the time I was in Angelique's parlor, but now I found that I was shaking. It was only just hitting me how close I had come to death or a fate worse than it. I was sorely tempted to give it all up and go back to the Lower East Side, where I felt safe. How could I possibly uncover any facts that the police hadn't already uncovered? And if Boyle was in some way involved in this murder, I was asking for trouble, showing up on his doorstep.

I pushed open the front door and started to climb the stairs. The stairway didn't smell a whole lot better than the one on Cherry Street. There was garbage piled in the first landing and something scurried as my footsteps approached. I had been told that Boyle lived on the second floor. How did that make sense? A man who seemed to be well known in the neighborhood, visited Angelique's parlor, who bought drinks for his friends in the local saloons yet lived in a place like this? Somehow he was earning more than an Ellis Island watchman's salary. I considered the nickname Bully. What had he done to earn it?

I had thought out what I was going to say before I knocked on the Boyle's front door. But when the door opened, and a sharp-faced woman demanded, "Yes? Whatda you want?" it all flew out of my head.

"Are you Mrs. Boyle?" I stammered.

"What if I am? Who wants to know?" She was scrawny and bony like a chicken and her chicken eyes darted around. She had her shawl pulled around her like armor.

"I'm sorry to trouble you. I wondered if your husband was home."

"So his fancy girls have taken to calling at the home now, have they?" she demanded. "One day that man's going to go too far and then you'll see. Just don't be surprised if you find his body floatin' in the Hudson River, that's all."

"I'm not a friend of Mr. Boyle's," I said. "I was calling because I need his help."

"Oh yes? If it's money you're after you can forget it."

"It's nothing like that." I laughed uneasily. "I'm trying to find out if he was on duty on Ellis Island the night that man was killed." I paused and waited for this to register. "You read about the murder on Ellis Island, didn't you? I'm sure I saw your husband on duty near the men's dormitory and—"

"You're trying to say that my man—"

"I just wondered if there was any chance he might have spotted the real killer." I finished hurriedly. "You see, the police think I had something to do with it, and I'm trying to prove my innocence."

"Boyle's on day shifts at the moment," she said flatly. "Gets home before seven, if he bothers to come home, that is."

"So you're sure he wasn't there three nights ago? He has been on day shift for a while, has he?"

"For the past year or so. But I wouldn't know where he was three nights ago. He didn't show up until morning."

"And when he did show up—" I tried to keep my voice calm—"how was he? Did he seem . . . uh . . . agitated, excited?"

"Drunk. Blind drunk as usual. How does he ever seem by the time he gets home here?"

I was dying to ask if she had noticed any blood on his uniform, but I wasn't about to do any more blundering, as Angelique had put it.

"So you've no idea where he spent that night?" I asked cautiously.

"Honey, I have no idea where he is most of the time. What do I care, drunken old fool. One day he'll cop it and the sooner the better as far as I'm concerned."

"Sorry to have troubled you," I said.

"Yeah." The door shut in my face leaving me in the cold and dark on the landing. I stood there for a while, listening. I wanted to hear voices inside the Boyle apartment. It occurred to me that maybe he was home all the time and maybe his wife's hostility was just an act to get rid of unwanted strangers. I waited but heard nothing, then I walked back down the stairs.

There was a saloon on the corner of the block, doing good business by this hour. I plucked up courage and went inside. Almost identical to the one before—dark, lots of mahogany woodwork, long bar, smell of stale beer and smoke. Everyone, it seemed, knew Bully Boyle. He stopped by almost every night— generous guy, bought drinks all around when he was flush. Was he flush often, I asked. It came and it went. He'd been in a couple of nights ago, though, acting like a Vanderbilt, treating everyone to whiskey chasers.

"And three nights ago," I asked. "Was he here then, can you remember?"

Puzzled frowns. Scratched heads. "I think he's been in every night this week, miss," the landlord said, "although I couldn't swear to it."

"Any idea what time he might have been here?"

"What's this about, then?" A man beside me demanded, shoving a beery face into mine. "Didn't he show up when he was supposed to for an assignation?"

"Oooh. *Assignation*. Big word." Ribald jokes rushed around the bar room. Someone tugged at my sleeve. "Don't let Ma Boyle cop you so close to his home, or you'll be in for it. She was in here once before, flailing her umbrella at some poor girl."

"Believe me, my taste in men doesn't include Mr. Boyle," I said haughtily. "I just needed his help about something that happened on Ellis Island. I won't trouble you any longer."

I tried to force my way out again. Hands grabbed at me. "Here, what's the hurry? Stay and have a drink. Come on, honey, don't be shy."

I had to give a couple of good kicks to the shins and stamp on a few toes before I made it past them. Enough. I had had enough of living dangerously for one day. Now I was going back to Daniel Sullivan. I didn't have much to go on, but I had found out that Boyle was a big spender and he hadn't been home all that night. Surely there ought to be something worth checking into in that.

"The young woman to see you again, Captain," a uniformed policeman announced with resignation in his voice. Daniel Sullivan looked up as I was ushered into his cubicle.

"Mrs. O'Connor. What a pleasant surprise. Is it too much to hope you've had a change of heart and you're here to tell us everything you know?"

"That's exactly why I'm here," I said, accepting the chair he offered me. "I've come up with several interesting facts you should be looking into."

"Such as?"

"For one, the blood on Michael's jacket and handkerchief. I remembered afterward where they came from. My boy got into a fight on board the ship. Michael brought him to me with a bloody nose. He had carried him away from the fight and lent him his handkerchief. So there you are."

"Nicely thought out. I credit you with great imagination."

"Imagination?" I demanded. "You think I'm making it up? Why would I bother to come here if I didn't think I'd be able to make you see that Michael Larkin did not kill O'Malley? That incident on the ship with the bloody nose—we were all in the big room together, you know. I could call you a dozen witnesses who saw it."

"Like mother, like son?" he asked, and for a second his eyes flashed amusement at me. "Both getting into very public fights?"

"That wasn't the main reason I came to you," I said, ignoring his goading. "I've been doing my own detective work and looking into Mr. Bernard "Bully" Boyle—the island guard I saw that night."

He held up his hand. "Mrs. O'Connor, please. No more suggestions that Boyle was responsible. I've got a sworn statement from two other watchmen that he was on their shift and took the launch back to New York with them."

"And I've talked to the boatman who said it was so cold that afternoon that everyone huddled together in the little cabin and it was impossible to see who was or wasn't there."

"But we've been through this before, Mrs. O'Connor. Why would an island watchman suddenly decide to attack one of the immigrants?"

"I'm not saying he did kill O'Malley. I just think that you should be looking into him a little more. He's a very interesting person, Captain Sullivan. He's known in all the saloons. He's generous. He shouts rounds of drinks when he's flush. He even visits prosperous houses of . . . ill repute."

"How the devil do you know that?"

"I checked it all out for myself." I gave him a triumphant smile, not admitting the precarious nature of my visit there. "And what's more," I finished before he could ask too many questions, "his own wife says that he didn't come home all that night."

"The man lives in Hell's Kitchen, doesn't he?" Sullivan demanded. "You went around there asking questions? You were taking a big risk, Mrs. O'Connor. These are not the kind of people you'd want to invite to take tea with you."

"I know that," I said, "but someone has to help Michael if you're not going to. And me—you still suspect that I had something to do with it, don't you? Somehow I have to clear both our names and I'll do what it takes."

"You're a gutsy woman, I'll say that for you," he said, "but have you ever thought what would happen to you if you were right and you did unearth the true killer? Someone who has slit a man's throat in a room full of other men is a reckless gambler. He's already taken at least one life. He'd make short work of you."

"I know," I said. He was looking at me with such concern that I felt tears stinging in my eyes. "But I have to keep trying, don't I—unless you'll do something to help us."

He reached out and placed his hand on mine. "Look, I'll do what I can," he said, then hastily withdrew his hand. "I'll have them run a thorough background check on Boyle if it will stop you from visiting Hell's Kitchen again. But I still don't see how he could have been involved. The men from the night shift would have noticed if he'd stayed on after the day shift left. And what could have been his motive? If it was robbery, he'd surely have been skillful enough to take what he wanted while the man slept. No, Mrs. O'Connor—the way O'Malley was killed, someone wanted to make sure he was silenced forever."

"Have you found out any more about O'Malley yet?" I asked. "Do the English police know who he really was?"

"Not much," he said. "He's been a wily bird. O'Malley is definitely not his real name but from what Scotland Yard can gather, it seemed he lived high on the hog and he might have been involved in some high-level blackmail in London, but beyond that . . ."

"So you don't know if he ever lived in Plumbridge, then?"

"Only you could tell us that, Mrs. O'Connor."

"And I swore that I never saw him before in my life. I still swear to that."

"He must have had a reason for carrying those newspaper cuttings, hidden in the lining of his trunk," Sullivan said. "They were the only items of any kind that tied him to a time or place."

"So the question is why was he coming to America," I said. "Was he fleeing to America because he was the unknown tenth man who betrayed the others? Was he coming to America to unmask the man who betrayed the others? Or was the motive nothing to do with the Plumbridge Nine at all? What if that wasn't even his trunk—he could have bought it secondhand, not even knowing what the lining contained."

"You certainly have the Irish gift of the gab, Mrs. O'Connor," he said. "Too bad you're a woman. You'd have made a good lawyer." He gave me an approving smile. I liked that. Let's face it, I liked him. I wanted him to like me.

"The cousin with whom we're staying made an interesting statement," I said. "He said the reason O'Malley was killed was simple. It was to stop him from coming ashore."

"Meaning what?"

"You say he was a known blackmailer in London," I went on. "Is it possible that he had been to America before and black-mailed here, too? If someone was on the lookout for him and found that he was coming back on the *Majestic*, that someone could have slipped to the island to wait for him and make sure he didn't get to New York."

"Not as easy as you make it sound, Mrs. O'Connor." He was still smiling. "The island is patrolled, day and night. There's just the one ferry slip."

"There would be a way, if someone was desperate enough."

"And how do you suggest we find this elusive someone, Mrs. O'Connor?"

I shrugged. "Until you find out more details of O'Malley's life, I can't help you there. But something might show up in your check on Boyle. Why is he flush from time to time? Where did he spend that night? Had he ever had a chance to meet O'Malley before?"

"All right, all right!" He held up his hands. "I promised you we'll look into it. Now if you don't mind, I'm a very busy man. Thank you for your suggestions, though."

"And what about Michael?" I asked. "Can't you let him go?"

"Not unless you want to come up with his bail money. It would be more than my job's worth to release him before I'd found a more likely suspect. The feds still want him handed over to them."

"If you send him back to Ireland, then there's no hope for him," I said. "You must know what it's like, coming from there yourself. It's hang first and ask questions afterward."

"Like the Plumbridge Nine?" He paused, giving me that searching look again. "Actually, I'm New York born and bred. Both my parents came over as children in the Great Famine. But I do get your point." He stood up. I took the hint and stood up, too. I wasn't about to let him tower over me. "I'm sorry, Mrs. O'Connor, I really am. I know you mean well and you've come up with some good suggestions. But they are just that—mere hypotheses, which means—"

"I know what hypotheses are, Captain. Strangely enough, I have read a book or two in my life. I won't be back until I can bring you concrete evidence."

As I walked out, I could feel his eyes boring into my back, all the way down the hall. I picked up my skirts, ready to go down the stairs.

"Kathleen," he called after me. "Please be careful."

❊ Sixteen ❊

This time my heart was racing but not from fear. I had heard the different tone in his voice. He had called me by what he thought was my first name. To know that someone in this new country cared about me was a strange and wonderful feeling. I was tempted to rush back into his office and tell him the truth. I wanted to hear him call me by my real name in that same gentle way. I had to remind myself very sternly that he was a policeman and even if I wasn't his number one suspect, then I was still on the list. If he found I was also a wanted felon in my own country, he would forget anything he might feel about me and do his job. All the same, it was a good feeling and I grinned to myself as I sped along the sidewalk with renewed energy.

Finbar opened the door to Nuala's apartment. He looked, as always, as if he had just awakened.

"Oh, hello there, my dear. Come in, come in." Gratefully I stepped into the warmth of the room. God forbid, but it was already beginning to feel like home. Well, it was the only place in the city where I could be warm and dry and expect something to eat, even if tongue-lashings came with it.

"You'd like a cup of tea, I expect," Finbar said. "There's a pot newly made."

I drank the tea gratefully and felt the warmth return to my

frozen limbs. Then I looked around. The place was awfully quiet. "Where is everybody?"

"The little ones went to meet their mother from work," he said. "They took your two with them. And Seamus isn't due back from the construction site for an hour or so. Eighteen hour days they're offering at the moment for men who want the work. And good pay, too. I'd do it if my health wasn't so poor. But right now a few hours at the saloon and helping here and there is all I can manage."

I nodded sympathetically. Poor health in anyone married to Nuala was understandable. There was bread on the table and I helped myself to a slice, spreading thick dripping on it. I could sense him watching me as I ate. He'd probably report to Nuala that I had been digging in to their food again, but I was so famished that I didn't care.

"I'm very glad that you came here," he said. "Very glad indeed. 'Twas a nice thing you did for Kathleen and the little ones. I'm sure we're all very grateful."

"I'm glad I could have been of help," I said. "And I really will make an effort to find a job tomorrow so that I don't overcrowd you any longer."

"There's no rush. No rush at all. In fact not everyone would be glad to see you go."

"No, I know Bridie still wants me around."

"And more than Bridie," he said. "A fresh, pretty young face like yours—'tis like a breath of Irish springtime."

"Don't tell me you kissed the Blarney stone in your youth," I said, laughing. Then the laugh faded. I saw the look in his eyes as he came toward me. Hungry, desperate almost.

"She won't be back for a while yet." He was breathing hard. "She won't let me touch her anymore, says three boys are enough to feed and she's not risking any more. But I'm a man, Miss Molly. I've got needs."

He grabbed at me. I dodged around the packing-case bench. "Oh no, Finbar. Your needs have nothing to do with me."

"But you've a lovely young body. I've been watching you,

the way you move. Lovely it is. I can't help it. I've just got to touch you."

He lunged at me again. "Steady on, Finbar." I was almost laughing. It was almost a comical scene. He was such a thin little person that I wasn't too afraid. "Just think what Nuala would do if she found you'd been bothering me."

"She wouldn't care. She'd be glad that I'd found someone so that I stopped pestering her."

"You're not going to be pestering me, either," I said. "What's wrong with men that they have to keep grabbing at us all the time? Get a hold on yourself, man. When I give myself to a fellow it will be my choice."

"You mean you're still untouched? Nuala said—"

"I don't care what Nuala said."

All the time we were talking we were still in a fencing match, dodging around the furniture, lunging and parrying. Suddenly he spun and, with a speed I would never have expected of him, thrust me against the wall. I could feel his beer-sodden breath in my face, his bony body pressing into mine.

"Let go of me this minute," I said, trying to struggle free. He was amazingly strong for one so skinny. Well, I suppose he had worked for years in construction until his accident. I should have remembered that. "Finbar, take your hands off me this instant or I'll scream the place down."

"Go ahead. Scream away. No one will care."

"Get away from me or you'll be very sorry." I was trying to maneuver my knee for an upward kick and cursed my stupid petticoats. Our clothing must surely have been designed by men to make sure we were hindered in matters of self-defense.

He was trying to kiss me, trying to grope at my bosoms. I was trying to make sure he did neither. Suddenly the door burst open and Nuala stood there, her vast shape blocking the doorway like an avenging angel.

"I knew it," she boomed. "I knew that girl was no better than she should be. I'm away five minutes and already she's leading my husband into temptation."

Finbar had dropped me like a hot iron at the sound of her voice. "I'm so sorry, my dear. I never meant any harm. I didn't know what I was doing."

"Of course, you didn't. She egged you on with her loose ways. I could tell it the moment I saw her."

"Just a minute," I interrupted, attempting to straighten my attire. "I did nothing to encourage his advances. I was fighting him off."

But Nuala was obviously not listening. She strode across the room, picked up my bundle, and thrust it at me. "Out of my house this instant, you hussy. Go on, get out with you and don't let me see you again you—you husband stealer, you home wrecker!"

"Don't worry, I'm going!" I yelled back. "I wouldn't stay in this hovel another second if you paid me. It's a wonder I haven't already caught the plague from this pigsty of a place. You should be locked up for trying to raise children in this filth. And I don't wonder your husband turns to other women for solace, either, when he's stuck with a bullying dragon like you for a wife!"

I grabbed my bundle and dodged as she swung a broomstick at me. "And that's about the only time that broom will be used in the next ten years!" I shouted up the stairs.

It was only as I opened the front door and was met by an icy blast of wind that I fully realized what had just happened. I was alone, in New York, at night, with no money and nowhere to go.

I thought of hanging around, waiting for Seamus to return from his work. At least maybe he could lend me enough money to find a room and something to eat. But my pride wouldn't let me. That was close to begging and Molly Murphy would never sink to that. I struck out into the darkness. There was a market in full swing on Hester Street—a Jewish market by the look of things. I lingered by the baked potato stand, enjoying the warmth of the brazier until the stall owner demanded, "Vell— you goin' to buy something or not?"

I moved among the crowd. The combined warmth of other people made it somehow less lonely. I had no idea where I was going next. Before long the market would end, the people would all go home, and I'd have to find somewhere to spend the night. The plush parlor at the brothel somehow didn't seem like such a bad proposition, after all. I made my way to the Bowery and visited each of the eating and drinking establishments in turn, asking if they needed any extra help in the kitchens. Nobody did. One of them made a suggestion that was not unlike Madame Angelique's. I moved on. Was there no employment in this town except for fish gutting and prostitution? If I could survive the night, I'd have to swallow my pride and go to the fish market in the morning, although probably that job was closed to me also, if Nuala was there to spread her poison.

I walked until I couldn't walk any more. One by one the gas lamps in the stores were extinguished. The last customers hurried home, wrapping scarves around their faces against the cold wind. The well heeled among them climbed into cabs and clattered away to unknown warm living rooms and roaring fires. At last I was the only person on the street. I tried a couple of churches, in the hope that they remained open all night, but they were firmly locked. I thought back to Ellis Island and it hovered in my memory as a haven of warmth and security. I was just trying a last church, for good luck, when I heard a voice behind me.

"It's no good trying to get in there, miss. They have to lock churches at night in a godforsaken city like this. You'd better come with me." It was a policeman, a chubby, middle-aged man with a round, innocent Irish face.

"I didn't mean any harm," I said as he took my arm and started to lead me away. "I wasn't trying to steal anything. I was just trying to find a place out of the wind."

"Just arrived, have you?"

"Yes, a couple of days ago. I thought I had somewhere to stay, but I wasn't wanted there."

We turned the corner and I recognized where he was taking

me. "Not the Tombs," I exclaimed. "Look, I haven't done anything. Captain Sullivan himself made sure I wasn't sent to the Tombs."

"Captain Sullivan?" he looked interested. "What's this about Captain Sullivan?"

"He questioned me about that murder on Ellis Island," I said. "But now he knows I had nothing to do with it, I'm sure. Ask him. He can tell you about me."

"Hold your horses, young woman," the policeman said, gripping my arm more firmly. "Nobody said anything about the Tombs and I'm sure I don't think you're New York's most wanted criminal. 'Tis the shelter next door where I'm taking you. The police shelter. You can spend the night there, if you've nowhere else to go. Stay out on the streets and you'll freeze, if you don't get your throat cut first."

We crossed the street and went down a flight of steps next to the jail entrance. There was an unwholesome smell of stale breath and unwashed bodies and the murmur of voices.

"Another one for ya, me darlin'," the policeman called and a large woman in a nurse's uniform and apron motioned for me to follow her. Well, it wasn't much better than a jail cell. There was a row of iron bunk beds, rather like the dormitory at Ellis Island, and a rough blanket on each. Heaven knows who had slept on it before me and what lurked in that mattress, but it was better than freezing. I lay down on the bed indicated by the fierce looking matron. The blanket did little to ward off the cold; I tried wrapping my shawl around me.

I jumped as I felt a tap on my shoulder. A woman who looked as if she had been one of the witches in Shakespeare's *Macbeth* was grinning at me—wild, unkempt hair, several missing teeth. "Here," she growled in a hoarse voice and thrust an old newspaper at me. "Go on," she insisted as I shrank away. "Take it. I've got enough. Wrap it around you under the blanket. It'll help keep the cold away."

"Oh . . . , thank you," I stammered.

"And if you've anything worth stealing in that bundle, I'd use it as a pillow if I were you," she muttered. "There's too many is light-fingered around here. They'd rob their old blind grand-mother for two cents."

I nodded my thanks, made a pillow of my belongings, and wrapped my feet and legs in the newspaper. Then I fell into a grateful sleep.

We were awakened by the matron at first light. There was a big pot of porridge on the table and mugs of hot coffee. I ate and drank as much as I could, then got ready to go out into the city. I decided to take the newspapers with me. I didn't know if they might come in useful again. As I straightened them out a headline caught my eye: MAYOR PAYS VISIT TO NEWLY BUILT ELLIS ISLAND. PARTY OF DIGNITARIES GET ISLAND TOUR. NEWLY ARRIVED IMMIGRANTS GET SURPRISE CONCERT. "His Honor, Mr. Van Wyck, mayor of New York, accompanied by aldermen and dignitaries of the city, made his first official visit to the newly opened Ellis Island facility. . . ."

I sat on my bunk, staring at the article. How could I have been so shortsighted? The immigrants and officials were not the only people on Ellis Island while I was there. The mayor's party had been there, too. Of course, they had paid an afternoon visit and then departed, so I had not thought to include them before. But what if one of them had spotted O'Malley sitting on a bench down below? What if one of them had something to hide and knew that O'Malley was a dangerous man who must not be al-lowed to enter New York City? I felt excitement surge through me. The paper was the *New York Herald* and the article had a byline. Reported by your correspondent, Jamie McPherson.

I got directions to the newspaper office and set off with a new spring in my step. I felt sure I was onto something that would finally make Daniel Sullivan sit up and take notice. Some-thing that might free Michael. I asked the matron if I could leave my bundle with her for an hour or so and she reluctantly agreed. The many blocks of Broadway seemed to flash by without effort. I got to Herald Square without incident and had to wait around until the newspaper staff arrived for the day shift. I had to convince the young man at the front desk that I was there on police business before I was sent up the stairs to a big room full of clattering typewriting machines. Jamie McPherson was a young Scot with an accent so broad I wondered how he ever managed to ask questions that New Yorkers could understand.

"Ach yes, I was there with the mayor and his party," he said. "What did you want to know?"

"The names of that party," I said.

"I didnae bother with them all, but I've got the most important ones written down here somewhere." He fished in a desk drawer for a notebook. "Let me see. Ah—here we are. Beside the mayor, there were two aldermen, McCormack and Dailey, and they had several Tammany men with them, too—you could get all the names from Tammany Hall if you wanted." He looked up, puzzled. "What was this about again?"

I couldn't let him know the truth. He was a newspaperman, after all, and this would be headline news. "I can't tell you at the moment," I said, "but if it works out the way I think it will, it could be big news and I promise I'll give you the scoop."

"Sounds suitably mysterious," he said with a grin. "You could get the names of the complete party from the mayor's office, I'm sure. I'd say it was a good representation of who's who in the city. Or a who's who at Tammany Hall, which amounts to the same thing."

"Thank you." I wasn't sure what to ask next. He was a young reporter who obviously thought that covering the mayor's visit was a boring assignment. I wished I could come up with a tidbit of information that would pique his interest, but lack of food and sleep had dulled my wits, and the terrible clatter of those typewriting machines made it impossible to think, anyway. How they managed to write stories in that room, I'll never know.

"So how did they get to the island?" I asked. "Did they come on a ferry?"

"Ach no. They traveled over in the government launch."

The government launch! If I'd only known I could have questioned the bad-tempered old captain. Now I'd have to seek him out again. "So you must have crossed with them."

"That's right. There were several of us pressmen."

"I suppose you couldn't tell if the whole party came back on the government launch. Nobody stayed behind, did they?"

"I didnae count them. It was so damnty cold, I was just waiting to get back to the city. They were all crowded into the cabin, swilling whisky, and they didnae offer any to us poor lads, either. We were left to freeze on the deck."

"Someone was taking photographs," I said. "They took a picture of my little girl with the mayor."

"Ach, so that's what's behind all this." He looked up with a knowing smile. "You want a copy of the photo of your wee bairn with the mayor!"

I smiled coyly and didn't deny it. It made an excellent excuse. I wish I'd thought of it first.

"Do you know who the photographers were? Were they with your newspaper, too?"

"Ach nae. They're all freelancers. They show up at events like this, hoping to sell their pictures to the weekly pictorials, or maybe to the mayor himself—he's vain enough to want to stick pictures of himself all over the walls."

"Would you happen to know the names of these photographers, and where I might find them?"

He shrugged and glanced down at his typewriting machine, wanting to get back to work. "I'm trying to remember who was there that day. I didnae pay particular attention. I know Simon Levy was one of them. Has a studio on the Lower East Side, in the Jewish quarter."

"That was the one who took the picture of Bridie," I said. "An old man with a beard. Thank you. I'll go and look for him then. You've been very helpful."

"Good luck ta yae." He gave me a half wave and the typewriting machine was clattering again the moment I turned my back.

❧ Seventeen ❧

The long trek back to the Lower East Side seemed to take forever. I had lost that initial burst of energy that drove me up Broadway with wings on my feet. As I walked back I noticed the big stores with elegantly decorated windows full of mannequins and flowers. One day, I told myself, I'd be that lady who climbed out of her carriage and went to shop there. Although on a fish gutter's pay, it was going to take quite a while.

The thought of fish gutting brought me up with a jolt. Poor little Bridie—what had they told her when I hadn't come home last night? I hated the thought of leaving the children in that place, with that terrible aunt, but, being homeless and penniless, there wasn't much I could do about it at the moment. Besides, I reminded myself, they weren't my children. I had delivered them to their father, which was what I had promised to do. All the same, the picture of those little faces haunted me all the way down Broadway. One day, I told myself again. Whatever happened I wasn't going to forget them.

My feet were dragging and the sole of my left boot was starting to flap as I came into the now familiar Lower East Side neighborhoods. The market on Hester Street was in full swing again. I looked longingly at the braided breads, the big pots of soup, the stall where a man was frying what looked like little pancakes. How was I going to get money to buy food for myself? How was I going to find a job if I spent my days chasing after photographers? I should go to Daniel Sullivan and let him follow up on my lead. That's what I should do. Then I could get on with my life.

But what if he didn't bother to follow up? My greatest fear was that I'd show up at his office one day only to find that Michael had been shipped off to Ireland. Of course, it was also possible that I could find myself dragged back and shipped home with him, if overzealous feds took over the case.

I stopped to ask a couple of street merchants if they knew Simon Levy. They did, and told me where I'd find his studio. I found it without difficulty, but it was shut with the blinds down. Out on Assignment. Back Later, the sign on the door said, in English and a couple of other languages I couldn't read. At least I knew where it was.

Hunger was becoming a problem again. It was lunchtime and the effects of this morning's porridge were wearing off. This is stupid, I thought. I'll be no use to Michael or myself if I die of hunger. I must find a job today. Which meant I should hand over my information to Daniel Sullivan and let him to his work. It made more sense, didn't it? He could go to the mayor's office and ask for an official list of everyone present that day. He could ask to see photos and nobody could deny him.

Reluctantly I made my way back to the police station. Captain Sullivan was out on a case, I was told, but I could leave him a note. I took the paper and pen offered and scribbled my hunch about the mayor's party and the name of the photographer who might have taken a group shot. I left it on Daniel's desk, lingered as long as I dared, then went down the stairs feeling dejected. I was unprepared for the disappointment I felt at not seeing him again.

As I passed city hall, I paused at the great hole in the ground they were digging to put in an underground train system. Steam and dust were belching out and it looked like the very gateway to hell itself. I stood there, warming my hands at a steam vent, until I found that the steam was also making me wet. As I went to move on, a whistle sounded. Men started to emerge from the depths, wiping the dust and grime from sweat-covered faces. I started to walk away, then heard a voice yelling, "Molly! Molly, wait!"

Seamus O'Connor clambered out of the diggings and ran to catch up with me. "Molly, I've been worried out of my mind about you," he said. "I got home to find you gone and Nuala wouldn't say where you were."

"That's because she drove me out with the broomstick," I said.

"She was ranting on about catching you with Finbar."

"She caught me fighting off Finbar, if you want the truth. I did nothing to encourage him. Believe me, when I want to encourage a man, he won't be a poor, sorry specimen like Finbar." And a picture of Daniel Sullivan flashed, unbidden, into my head.

Seamus touched my arm. "I'm so sorry, Molly. After all that you did for us, too. Please come back. I'll make it all right with Nuala, I promise."

"Oh no thank you, Seamus. Not in a million years would I set foot inside that place again."

"But the children—they need you."

"I know. I feel bad about walking out on Bridie, but they've got to get used to living without me," I said. "I'm not a relative, Seamus."

"I'll find a place of our own, if you'll say you'll come and stay with us."

I remembered how easily Finbar had succumbed to temptation. And it appeared that all men had the same weakness. I wasn't going to give Seamus any ideas, that was for sure, however much I cared about those children. "That wouldn't be right. Me an unmarried woman and you a married man. I've a reputation to consider."

He nodded. "You're right. It was wrong of me to ask you."

"But get your own place as quickly as possible," I said. "It's not healthy for the children in that flea pit." He was looking dejected. I reached out and touched his arm. "Look, I'll stop by and help you with them as much as I can—once I've found myself a job and a place to stay. Tell Bridie I haven't forgotten her, will you?"

"You've not found a place to stay yet? Where did you spend last night?"

"In the police shelter," I said. "I've no money until I find work." It just spilled out. I bit my tongue but it was too late.

Seamus fished into his overall pocket. "No money? Here— let me see what I have."

"I can't take money from you. Don't worry. I'll be fine."

"But I want to help. You helped us. You took care of my children. Here." He held out a handful of coins. "There must be a couple of dollars here. Take it."

"I'm not taking charity."

"It's not charity. You earned it. Go on. Take it."

He grabbed my hand and thrust the coins into it, closing my cold fingers around them. "And let me know when you find a place to stay, so that we can keep in touch. The children will miss you. Bridie cried herself to sleep last night when you didn't come home."

"I'll keep in touch," I said. "I promise."

He looked around. "I better go. If I don't get a meat pie down me in the next ten minutes, I'll have to work all afternoon with no food. Take care of yourself."

"You too, Seamus."

He hurried off and I stood clutching that handful of coins. I went and sat on the steps of city hall, under the watchful eye of two policemen, and counted them: almost two dollars. The first thing I did was to go to the nearest eating house and squander five cents on a bowl of soup and a roll. The proprietress was a large, jolly-looking woman so I asked her advice about finding a room. She looked horrified.

"A young woman on your own? You're surely not thinking of renting a room? Mercy me."

"Why not?"

"On your own with no man to take care of you? If you'll take my advice, my dear, you'll get yourself settled somewhere respectable. I hear there's a very nice hostel for young women down close to Battery Park. It's run by the ladies of the Bible Society and they don't stand any nonsense."

I wasn't sure whether the ladies of the Bible Society would welcome a Catholic like myself and was even less sure that I wanted to be in a place where they didn't stand any nonsense, but it would do for now. I retrieved my bundle and started to walk down Broadway. It was all hustle and bustle and any other time I would have enjoyed watching the fine carriages and the trams going up and down. But now my feet hurt and I just wanted to get settled somewhere where I could relax for a while.

There was something happening across the street. A crowd was gathering on the sidewalk and there were several fancy carriages and automobiles lined up outside a building I now saw was a pretty little church, tucked in between the massive squares of brick and stone. Being curious by nature, I went over to look. A wedding party had just come out and was standing on the steps. The bride was wearing the most stunning white hat, trimmed with egret plumes and a cunning little veil. The groom was handsome in military uniform. The rest of the party was composed of two adorable little bridesmaids in white fur capes, elegant ladies, draped in furs and distinguished-looking gentlemen in top hats, with impressive gold chains dangling from their waistcoats.

I stood daydreaming for a moment, putting myself in the place of that bride. Strangely enough, the groom bore a remarkable resemblance to Daniel Sullivan.

"I heard someone say, "It's an honor, Mrs. Vanderbilt," and someone else call out, "Hold still, please, if you would, ladies and gentlemen." There was a flash and the smell of sulphur. Then I noticed the photographer. I ran up to him. "Mr. Levy?"

He didn't look up. "Just a minute, my dear. Stand back, please." There was a click and a flash. The air filled with acrid smoke. As it cleared, he looked up, smiling with satisfaction. "That will be a very good shot. Got the whole group of them together. I've no doubt the *Weekly Illustrated* will pay good money for that one. Now, what was it you wanted?"

"You were taking photographs on Ellis Island the other day."

His eyes twinkled. "I know you. You had the adorable little girl who wouldn't smile for the mayor." He had a slightly foreign accent, but his English sounded cultured. He looked cultured, too—dark suit, high white collar, polished shoes. I guessed that this was a man who had been somebody back in his own country.

"Right. That was me. You have a good memory."

"Listen, my dear. In my line of work you have to have a memory like a filing cabinet. So what can I do for you? Wait, don't tell me. I know. You'd like one of the photos I took as a souvenir. Am I right?"

"I'd love to see it," I said. "I can't afford to buy photographs at the moment. But I wondered if you also took a group shot of the mayor's party?"

"Yes, I did. And he hasn't paid me for it yet, either."

"Do you think I could see that one, too? It's possible that a distant cousin of mine is now working for the mayor. I'm sure I recognized him." I winced as the lie came out. Lying was becoming so easy for me. If I was hit by one of those electric trams before I got to confession, it would be straight to hell, for sure.

"Come to my studio, by all means. I should be back there by the time it gets dark. Do you know where to find me?"

"I went there earlier today. I'll come back around five, then, shall I?"

He reached out, took my hand, made as if to bring it to his lips, then thought better and patted it. "I shall look forward to it, my dear."

I found the women's hostel soon after. It was in an austere brownstone building positioned on a corner to catch the wind from the harbor in two directions. The lady in reception looked me up and down for a good minute before deciding that they might have a bed for me. "You don't have employment yet?" she demanded.

"I only arrived this week. It's impossible to look for a job before I have a place to stay," I said. "I stayed a couple of nights with friends but it was too crowded and I had nowhere to wash properly."

She nodded as if this was the right answer. "Very well. We charge a dollar a week, which includes your breakfast and evening meal. You are expected to be present for our communal evening meal at six o'clock sharp. You are expected to attend morning prayers before breakfast—six thirty sharp, with breakfast at seven. You are not permitted to loaf around the hostel during the day. You are expected to be out looking for work. The hostel is locked for the night at nine o'clock. No gentlemen callers are allowed. Is this all clear?"

"Yes, ma'am." I nodded in what I considered a suitably humble way.

"Very well. I'll have you shown to your room. I hope you'll be happy with us, Miss Murphy."

It was wonderful to be in a place with clean sheets, a bathroom with hot water, and a mirror to fix my hair, even though there were texts all over the walls to remind me that vanity was a sin. I straightened my attire, washed out some smalls, and felt almost human by the time I went out again. I tried several more establishments, looking for work, but with no success. Reluctantly I decided to go to the fish market in the morning.

On the way to see Mr. Levy I came up with a crazy idea. I would ask him if he needed an assistant. I was quick. I learned fast and I liked him. I could also learn how to take pictures and maybe I could set up my own photography business some day. It was dark and cold and starting to rain by the time I walked back to Hester Street. The distance I had walked in the past few days must be equal to the whole of Ireland, from south to north.

There was no light shining through the blinds of Mr. Levy's establishment, but the door was slightly ajar. I reasoned he was probably working in a back room somewhere, developing those pictures he had taken today. I pushed the door open and stepped inside.

"Mr. Levy? Are you here? It's Molly Murphy, come about the picture you took?"

There was a strong chemical smell about the place. I had only taken a couple of steps when my foot struck something. I bent to pick it up. It was a heavy square metal object and it took me a moment to realize it was a camera.

Something was wrong. Mr. Levy wouldn't leave his precious camera on the floor to be trodden on. I opened the door wide, to let in as much light as possible from the gas lamp outside. It shone on a place in utter disarray. Papers were strewn everywhere. Bottles lay smashed with their contents all over everything. And there was a dark shape sticking out from behind the counter. I stepped gingerly over the broken glass and debris and saw what it was. It was a man's leg.

"Mr. Levy!" I bent down to him. "Are you all right?"

As soon as I tried to move him I knew that he wasn't. Where I expected to feel the fabric of his coat, my hands touched something sticky. I recoiled in horror.

At that moment I heard footsteps and someone came in through the front door. I cowered behind the counter, holding in breath. I didn't know whether to call out for help or stay hidden. A torch was turned on and its beam strafed the signs of chaos before settling on me. The owner of the torch came closer.

"What has been going on here?" asked Daniel Sullivan's voice.

❦ Eighteen ❦

Daniel—Captain Sullivan," I called. "Thank heavens it's you. How did you know?"

"I was checking out the list of photographers you left for me," he said. "What's happened?"

"Over here, behind the counter. It's Mr. Levy."

Glass crunched under his feet as he came toward me. His flashlight was blinding me and I put up my hand to shield my eyes.

He knelt down beside me.

"He's dead, I think," I said. "I can't move him and . . ."

He was shining the flashlight on the hand I was holding over my face. As I lowered it I saw that it was covered in what had to be blood.

"Are you all right?" he asked sharply.

"Me? Yes, I'm fine. I just got here. The door was open and he didn't answer."

Daniel got to his feet again. "In here Briggs, O'Hallaran," he snapped. "Briggs, you get to HQ as quick as you can. Tell Sergeant O'Neil there's been what looks like foul play and have him bring a backup team here. You, O'Hallaran, see if you can get us some light going, then keep the crowd away."

I got to my feet, too, feeling cold and shaky. I was about to hug my arms to myself when I remembered the blood on my hands. There was a hiss and a pop and the gas bracket on the wall glowed, throwing grotesque shadows over the chaos and illuminating the body enough for me to see the eyes open in horrified surprise and the big dark stain covering the front of his jacket.

"You're sure it's too late? He's already dead, is he?"

Daniel was looking at me, hard. "He's dead, all right. Whoever did it made damned sure of that."

"Poor man," I said. "He was so nice."

He had taken out a notebook. "So do you mind telling me exactly what you were doing here, alone with the body, in the dark?"

"I met him this afternoon. He invited me to his studio. He said he'd be back as soon as it got dark." The words were spilling out in a torrent. "The door wasn't shut properly but there was no light on. I thought he might be in the back somewhere, working on his pictures. I called out and then I kicked something." I stepped gingerly across the debris and pointed to it. "It was his camera. Then I knew that something had to be wrong. His camera was his livelihood. He'd never leave it on the floor."

"Why didn't you light the gas?"

"I couldn't find it. I—," I stammered. "I'm not used to these new-fangled inventions yet. We only have oil lamps and candles at home."

"So you went forward in the dark?"

"I opened the front door as wide as it would go so that some light came in. That's when I saw that the place was ransacked. And then I saw a leg sticking out. I came around the counter and I found him."

"You kept going into the room in the dark, even after you saw the man's leg?" He sounded incredulous. "Either you are very brave or very stupid, Mrs. O'Connor. I can't decide which. Did it not occur to you that you might have walked in on the killer and he might still be here, hiding in the shadows?"

"I'm stupid, I suppose. It never crossed my mind. I only wanted to get to Mr. Levy and see if I could help. I thought for a moment he might have been taken ill and knocked things onto the floor when he fell."

Daniel Sullivan was staring hard at me. "It's amazing how people manage to get murdered whenever you're around and yet you have nothing to do with it."

"Wait a minute," I said, anger now competing with fear. "You don't mean to tell me you think I might have had something to do with this poor man's death?"

"I wish I had an instrument to see into your head," he said. "I don't want to think that you're lying to me, but you have to admit it doesn't look good for you. I catch you here with the man's blood all over you, in the dark."

"I've just told you what I was doing here," I said. "And why on earth would I have wanted him dead? He was the one person I wanted to see, the one man who could possibly have freed Michael. He said he had a group shot of the mayor's party. He was going to show it to me."

"And how exactly did you think this group shot would help you?"

"It might have showed me the real killer, of course," I retorted.

"The real killer?"

"Supposing someone in the mayor's party saw O'Malley and knew that he must not be allowed to come ashore. That person took a huge risk, did not ride back with the others, borrowed a guard's jacket and cap, sneaked in, and killed him during the night. And if nothing else proves it, then this surely does." I pointed down at Mr. Levy's body. "Somebody must have found out we were onto this. He hadn't thought about photographs before. Now he had to make sure that Mr. Levy's photographs were wrecked before I got here."

Daniel was still looking hard at me. "In which case you could be in a lot of danger yourself. You're looking at the actions of a very violent person, Mrs. O'Connor. Do you actually enjoy courting death? What can I say to make you realize that you have to stay out of police business?"

"I'm trying to help Michael," I said. "I'm trying to make you see the truth that you're too pigheaded to see for yourself."

"And in the process you've just wrecked a perfectly good crime scene with your blundering. You've probably trampled and contaminated any evidence in this room."

"No more than you have!" I said. "You did your own share of blundering. I heard you."

He looked at me for a long moment, then shook his head. "What am I going to do with you? You realize, of course, that I'm going to have to take you down to headquarters to get a statement. What can your family think about you being out playing detective all the time—it's not wholesome for a married woman."

I was just realizing something. If I didn't turn up for communal supper and prayers at the Bible hostel, I'd be thrown out come morning. And I certainly didn't want to waste more precious time looking for a place to stay. So I did what every self-respecting woman does in such situations—I fainted.

Looking back on it, I don't think the faint was all put on. The delayed shock and lack of good food suddenly overtook me. I think I really did lose consciousness. The next thing I knew I was sitting up on a chair with my head between my knees and a strong hand on the back of my neck. My first reaction was that the killer had got me, and I struggled to sit up.

"Just relax, Mrs. O'Connor. You'll be fine." The voice was Daniel Sullivan's. Which meant that the warm hand on my neck must also belong to him. He raised me to a sitting position. "All right now?"

I nodded. "I think so."

"You had a nasty shock." He was looking at me with the same tenderness I glimpsed that time in the police station hallway. "Look, you can't go on acting like this. I forbid you to do any more investigating without telling me first. Is that clear? If I have to have you locked up for your own good, I will. Now I'm going to have one of my men take you home and give your husband a good talking to. He should know that his wife is out wandering round a strange new city at all hours, taking terrible risks. Maybe he's the one who can get you to start acting sensibly and make you stay home with the little ones, where you belong."

Now it was all going to come out. Nuala would spill the beans if nobody else did. They already had my address. I tried to come up with another glib lie, but none would come. To tell the truth, all I felt like doing was going somewhere warm and safe and curling into a little ball.

"All right," I said. "I've had enough of danger, believe me. And I haven't gone looking for it, whatever you may think. It's just sort of followed me. I'll go home and stay quiet. You have enough to go on now, anyway—find out who was in the mayor's party. Find out who didn't return with them. Match the fingerprints to something in this room."

"You're telling me my job again," he said, but he was grinning. "Although I rather fear that we're too late. Any useful evidence has been destroyed. If there was a group shot, the killer has done away with it."

More policeman had arrived on the scene. A crowd had assembled outside the door and there were angry murmurs. "I saw her the other day," I heard one of them saying to the arriving police. "She was hanging around the market on Hester Street."

"She was asking questions about poor Mr. Levy earlier today."

Daniel gave me an amused glance. "You're lucky I'm here, aren't you? You're the prime suspect in their eyes. You'd be facing a lynch mob." He took my arm and helped me to my feet. "Come on. I'll have my constable take you home now. Cherry Street, isn't it?"

"Look, Captain Sullivan," I took a deep breath. "I'm not living there. I—I moved out. I'm living in the ladies' hostel down by the Battery Park."

He moved closer to me, so that the other policemen couldn't overhear. "What happened?"

"Uh—things weren't going too well, between me and my husband."

He nodded with understanding. "It's not always easy after

such a long separation, is it? People change over the years. I've seen it happen before."

I managed a small, suffering smile, thinking it better for once to be silent.

"And what about the children? Are they at the hostel with you?"

"They're staying for now with his cousin's family. It's better for them to be with a family while I find a place and work." These lies were becoming positively stupid now. Stop before it's too late, Molly.

"And you? What will you do now?"

"Find a job. Get on with my life. See how things turn out."

"On your own? Get on with life on your own?"

He sounded shocked, and I realized that it wasn't going to be easy to free myself of my mythical husband. A woman who left her husband and children would be frowned upon and considered loose. I needed to change the story.

"Very well, if you must know the whole story. I've discovered my husband has taken up with another woman. So the sooner I find a decent situation for myself and the children, the better."

He nodded. He was trying to look sympathetic and sad, but he wanted to grin. I can't tell you how much that lifted my spirits.

"I'd take you home myself," he said, "but I have work to do here."

"That's all right. I'll be sensible and go straight home, I promise."

He smiled. "I'm going to make sure of that. Take Mrs. O'Connor home, Constable. She's staying with the good ladies of the Bible Society. She surely can't come to any harm there."

I turned back to look as he ushered me out of the door. He was staring after me.

The constable ushered me through the crowd, who muttered and glared at me. Someone spat at my feet.

"I had nothing to do with it," I started to say, but the constable grabbed my arm and shoved me through the crowd. "Come along, ma'am. Better not say anything right now when they're riled."

He took me through backstreets and alleys until I saw the twinkle of bright lights ahead and realized where we were. "Oh, this is the Bowery, isn't it? Look, you don't have to come all the way with me. I'll be just fine from here." I was imagining the look on the receptionist woman's face if I arrived with a policeman holding my arm. She'd probably take me for drunk and disorderly.

"The captain told me to take you home," the constable insisted.

"It's only just down this street, isn't it?" I said. "And what could happen to me with all these people around?"

He was still looking worried. "Look, Constable," I said. "I'm staying with the Bible Society ladies. I'm afraid they'd get the wrong impression if a policeman brought me home my first night."

He smiled. "Oh, I see what you're getting at. All right then. I don't suppose much can happen to you between here and there. If you get worried, you'll find plenty of our men patrolling this street. Lots of Irish saloons and Italian taverns, and when they meet . . ." He tipped his hand to his helmet. "I'll say good night then, ma'am."

"Thank you, Constable. I'm most grateful."

He swung around to the right and I turned left, into the Bowery. It was the height of evening traffic. Customers were pouring out of cabs and into eating houses and theaters. Shoppers were coming out of stores with laden baskets. All in all a merry scene. I hurried through the crowd, admiring, every now and then, a particularly fine bonnet. Maybe I'd have an ostrich feather like that on my hat some day. . . .

They say the Celts are born with a sixth sense. I'd never given much thought to it until now, but gradually I was aware that I had become tense and vigilant. I stopped and turned around. The merry throng swept by me. I turned back and walked on. I could feel the back of my neck prickling. I don't know how I knew, but I did. My sixth sense was telling me that I was being followed.

I swung around again, but I saw nothing to alarm me, nobody I recognized, in that crowded street. And yet the feeling wouldn't go away. I was sure someone was following me. I quickened my pace, but the feeling didn't ease. Someone was keeping pace with me. It would have been easy enough to mingle with that crowd, to duck into stores and behind awnings if I looked around. I tried to remember—was it all lights and business right down to the ladies' hostel? If so, I would be safe. But if there was a length of street with no crowds and no lights, then I would have real trouble. How stupid I had been to send the constable away. Daniel Sullivan knew this city better than I and he had been concerned about my safety.

Not to worry, I thought. The constable said that policemen always patrol the Bowery. I'd find the nearest policeman and ask him to escort me home. But was that such a good idea? If the man who had murdered O'Malley and Levy didn't know where I lived, was I stupid to show him now? All he'd have to do was wait for a suitable moment. At some stage I would come out of the building alone and unprotected and then he could strike. Somehow I would have to lose him.

I picked up my skirts and ran, dodging in and out of people. Then I ducked into the nearest shop. It was a butcher's, with carcasses hanging in the window and sawdust on the floor. The sight of the blood spatters and the smell of raw meat made me feel hot and clammy again. I held onto the edge of the glass-fronted counter, hoping that fainting wasn't going to become a regular event with me. Until now I had always suspected that young women pretended to faint when convenient. The way the blood was singing in my ears at this moment made me decide that my prior judgment could have been harsh.

"Can I help you, miss?" the man behind the counter asked.

I made a supreme effort and stood up straight. "I'm still trying to make up my mind, thank you," I said. I appeared to be studying the various cuts of meat, while at the same time watching the street out of the corner of my eye.

The butcher was tapping the counter impatiently.

"I'll have—one of those, please." I pointed at the smallest sausages down at the far end of the counter.

"One? One sausage?"

"That's what I said. One sausage." I returned his stare defiantly. "Is there any law about only selling sausages in twos?"

"No ma'am," he growled and savagely hacked one sausage from the string before wrapping it in paper for me. "That's two cents."

As I fished in my purse for the money I stiffened. Bully Boyle had just walked past the store without looking in. I put down the money, snatched up the wrapped sausage and hurried to the doorway. I could see the back of Boyle's head. He wasn't in uniform but in a blue suit and smart derby. I moved out into the crowd and followed him. I wasn't going to let him out of my sight. He was moving fast now, looking around him. Was he looking for me? He crossed the street. I crossed too, dodging the streetcars and carriages. Then he went into a dark-fronted store. It had three golden balls hanging over the door, a universal sign that even I, from a little village across the world, knew to be a pawnbroker's establishment. I moved behind the awning of the fish shop next door and pretended to examine some eels.

A few minutes later he came out again. I muttered, "Not fresh enough" to the angry fishmonger and followed Boyle. This time he crossed back to the original side of the street and went into the Irish Variety Theater we had just passed. I watched him long enough to see him buy a ticket and go inside. Was he really going to spend the evening watching the clog-dancing sisters and listening to the men who were the pride of old Ireland, or was this just a ploy? Had he seen me through the butcher's window, after all? At this very moment he could be sneaking out through a side door of the theater. I waited and watched. Time passed but he didn't reappear.

I knew I should be sensible and go straight home while I had the chance, but I had to know what Bully Boyle had been doing in the pawn shop across the street. I crossed and pushed open the pawn shop door. A bell tinkled and an old man sprang up from behind the counter.

"Hello," I said. "I'm looking to buy something nice for my little sister. It's her twenty-first birthday. I don't have much to spend but I want it to be nice."

He smiled a toothless smile at me. "It just happens I've got some nice stuff come in," he said. "I haven't even had time to price it all, but I'll let you make me a fair offer."

He brought out a velvet-lined tray from behind the counter. It was full of pretty things—brooches, hair clips, pearls, and one thing that particularly caught my eye—a muff chain made of amethyst beads. I had seen that chain before, a few days ago. It had been around the neck of a little German girl waiting to enter Ellis Island.

❦ Nineteen ❦

The next morning we had just finished the Bible reading and I was filing downstairs to breakfast with the other inmates when I heard a raised voice coming from the reception area.

"I'm sorry. I've just told you. We have no Mrs. Kathleen O'Connor staying here."

I glanced down the stairs. A large policeman was standing there—the same constable who had escorted me home the night before. The moment I spotted him he happened to look up the stairs and saw me.

"There she is. That's her, with the red hair," he said, loudly and dramatically.

Every head in the place turned in my direction. I pushed past the other women and got to him before he could do me any more damage. Why had I been stupid enough to register here under my own name? Mainly because it was a hostel for unmarried women, I suppose, and because I had hoped I could finally give up the pretense of being Kathleen O'Connor.

"I'm sorry, Constable," I muttered to him so that the Bible lady couldn't overhear. "I didn't want to be traced. Just in case anyone was following me."

He nodded. "I understand, miss. Good thinking. And I'm really sorry to trouble you so early, but Captain Sullivan would like to see you right away."

No other summons would have made me miss my breakfast so willingly. "I'll just get my wrap," I said.

When I came down again, the constable was waiting outside, but the dragon Bible lady was hovering at the foot of the stairs, blocking my exit.

"This is a respectable establishment, Miss Murphy. I don't know what you have been doing but you should realize that anyone who finds herself in trouble with the law is not welcome here."

"I'm not in any trouble with the law," I said haughtily. "I witnessed a crime yesterday. The constable wants me to come to headquarters to make my statement."

"So are you really Murphy or O'Connor? Deceit is a tool of the devil, you know."

I'd thought this one out on my way upstairs. "Murphy is my maiden name," I said. "I've gone back to it, since I arrived here to find my husband run off with another woman."

She looked at me with sympathy then, which made me feel guilty. Lying to a Bible lady was right up there with the seven deadly sins, I'd imagine.

"I understand," she said, patting my hand awkwardly.

"I have to go. The policeman is waiting," I said and hurried out through the front door, my cheeks burning.

This time we took a cab. I was glad the dragon at the hostel didn't have to witness my being driven away in a paddy wagon.

Daniel Sullivan was sitting at his desk, sleeves rolled up, vest undone, collar undone, unshaven, looking somewhat the worse for wear.

"You look terrible," I blurted out. "Don't you ever sleep?"

He looked up with a tired smile. "Thanks for the compliment and no, not much while I'm on a case." He motioned to the chair beside him for me to take a seat. "And I seem to be on a permanent case since I met you."

"Don't go blaming it on me. I'm not enjoying it too much, either, you know." I spread my skirts and tried to sit gracefully. "Four days I've been in New York now and every one of them has been full of policemen and dead bodies. I'd just like to get on with my life."

He smiled again. "I'm sorry," he said. "I'm sure you do have plenty of worries of your own at the moment. These days can't have been easy for you."

They haven't been all bad, I wanted to say, and had to remind myself that it wasn't proper to start flirting with policemen—especially when I was still officially a married woman and only a hair's-breadth away from being a suspect myself.

He straightened the pile of papers in front of him. "Look, I'm sorry to call you in so early, but I wanted to get working on this right away. I thought over what you said last night and I had to admit it made sense." I tried not to grin and looked down at my hands.

"Who would have more to lose than a prominent New Yorker?" he went on. "So I had my men round up everything they could from the studio and we were in luck. Levy was an old-fashioned kind of photographer. If he'd been modern and used celluloid film in his camera, we'd have been out of luck. But he still used plates. We found an undamaged plate of the mayor's group and we've had a print developed. I want you to take a look at it."

He put the photograph on the desk between us. I bent over it, trying to concentrate, half conscious all the time of his head close to mine. Two rows of ladies and gentlemen, all looking rather pleased with themselves. I recognized the mayor, standing in the middle, flanked by the entertainers, the Italian opera star taking up more than her fair share of space. Then in the back row, at the end of the line . . .

"That's him!" I tapped excitedly at the photograph. "That man at the end on the right. I'm almost sure that's him. Same bushy whiskers and large stomach."

Daniel Sullivan gave a nervous laugh. "I don't think you're right this time. That's Alderman McCormack. He's one of the big wheels at Tammany Hall."

"So who would have more to lose?" I demanded. "If he's a

big wheel at Tammany, then the Irish people in the city must love him and respect him. If he was the one who betrayed those boys in Plumbridge, he'd lose everything he'd gained here, wouldn't he?"

Daniel was shaking his head. "But you don't understand. When I call him a big wheel, I mean a really big wheel. Men like him don't do their own killing. Tammany owns half the gangs in the city. He'd have found it easy enough to have a band of thugs waiting for O'Malley the second he stepped ashore."

"But what if O'Malley had blurted out the truth about the alderman before he was killed? His bully boys wouldn't be so anxious to work for him then, would they?" I hesitated, my brain racing at the word *bully*. "Wait a minute, though. Maybe I have got it wrong about Alderman McCormack. Maybe my first hunch was right, after all. I forgot to tell you what happened to me last night. I saw Boyle, the guard, down on the Bowery. I think he was following me. He's definitely a crooked one, you know. He steals from immigrants and then pawns the stuff."

"He wouldn't be the first to do that," Daniel said, then stopped short. "You said you were followed last night? But I sent you home with a constable."

"I know." I felt myself flushing at his stare. "I thought I could do the last bit on my own. I didn't want the ladies at the hostel to see me being escorted home by the police."

"And would they have thought better of you if you'd arrived in a hearse?" he demanded.

"It's all right. I shook him off easily enough. I ran through the crowd and ducked into a butcher's shop. That's when I saw Boyle going past." My brain was racing again. "And that might make sense, too. One of those big wheels, as you call them, could have paid Boyle to stay on the island overnight and do the actual killing."

Daniel sighed. "I've told you before—we have sworn statements by other guards that he went back to the city with them on the last boat. The pilfering I'd believe. It's very common, so I understand. But he wasn't on the island that night."

"Then it had to be the alderman," I said. "There's a distinct resemblance between them and I saw a guard with big, bushy whiskers, a big paunch, and a big, booming voice."

"But he can't be the one," Daniel said. "It doesn't make sense. He's been in the city for as long as I can remember and I'm sure he comes from southern Ireland. Nowhere near Plumbridge."

Daniel picked up his half-full coffee cup, took a sip, made a face, and put it down. "Stone cold," he said. "Would you like a cup of coffee?"

"Thank you, that would be wonderful. The constable dragged me out before I had a chance to eat my breakfast. And I'd already spent an hour listening to the Bible, too."

"That's what happens to you when you mix with Protestants." He gave me a grin. He really had the most enchanting smile.

A young policeman was dispatched to bring us coffee and rolls.

As soon as he had gone, Daniel's face became serious again. He leaned closer to me, as if he didn't want anyone to overhear. "If by any chance it were the alderman," he said, "we'd never be able to prove it. This is a man who has every branch of the city in his pocket, including the law. I would be a fool to even try and pursue it. I'd find myself out on the streets with no job, if I managed to keep my skin. And the same goes for you. If you were the one person who could identify the alderman in court, I'd start ordering your coffin."

"But if you got proof of who he really was," I insisted, "If you sent off to Ireland and had them check into his background?"

The young policeman returned with our breakfast. Daniel took a swig of coffee and waited a moment before continuing.

"And if he found out I was doing it?" He lowered his voice. "Don't you realize this place is full of his spies? The police love him. He gets them their pay raises and gives them carte blanche to extort bribes and kickbacks from every shady operation in the city." He paused. "Oh sorry, carte blanche means—"

"I know what carte blanche means. *Je parle Française très bien.*"

Again he looked at me with surprise. "You're an interesting woman, Mrs. O'Connor. How did someone from a small village in the back of beyond get an education like yours? Most of the Irish who come here are lucky if they can write their own names."

"I was educated with the young ladies at the manor house," I said. "Their mother thought me worth educating."

"And why was that?"

"I—told her land agent what I thought of him when he tried to raise my parents' rent. She found it amusing."

"How old were you?"

"About ten."

"I see. Making trouble even then?"

"From the moment I was born, according to my mother."

"No wonder your husband found you too hard to handle," he chuckled, then checked himself. "I'm sorry, that was a tactless thing to say."

"It's all right. I'm sure it's true."

"Do you think you'll go back to him?"

I was so longing to tell him the truth. I'm free. I'm available. I'm yours for the asking. But he still had Michael Larkin locked in his jail. He was still the law.

"I'm not sure what will happen next," I said.

"Does he want you back? Do you still—I'm sorry, I should shut up. I've no right to pry."

This was becoming awkward. "If you'd hurry up and get this case sorted out, I could think about getting on with my life," I said. "It's like walking on eggshells. But at least I get the feeling that I'm not a suspect anymore—" I broke off as I realized something—"and Michael can't be your number one suspect, either. He was locked in your jail when poor Mr. Levy was killed last night. Won't you let him go now?"

"What is he to you?" Daniel asked. "He's only a boy. Surely there's nothing more than—"

"Nothing more than concern for a friend, I assure you."

"I let him go, last night," Daniel said. "I came to the same conclusion. It seems that you and Michael being on the same ship as O'Malley was just a horrible coincidence."

"Thank you." A wave of relief swept over me, as if it were I who had been set free. In a way it was. "You don't happen to know where he is now?"

Daniel shrugged. "No idea. I'd imagine he spent the night in the police shelter. We have a place for indigents to sleep, next to the Tombs."

"Oh, really?" I pretended to be interested in finishing my roll. I wasn't going to let him know I had also spent the night there. "I'll try and track him down. And then I must find myself a job. Do you know how hard it is to get work in this city?"

"With your education I should have thought you could find employment as a governess. Although you'd have to live in and they probably wouldn't want a woman with children."

"But it's a thought," I said. "Better than the only things I've been offered so far." I refrained from mentioning that they were fish gutting and prostitution.

Daniel drained his coffee cup. "For my part I'd be very happy if you got yourself settled, preferably as far away as possible."

"Oh." It felt like a slap in the face. He wanted me out of his hair. I was a nuisance to him.

"You're still in danger, you know. Unless I make an official statement that I'm dropping the case, due to lack of evidence. And if Alderman McCormack is involved, I might just have to do that."

"I hate to let anyone get away with murder," I said. "I'd be prepared to take the chance for myself. You can't just leave someone out on the streets free to kill more people. And it's possible that he was the one who betrayed his friends in Ireland, too. Who let those boys all hang."

"Sometimes my job isn't pleasant," he said. "My hands are tied when I'd like to act. But I will send off to Ireland and get confirmation on the alderman's background if that will keep you from doing any more stupid things."

"Don't worry. Now Michael's free, I've done my part. I'm off job hunting." I stood up and brushed the crumbs from my shawl. "Wish me luck."

"I wish you all the luck in the world," he said.

I floated down the stairs.

Now I had some objective. A governess sounded like a good idea for a start. At least it would mean a roof over my head, enough to eat, and a place well away from the Bowery, should Boyle, or whoever it was, want to follow me again. I went back to the hostel and asked the ladies how I should set about it. They were instantly helpful. A governess was the sort of profession of which they approved—suitably humble and austere.

"There is a very trustworthy Christian agency on Park Avenue that specializes in placing domestic employees. Some of our more refined and educated girls have found an entrée into domestic service there. Put on a fresh white blouse before you go. They are very strict about appearance. And of course you'll have your references from home with you."

Of course I would. I went back to the dormitory to change into the one white blouse I had luckily brought with me, to spruce myself up, also to write myself a couple of glowing references on notepaper I had stolen from the office downstairs. I decided that the occasion warranted that I didn't arrive looking hot and disheveled, so I wasted five cents on the elevated railway up Third Avenue. What a wonderfully exciting view of the city it was, peering into all those windows as we went past. It was interesting to watch packed tenements give way to streets with trees in them, then to squares and parks and tall brownstones. I was truly going uptown! I was bubbling with energy. Soon I'd have a good job and I'd be able to start on the next stage of my life.

I found the agency, among smart dress shops and professional offices just off Park Avenue. A middle-aged woman in a severe high-necked black dress, her graying hair scragged back into a high bun, was seated at the desk. She looked a little like Queen Victoria on the old pennies, and just as little likely to be amused.

"Yes? Can I help you?" she asked in a clipped English accent that may or may not have been put on. She was eyeing me up and down as if I was something that the cat had brought in. I was conscious of my travel-stained skirt that needed a good washing and ironing, and my old woolen shawl which had certainly seen better days.

"I've come about a position," I began.

"Oh yes?"

"A governess position," I said firmly.

Now she looked surprised. "Governess? I hardly think—"

"I have just arrived in this country," I said. "I may not be looking at my best, but I can assure you I have a high quality of education, and I'm good with children. I was just hired to escort two young children across the Atlantic." This was a flash of inspiration and I saw it register in her eyes. "I was educated with the daughters of gentlefolk," I went on. "I know Latin and French and I'm very well read in the classics."

"I really don't think—" she went on, but I didn't give her time to say what she didn't think. "And I have references," I finished triumphantly. "From the best families—from titled families."

That clinched it. "Really? Well in that case we may be able to help you. Please take a seat, Miss? . . ."

"Murphy. Molly Murphy."

"I am pleased to make your acquaintance, Miss Murphy. I am Miss Fortescue. May I see the references?"

I handed them to her. She read them, then nodded approvingly. "Most satisfactory," she said. Of course they were. I had a fine way with words when I chose. "I'm sure we'll be able to place you in a suitable position," she said. "Just as soon as we've had a chance to check on those references."

"To check on them?" I blurted out. "But they're all the way over in Ireland. It could take weeks before you get a reply. The viscount and viscountess travel a lot. They usually spend the winter in the south of France."

She gave me a patronizing smile. "This agency prides itself on the meticulous checking of references. We would never risk our reputation on sending out a girl before she was thoroughly vetted. I'm afraid you'll have to be patient if you wish to work through us."

"But I can't afford to wait for weeks before I'm hired." I took the references back from her. "I have to pay for my room and board with no money coming in. I'm afraid I'll have to look elsewhere for a job. Maybe I should try finding a position through the advertisements in the newspapers."

"As you wish," she said, "although I assure you the best families will be as meticulous in their hiring procedures as we are. Of course, if you choose to leave New York and go out West, then you might find standards are considerably laxer. In California, or Colorado, so I understand, they will hire just anyone."

"Thank you, I may do that," I said.

I rose to my feet. So did she. "If you change your mind . . . ," she began when another woman, slightly younger but no less severe looking, came scurrying out of a back room and beckoned fiercely to Miss Fortescue.

"That was the alderman's butler on the telephone," I heard her mutter. "He said they are desperate. The alderman has a dinner party tonight—"

"The alderman will just have to wait his turn like everyone else," Miss Fortescue said. "Trained parlor maids do not grow on trees."

"So what should I tell him?"

"That we will do our best to find him a speedy replacement. I have some more girls arriving from England at the end of the month."

"He won't be happy."

"I'm sorry, but that's the best we can do."

The younger woman scurried into the back room again. Miss Fortescue looked around and saw me still standing there.

"Thank you for stopping by, Miss—uh—. So sorry we couldn't help you," she said with a dismissive wave.

"By any chance, would that be Alderman McCormack?" I asked.

"We never discuss our clients," she said in a horrified voice. "Good day to you."

I came out into the crisp cold air and stood on the sidewalk, trying to collect my thoughts. My heart was racing at the preposterous idea that was forming in my mind. If it was Alderman McCormack who was desperate for a new parlor maid, then maybe I had found him a suitable replacement.

❧ **Twenty** ❧

I couldn't believe my luck. If only I could gain access to the alderman's household, I might have a chance to find out the truth for myself. It shouldn't be hard to discover whether the alderman came home on the night of the Ellis Island murder. It might not even be hard to find out about his background in Ireland. Even if it turned out that he wasn't the alderman who needed a new parlor maid, I'd have an excuse to chat with his servants. I imagined the satisfaction I'd feel when I presented Daniel Sullivan with the truth. I was so impressed with my own cleverness that it never crossed my mind that I could be putting myself at considerable risk.

It wasn't hard to find out where Alderman McCormack lived. The first person I asked, a greengrocer delivering produce, pointed me up Park Avenue. "You can't miss it—bloomin' great castle it is, turrets and all."

As I walked up Park Avenue the houses grew ever grander until they were nothing short of mansions. On my left a glorious park opened up. It was still dotted, here and there, in patches of snow and made a most charming scene. Among the snowy lawns and snow-draped trees I saw prim English nannies in their starched bonnets wheeling their youngest charges, while the older children ran laughing ahead, dragging wooden wagons or pausing to throw snowballs when their nannies weren't looking. Ladies in sweeping fur capes walked little dogs while a hurdy-gurdy man played a lively Italian tune. It might have been half a world away from the New York I had just left. This was finally life in the city as I had pictured it in my dreams. With a little bit of luck, I might be living here.

Alderman McCormack's house was the grandest mansion of them all. It was, indeed, a bloomin' great castle with turrets rising at each corner. Luckily I knew from my training with the Hartley family that humble people like myself should never use the front entrance. I had only done that once before the Hartley's butler put me firmly in my place. Now I behaved like a good parlor maid and followed the sign to the tradesman's entrance around the side of the house.

The door was opened by a young maid with a scrubbed, fresh face. I had tried to think out what I should say as I walked up Park Avenue. I couldn't very well lie and say that the agency sent me, but I might be able to hint it and they might be desperate enough not to ask too many questions. And if it turned out that I'd come to the wrong house, then they might at least offer me a cup of tea and a chat before I went.

"You're needing a parlor maid, I understand." I decided to tell no lies and state only facts, at least until I got my foot in the door.

"Wait here. I'll get Mr. Holmes," she said, and shut the door in my face again.

The next time it opened a tall and gaunt distinguished-looking man in a black frock coat was standing there. I took him for the master and wondered, for a moment, whether I'd come to the wrong house.

"So the agency found someone for us, after all? Splendid. I knew they wouldn't let the alderman down." He had a very superior English accent, quite as aristocratic as the Hartleys'. Was the entire domestic service profession run by the English over here? "I am the alderman's butler. You will call me Mr. Holmes. Well, don't just stand there, there's work to be done."

I was half dragged into a dingy back hallway and the door behind me closed with a bang. The sound of that door slamming brought me to my senses for the first time. The butler shot the bolt across the back door. "Follow me," he said. "The sooner we get you out of those unsightly clothes and into a respectable uniform, the better."

"Just a moment," I said. I could hear my voice rising. "My things are still down at the ladies' hostel. Shouldn't I go and fetch them first?"

"They will be collected for you when the coachman has time. You will not be needing them in a hurry." He walked down the hall ahead of me, not looking back. The uneasiness grew. I wasn't going to be allowed to leave again. Don't be stupid, I told myself. He couldn't possibly know who I am. I was perfectly safe—at least for a couple of days. I knew the agency had no available girl to send. I'd stay for the weekend, glean all the information I could, then find an excuse to leave again. And even if I happened to pass the alderman in a hallway, nobody ever looks at servants. I'd be just another girl who worked in his house. I had nothing to worry about at all.

I was taken into an enormous warm kitchen. Pots and pans hung over the largest kitchen range I had ever seen. The center of the room was filled with a scrubbed wooden table where a girl sat chopping onions, occasionally lifting her sleeve to wipe her eyes. A round woman dressed in black was talking with another woman who was stirring a pot on the stove.

"Excuse me, cook. I'm sorry to interrupt. Mrs. Brennan? A word please?" the butler said and the woman in black turned around.

"The agency has sent a replacement for Eileen."

She looked me up and down critically. "What's your name, girl?"

"Molly, ma'am."

"Molly, eh? Well, Molly, I am Mrs. Brennan, the housekeeper. You get your orders from me. I hope you're used to hard work. The mistress expects the highest standards in this household. No cutting corners. No slacking off when nobody is watching."

"Oh no, ma'am. I'm used to hard work."

She nodded but her expression was skeptical. "Very well then. We'll see how you do. We're at sixes and sevens today because the master is hosting a large dinner party tonight—he always does, the week before St. Patrick's Day. And with a girl short, we've all been run ragged. I'll find you a uniform and have Daisy show you your duties. Follow me."

She led me out of the kitchen, along a dark hallway, and into a small office. The shelves were lined with folded linens. She took a black dress from a closet, held it up, then nodded to herself. "That was Eileen's dress, it will have to do, near enough for now. And here's your apron and cap. Make sure you don't spill anything on your apron. It won't get laundered until next Friday."

Then she was off again, along the hall and up a flight of uncarpeted stairs. She pushed open a swing door and we were in a different world. It was an entrance hall with a marble floor, adorned with life-sized marble Greek statues and potted palms as big as trees. To our right a curved marble staircase swept up to the next floor and the chandelier over it was sparkling even though I could see no candles. It took me a second to realize that it was lit with carefully hidden electric lights. The house-keeper hurried me across the hall and opened a door on the far side. It was a dining room, far grander than anything in the Hartleys' house. Two maids and a footman were standing at a table long enough to host the Last Supper, giving a final polish to candelabras before placing them on the center of a long white cloth.

"Daisy?" Mrs. Brennan's voice cut through the silence. "Leave that for a moment. This is the new girl, Eileen's replacement. Take her up to your room, help her into her uniform, and then she can finish laying the table for you. Go on, girl, get a move on. There's work to be done."

Daisy gave her a frightened look, scurried across the room, and out of the door. I followed. We ducked through the swing door again and she led me up a narrow wooden back staircase. Up and up. Those turrets that looked as if they reached into the sky? We were sleeping in one of them. My legs felt like jelly by the time she pushed open a door on the final landing. It was a narrow, cold room with just one bed in it.

"Here we are," she said. "I'm Daisy, by the way."

"And I'm Molly." I smiled at her.

"When your belongings come you can put them in the bottom drawer. I've got the top one."

"Where's your room, then?"

"This is it."

"And mine?"

"We'll be sharing the bed," she said in an Irish accent thicker than my own. "I hope you don't snore."

"Sharing the bed?" I demanded. "They can afford all those marble statues and they can't buy enough beds for their servants?"

"Hush!" She put her fingers to her lips and glanced at the door, although how she thought anybody would hear us all the way up here, I don't know. "For the love of mike, don't let them hear you talking like that or you'll be out before you start. Alderman McCormack is known for being very good to his servants."

"Where I come from only the Kane family had to share beds, and they were as poor as dirt, and had more children than rabbits," I said.

"Stop talking and hurry up," Daisy said. "Mrs. Brennan will start yelling if we're not down again before you can blink. She gets so nervous when the master has a dinner party. The mistress is very fussy, you know. Everything has to be quite perfect."

She started trying to undo the buttons on my blouse for me. "I can do it, thank you," I said, hastily. "Is that why the last girl was fired?"

"Fired?" A look of amusement spread across her face. "Who told you she was fired? Ran away she did—her and Frederick, the under footman. Oh, you should have seen the fuss! A parlor maid and a footman running away to get married, just like their betters? Never heard of!" She held the black dress over my head and pulled it on to me. Then she buttoned it down the back. It was scratchy wool. She helped me tie the apron and held out the cap.

"You've too much hair," she said. "They'll probably want you to cut it off. No signs of vanity allowed around here."

"I'm certainly not cutting off my hair," I said indignantly. "I like my hair the way it is, thank you."

"Don't let Mrs. Brennan hear you talking like that. You have to look the way they want you to. What kind of household were you in before?" She was looking at me with horrified fascination as if I was a dangerous new type of animal.

Shut up, I reminded myself. She might report everything I'd just said to the housekeeper and then I'd be fired before I could find out anything useful.

"My mother always used to say I had too much pride," I said, laughing. "I don't think it will ever get stamped out of me."

"It will here, if you stay long enough," Daisy said. She ran a brush savagely through my long curls. "Anyway, for now we'll try to hold it back with pins. The mistress hates to see any hair poking out from under a cap." Together we managed to tame my hair and she tied the cap so tightly across my forehead that it hurt my eyes.

"Ow," I said. "Not so tight."

"It has to be tied as tight as that or it slips. And you'll get in awful trouble if they see you with your cap crooked." She turned me around. I caught a glimpse of a severe white-faced stranger in the mirror on the dresser. "Right. You'll do. Now we'd better get down there or we'll never hear the end of it."

Back down all those stairs, our feet clattering on bare boards. The candelabras were now in place, and between them large bowls of fruit and flowers. Daisy showed me the open chests of cutlery lying on a sideboard. "Do you know how to lay a table properly?"

"Only the Irish way," I said, not wanting to admit that I'd

never seen a table laid properly in my life. Refreshments at the Hartleys' house had been limited to milk and a biscuit taken in the nursery.

"George, put out one place setting for her, then she can follow," Daisy said to the footman.

"I'm still busy polishing," George said. "Whoever put these away didn't do a good enough job at wrapping them. They've started to tarnish."

"Oh, all right. I'll do it." Daisy grabbed a handful of knives and forks. "Now, you start from the outside and work inward, as I expect you know," she said. "The little knife and fork are for the entrée, then the soup spoon on the right, then the fish knife and fork are in that box, then the meat—"

"Holy Mother," I said. "How many courses are there?"

"Seven, as usual. It's only for special occasions that they have twelve. This is just regular entertaining that they're always doing."

"They entertain a lot, do they?" I asked, putting out knives and forks as she had demonstrated.

"Oh, all the time. The mistress likes to think of herself as the number one hostess in the city. She's always entertaining the Vanderbilts, and the Roosevelts—all the hoity-toities come here."

My brain was working fast. Today was Saturday so if I counted back . . . "I suppose they only entertain at weekends? They don't do this sort of thing on a Monday, say?"

"Oh, sometimes they do. They're either out to dinner or they've got somebody here all the time."

"What about last Monday? Did they have anybody to dinner then?"

"What would you want to know that for?" she laughed. "How can I remember back to last Monday?"

"I remember last Monday," George said without looking up from his polishing. "They were out. I know because Sunday's usually my evening off but they had the mayor over then and Mr. Holmes told me I could take Monday instead because they'd be dining out."

So the alderman was not at home on Monday evening.

"I bet they come home at all hours when they've been out," I said. "Do they wake you up when they come in? They don't want to be waited on, do they?"

Daisy looked up from the place she was laying across the table. "Only the master and mistress's personal maid and valet have to help them get undressed. Mr. Holmes always stays up until he can lock up for the night. But we don't have to worry about that. We're sound asleep at the top of the house. They could let a herd of elephants run through the place for all we'd hear."

"Do you always chatter like this, Molly?" George demanded. "The mistress doesn't like servants chattering when they're supposed to be working."

"Sorry," I said. "I just like to get the feel of a new place. I won't say another word."

I went back to work. I was pleased to notice that I was quicker than Daisy and even Mrs. Brennan nodded approvingly when we'd finished. "This table looks a treat," she said. "And I must say your appearance is a big improvement over the last time I saw you, Molly. You look quite civilized now. Run and get yourselves a cup of cocoa, girls, before you put the carpet sweeper over the living room and the main staircase."

I followed the others back to the warmth of the kitchen. There were mugs of hot cocoa and big slabs of fruit cake waiting and I fell on them eagerly. It felt like days since I had had a decent meal. While we ate I was wondering how I could find out if Alderman McCormack had not come home on Monday night. Mr. Holmes looked like a meticulous kind of person. Perhaps he kept a diary or appointment book. I'd have to get a feel for the rhythm of the household to know when might be a safe time to go into the butler's private quarters. I couldn't afford to make any mistakes.

As soon as the cups were drained Daisy nudged me. "Come on, we've got sweeping to do." She took me to a broom closet and handed me a square box on a long handle. "Go on, take it," she said impatiently. "Have you never seen a carpet sweeper before? What kind of households have you worked in?"

"We're not as up-to-date in Ireland," I said, "What do I do with this?"

"Oh, it's like a miracle. You just push it over the carpet and it picks up all the specks. You'll never want to go back to sweeping with a broom again."

We went up the stairs again and back into the bright, sparkling light of the front hall. They kept the electric lights in the chandelier running all the time, even when nobody was around!

"I'll do the drawing room," Daisy said. "The mistress is more likely to notice specks when they're having coffee in there after dinner. You can do the stairs." She pointed at the curved staircase. "And make sure you do each step thoroughly. And if you hear any family members coming, try to get out of the way until they've passed. They don't like seeing servants in the main part of the house. They like to pretend the house runs itself with no human help!"

I took my sweeper and started on the bottom step, feeling quite exposed in the front hall. The sweeping might have been easier than with the brush and dustpan we used at home, but there were an awful lot of those steps and they became so narrow at the center that it was impossible to get that sweeper to work properly. I was feeling hot and tired by the time I reached the top. But a fascinating new hallway stretched out ahead of me. This might be a good opportunity to do a spot of scouting. My sweeper gave me a good excuse for being there. I started along the hall until I reached the first door. I glanced around, then knelt to put my eye to the keyhole. I was just focusing when the front door opened, letting in a blast of cold air. As I scrambled to my feet and grabbed the carpet sweeper, I got a brief impression of a large man with bushy whiskers depositing his hat on the hall table. Footsteps came up the stairs toward me. I shrank to the side as large feet came past me.

"You, girl. Go and tell Holmes that I'd like a whiskey and soda in my study straight away and then let cook know that I'll take my lunch on a tray up here while I'm working. Nothing fancy, tell her. A slice of her pork pie and some pickles will do."

"Very good, sir." I bobbed a curtsy, as I'd seen the maids at the Hartley's do, and kept my eyes firmly on my feet.

"You're new here, are you?"

I had to look up then. "Yes, sir." Was the face the one I had seen that night? It was hard to tell. Same impressive whiskers and rounded paunch with a vest stretched across it. I realized that I had never taken in the features beneath those whiskers. Hadn't the nose been larger? If it was he, then surely he must recognize me by now.

"What's your name, child?"

"Molly, sir." I lowered my face rapidly again until he was looking at a cap.

"You don't have to be nervous with me, young woman. This is a happy household. If you do your work well, you have nothing to be afraid of."

"No, sir. I'll go and find Holmes for you, sir." I made a bobbing curtsy, grabbed my sweeper, and ran down the stairs. I was pretty sure he hadn't recognized me. The question was whether I had recognized him. He had spoken to me in a soft, rumbling voice. I'd have to wait to see how his voice sounded when it was booming.

I found Holmes without any trouble and passed on the instructions. He turned very pale.

"The master came home and I didn't even hear him come in? That makes twice in one week now. Dear me. I must be slipping. Very well, girl. You can go back to your duties."

I left him and went into the kitchen to pass on my message to the harried cook. She now had several pots on the stove and was moving from one to the next.

"Oh, blast him, right when I'm in the middle of waiting for this sauce to thicken," she muttered. "And Ruby still has all those potatoes to peel."

"I could take it up for you, if you'd like," I said.

"You? You're the parlor maid. It's not your job. Don't be ridiculous."

"I just wanted to help. I've finished doing the stairs."

She glanced around as if she was committing a crime. "Well, I won't say no this time," she said, "and if the master doesn't like it, you can tell him I didn't want his favorite sauce to curdle."

She pointed out the pie and pickles to me, then gave me step-by-step instructions on which cloth to put on the tray, which napkin to go with it, and which salt cellar to use. When the tray was finished to her satisfaction she sent me off with it. "Up in his study. Third door on the left as you go along the upstairs hallway. Don't linger now and come back down the servants' stairs."

I carried the tray up the stairs and was just approaching the study door when I heard the master speaking.

"I told you, Bertie, there is nothing to worry about."

I paused in the hallway. The study door was half open and I got a glimpse of the alderman speaking into a telephone. "Who could find out? We are the only two who know and everything will be fine if you don't blab. . . . Yes, I'm aware of the newspaper man, but, in my opinion, he was just fishing. He can't know anything . . . No, that wouldn't be a wise move at this stage. Only calling attention to you, which then calls attention to me. Just sit tight and shut up, Bertie. This will all pass over and everything can go on as it was before. Of course I still plan to be the grand marshal of the St. Patrick's parade. Why shouldn't I? The people love me."

I watched the speaking part of the telephone being hung back on its hook. I was about to knock on the door when I saw him open a drawer in the top part of his desk. He pulled that drawer all the way out, then reached in and opened another drawer behind it. He removed papers from it, went through them quickly, then nodded in satisfaction and put them back again. I tiptoed back down the hall, waited a suitable amount of time, then made another approach, before tapping on the door.

"Your lunch, sir."

"What? Oh yes. Put it there." He indicated a spot on a side chest of drawers where a tray containing a whiskey decanter and soda siphon already stood. I put the tray down and made a hurried departure.

❧ Twenty-one ❧

W e servants took our midday meal together at the big scrubbed kitchen table. I came into the kitchen to find Daisy, George, and a couple of others I hadn't seen before already seated. I pulled out a chair beside Daisy.

"Where do you think you're sitting, girl?" Mrs. Brennan demanded. "You're a newcomer. Your place is at the bottom of the table, beside Ruby."

With all those eyes on me, I moved to the bottom of the table and tried to look humble. I picked up my fork and was about to reach for the nearest plate when Ruby dug me hard in the ribs.

"We have to wait for Mr. Holmes to say grace," she whispered.

We sat and waited until Mr. Holmes made a grand entrance and took his place at the head of the table. "For what we are about to receive may the Lord make us truly thankful and ever mindful of the wants of others," he intoned. Then we all fell upon our meal.

The food was better than anything I had eaten in my life before—a joint of cold ham, cold roast beef, another large round pork pie, hot-jacket potatoes, a big slab of cheese, pickles. I wondered if we were celebrating our own special occasion until the cook said to the butler, "I'm sorry for such meager fare, Mr.

Holmes, but I've been so run off my feet this morning that I didn't have time to cook for us today."

"I quite understand, Mrs. O'Leary," the butler said. "I'm sure we can all make do with leftovers for once."

Make do with leftovers? If it turned out that the alderman had nothing to do with the events on Ellis Island last Monday night, I might do well to stay here for a while—if I could ever learn to be humble and behave like a proper servant, that was. But what I had seen and heard in the upstairs study made me think that I was on the right track. The alderman had something important to hide—something that had piqued a newspaperman's interest and the Irish community shouldn't know about. What else could it be? He had obviously confided in one other person and it sounded very much as if that person—Bertie, wasn't it— had been prepared to kill on his behalf. I was dealing with a dangerous man all right. I would have to tread very carefully indeed.

I wondered if parlor maids had any duties during dinner parties. If they were all busy cooking and serving food, I might just have time to slip up to the master's study and see what I could find. At least I'd be reasonably safe, knowing that the alderman and his wife were in the dining room, eating with guests.

As soon as lunch was over the cook and senior servants went for an afternoon rest. Holmes, it turned out, went out for a walk. I was instructed to wipe off all the best china, then place it in the little lift they called a dumbwaiter to be taken up to the storage area behind the dining room. There was an anteroom, hidden to one side of the dining room, where the plates were stacked in the correct order. Food would also be sent up in the dumbwaiter. Two footmen would carry it through and serve at table. Apparently female servants were too lowly and clumsy for such tasks. Which might mean I had some time and opportunity to do a little scouting.

I worked fast, polishing all those plates, sixteen of each, then sending them up for the footmen to lay out above. Mrs. O'Leary, the cook, sat in a rocking chair beside the kitchen range, snoring.

Ruby, the scullery maid, was still out there washing up the plates from our meal and the pots that had been used that morning. No sign of Daisy—I presumed she was up helping the footmen. I was all alone. I darted out of the kitchen. If Mrs. Brennan had an office, then Mr. Holmes must have one, too. Cautiously I opened one door after another until I came to a door that was locked. By peeking through the keyhole I saw a tidy desk, a large bunch of keys hanging on the wall . . . it had to be Mr. Holmes's office, but unfortunately he seemed to be the one person in the household who locked his door when he went out.

I went back to the kitchen, just in time, as it turned out. As I stepped in through the door a bell started jangling on the far wall. Mrs. O'Leary woke with a start. "The mistress's sitting room," she said. "She must have returned from lunch, and Mr. Holmes isn't back from his walk yet. You'd better go and see what she wants, girl."

"Which room is it?"

"First floor, at the far end of the hall, past the master's study. Go on, run. She hates to be kept waiting."

I ran up the back stairs, past the master's study and tapped on the far door before entering. An exquisitely lovely young woman, with blond curls piled on a doll-like face, was reclining on a pink silk chaise longue before the fire. I couldn't have been more surprised. The alderman was a middle-aged man. His whiskers were already graying at the sides. If this was his wife, then she was a good twenty years younger, and very lovely. She was reading a letter and didn't look up as I came in.

I waited a few moments and then cleared my throat. "You rang, madam?" I asked.

She glanced up, then went back to the letter. "When I am ready to talk to you, I will," she said, her voice matching the coldness of her expression. Then she looked up again. "You're new."

"Yes, madam." I hoped my own expression looked suitably chastened.

"And your name is?"

"Molly, madam."

"In which case, Molly, the first thing you should learn is that servants are here to wait on their masters. When I am ready to give you an order, I will do so. Is that clear?"

"Yes, madam, only I thought that perhaps you hadn't heard me come in. I just wanted you to know I was there."

Her delicate cheeks flushed. "And you do not answer back. Servants in this house speak when they are spoken to."

I hung my head, not sure whether saying I was sorry might constitute speaking out of turn again, and tried to look like a mortified parlor maid.

"It's all right. I'll overlook it this once, seeing that you're new and haven't had a chance to be properly instructed yet." She gave me an enchanting smile. "Please tell cook that the dressmaker will be arriving at four for a final fitting for tonight's dress. We will have tea and suitable cakes in my dressing room at four fifteen."

"Yes, ma'am."

"I hope you'll be happy with us, Molly. You may bring the tray up to my dressing room at four fifteen. Make sure you don't spill anything."

I was getting good at curtsys. Humility was going to take a little longer.

Mrs. O'Leary sniffed when I passed on the instructions. "Tea and cakes. As if I haven't got enough to do with cooking seven courses for sixteen. If she doesn't watch what she eats she'll lose that lovely figure and then the master will lose interest. It wasn't for her brains he married her."

"Have they been married long?"

She leaned toward me confidentially. "Only a year. His former wife died suddenly and he married this flibbertigibbet before the poor woman was cold in her grave. She was one of the original Floradora Six."

I had heard enough about the Plumbridge Nine, but the Floradora Six? She saw the surprised look on my face. "You know, the Broadway show, 'Floradora.' They say all the girls in that original sextet married millionaires. We're in the wrong job, girl.

194

But then I never did have Mrs. McCormack's figure, even when I was young." She chuckled, ran her hands over her ample stomach, and went to check something in the oven.

I had even more to think about. If the alderman was the monster I thought him to be, then maybe his wife's sudden death was no accident, either.

At four fifteen on the dot I carried the mistress's tray upstairs to her dressing room and I made sure I knocked. Loudly. Her personal maid took the tray from me at the door. "Zay are busy and do not wish to be interrupted," she said in a very French accent. Even so I managed to catch a glimpse of the most gorgeous burgundy velvet gown that clung to her figure like a second skin. As the door was closed behind me I heard her say, "And I think the rubies tonight, don't you, Francine?"

Back in the kitchen, tea had been laid on the table for us. Loaves of bread, slabs of butter, pots of jam and honey, and two different cakes. Was it only yesterday that I had wondered whether I would die of starvation? Now I was worried about whether the tight waist of my uniform dress would stand yet another meal.

Mr. Holmes and Mrs. Brennan joined us for tea.

"Final instructions, everybody," Mr. Holmes said. "George and Hamish, you have clean white gloves ready for tonight? Bring them to me for inspection. Daisy, you will be positioned in the anteroom before the guests take their places, ready to take each course from the lift and place it on the hot plates. You will then take the dirty plates from George and Hamish and send them down in the lift for Ruby to wash up. You girl—what's your name? Yes, Molly. You will act as go-between. You will be available at all times to take messages to the kitchen as necessary, bring up items that didn't make it into the lift. You will use the servant's staircase and make sure you are, at no time, seen by the master's guests. Is that clear? Good. And I don't need to remind you that any dish dropped and broken will be paid for from your wages—and we are using the best Wedgwood tonight."

So I was going to be occupied, after all. At everyone's beck and call all evening with little chance to explore the alderman's study. If I disappeared for more than a moment, I'd be missed. I reminded myself there would be other occasions. I didn't have to accomplish everything in one day. But I felt a terrible sense of urgency, a nagging voice in my head that if I didn't act now it would be too late. Maybe it was that Celtic sixth sense working again, because I also sensed the presense of danger.

At six thirty the first guests started arriving. Mrs. Brennan and George were in the hallway to take coats and hats. Holmes was in the drawing room, stationed at the drinks table. Daisy was to take the trays of hot hors d'oeuvres upstairs as they came from the oven. And I found myself jobless for a moment. Suddenly I realized that this was my big chance. The alderman would be in the drawing room with his guests. The butler and housekeeper were otherwise occupied. There was nobody to see me flit into the alderman's study.

My pulse was racing so violently that I found it hard to breathe as I came out of the servants' door on the first floor. I could hear the sound of voices and laughter floating up from the floor below. There was a knock at the front door, a gust of cold air wafted up to me, and voices echoed from the marble tiled hallway. More guests were arriving. I waited until I heard Mrs. Brennan escort them to the living room before I tiptoed down the hall and tried the study door. It was unlocked. I opened it and went inside. I wished that I had a torch, like Daniel Sullivan had used that night in the photography studio. The electric light, after I located the wall switch, was so very bright and visible. But the window faced the side of the house and I doubted if anyone would have need to go around there tonight.

I scanned the room quickly, not sure of what I wanted to look at first. There were several framed diplomas on the wall. One was a proclamation bestowing the keys of the city to the alderman for his outstanding leadership and philanthropic works. One was likewise the keys to the city of Dublin, for the alderman's great contributions to the Irish cause. Another was a diploma from Dublin University. Joseph William McCormack, of Waterford, had graduated with a B.A. in theology in the year 1873. And lastly a certificate of citizenship of the United States, dated 1885.

That changed a lot—unless the diploma was a forgery, Joseph McCormack really was from the far southern part of Ireland. And he had already been residing in the United States when the Plumbridge Nine were attacking the land agent in Northern Ireland. It looked as if I had been following the wrong man. No wonder he hadn't recognized me. But there was still that little matter of the secret drawer. What secret was he sharing with someone called Bertie? Why did Bertie think he might not want to show his face at the St. Patrick's Day parade? And what secret could be important enough to make Bertie think of disposing of a newspaperman? I had to know. My mother had always maintained that if my big mouth didn't kill me, my curiosity would.

I crossed to the desk, opened the front, and took out the drawer. The long, slim drawer behind it slid out easily. I started looking at the papers, not knowing what I was expecting to find. They all seemed harmless enough—receipt for a donation to the Irish Home Rule Fund from a wealthy benefactor in Boston. Letters of gratitude for donations made to various Irish freedom-fighting organizations. So the alderman was acting as middleman, taking in donations and forwarding them to freedom fighters. Obviously not very popular with the English if they found out, but what Irishman would not approve? It wasn't until I stopped reading the words and started doing the math that I got an inkling of why all these letters were kept in the secret drawer. There were too many examples of ten thousand coming in from donors and five thousand going out to freedom fighters. The alderman was taking a nice cut from every single donation. No wonder he could afford such an extravagant lifestyle!

I refolded the papers exactly as I had found them, slid the drawer back into place, and was just replacing the outer drawer when I heard footsteps outside the door. I shut the desk but had no time to hide before the door was hurled open and the alderman stood there, his eyes blazing.

"What the devil are you doing, girl?" He demanded, and his voice was, indeed, big and booming. "I happened to look out of the window and I saw the light shining on the building next door. Do you mind telling me what you're doing in this room?"

"I'm sorry, sir," I stammered. "I meant no harm."

"Meant no harm? Sneaking into my private room and you meant no harm? Come on, out with it. Did you think you'd find something worth stealing?"

"Oh no, sir. I promise you I wasn't thinking of stealing anything."

"Then what?" He came closer and closer until I could feel his hot, alcohol-laden breath on my forehead. He grabbed my wrist and twisted it backward, making me cry out in pain. "Come on, tell me. Who sent you? Who's paying you?'

"Nobody, sir. I've just arrived from Ireland. I know nobody in this city. I meant no harm, I tell you."

My eyes scanned the room, trying to come up with a plausible answer. Could I have left something there this afternoon? Dropped a key? Left my mop in the corner? My eyes fell upon the diplomas. "All right, I'll tell you," I said, and he dropped my wrist. "I saw your diploma this afternoon, when I brought you your lunch. I wanted to sneak another look at it, to see—to see if you came from the same part of Ireland as me. I thought I caught the same accent that I have, sir, so I just wondered . . . I'm sorry. It was stupid of me, but I'm new here, sir, and I'm feeling homesick."

It was the weakest of excuses. He was staring so hard at me that I could feel his eyes boring into my head. And my mother always said I was a terrible liar. He'd only have to look at me long enough and he'd know. And then what? Daniel had told me that he was a ruthless man. He couldn't risk my staying alive, knowing what I knew.

He grabbed my chin and forced it up, so that he was staring straight into my eyes. "There is no place for snoops in this household, young woman," he said. "I don't care how innocent your motives were, I don't like servants I can't trust. I won't fire you tonight, because I want my wife's dinner party to go smoothly, but first thing in the morning you pack your bags and you are out of here! Do you understand me?"

"Oh yes, sir. I'm so very sorry, sir." I hung my head and played the role of the penitent. At least he had decided I was merely stupid and not dangerous.

"Now get back to your duties!" he thundered and waited until I was in the hallway before shutting the door behind me.

A blast of cold air announced the arrival of yet another guest. The alderman left me and headed down the stairs. "Daniel, my dear boy. How good of you to come!"

"I wouldn't have missed it for the world, Alderman. So good of you to ask me."

I tiptoed to the top of the stairs and peeked down. Daniel Sullivan had just arrived at the party.

Twenty-two

S omehow I made it back to the kitchen. How could I have
been so stupid, so naive? He must have known about the
alderman all along! Since the moment I arrived here I had
heard that the police were in the pay of Tammany Hall, but I
had never thought to include Daniel. Of course, considering I
had been smitten with him from the beginning, I had only seen
what I wanted to see. And to be fair, Daniel had tried to warn
me off enough times. He had tried to keep me from getting into
a situation I could not handle.

Now I saw that I had got it all wrong—the newspaper article
about the Plumbridge Nine had nothing to do with the reason
O'Malley was coming to New York. O'Malley was a known
blackmailer. Obviously he had caught wind of Alderman Mc-
Cormack's skimming the cream off donations intended for the
freedom fighters in Ireland. What a plum for a blackmailer—the
darling of the Irish in New York, the great philanthropist, rob-
bing the very people he claimed to champion? He must have
contacted the alderman to make his demands and then he was
stupid or presumptuous enough to come to New York in person.
Of course he had to be silenced instantly. The alderman couldn't
risk his coming ashore to New York. He couldn't risk delegating
the job. He had to take on the task himself.

In which case—I went one step further—it was he that I saw
that night. If he hadn't already recognized me, he soon would.

I must get out while I still had a chance. And go where? I asked myself. A man as powerful as Alderman McCormack could hunt me down wherever I went. And I could no longer rely on Daniel Sullivan to protect me. I felt tears stinging in my eyes and I wasn't sure whether they were tears of anger or disappointment. I had no choice but to bluff it out. There was the smallest chance he hadn't put my face to the woman with the child he had encountered on Ellis Island. There was also the smallest chance that he hadn't suspected me of finding the secret drawer. In which case I could disappear in the morning and go as far away as possible—which wasn't very far, seeing the amount of money I had.

"You, girl. Look lively!" The cook's voice jarred me back to reality. "The entrée is ready to be put into the dumbwaiter. Carry it carefully."

I carried the platter of smoked salmon, caviar on tiny triangles of toast, deviled eggs, and kidneys wrapped in bacon across to the lift without mishap, no small feat given my trembling hand. Cook was already ladling soup into two tureens. It took all my concentration to carry them successfully to the lift. After that I was so busy I didn't have time to think. Plates came down and had to be ferried to the sink in the scullery. Warm plates were sent up for the fish course. Covered silver salvers with fillets of sole followed them. Then Cook grabbed my arm.

"Here, girl. This is the caper sauce. Run it up to them and keep stirring all the time. I don't want a skin to form. Go on, up you go."

I ran up the back stairs, stirring the sauce as I went. There was loud conversation coming from the dining room. As I reached the serving room and handed the sauce boat to George I heard the alderman tap his knife against his glass. "If I might have your attention, ladies and gentlemen," he said. "I think it's time to propose a toast to our distinguished guests. Looking at you all, I can see that we've garnered the flower of the Irish in America at this table. I want to tell you how proud I am of you all. All of us came from humble backgrounds with no prospects in the old country and each one of us has made our mark on society in the New World. This just goes to prove there is no stopping the Irish!"

A loud cheer from the table.

"And to you, Daniel, my boy, on behalf of New York's finest, a special toast. You all know Daniel Sullivan, don't you? Ted Sullivan's boy—finest cop to ever walk the beat. Daniel hasn't even turned thirty yet and he's already a captain. We expect great things of you, Daniel. And you can tell your men that there will be a special bonus for working the St. Patrick's Day Parade. And drinks all around from me for the officers on duty that day."

"Thank you, Alderman. You're very generous, as usual."

I tried to spot Daniel through the crack in the door. Instead I caught a glimpse of other faces I recognized. The famous Irish tenor who had sung on Ellis Island, and Billy Brady, the comedian, too. They were sitting on either side of Mrs. McCormack, who looked like royalty in her velvet gown and rubies. On any other occasion I would have loved to witness such a grand festivity. Instead I crept back down the stairs to the safety of the kitchen.

I didn't have to go up again during the rest of the meal. I obeyed orders in a daze. It was better not to think, because I couldn't come up with a good solution, anyway. I helped Daisy put away the clean dishes as Ruby finished washing them. Then Daisy was sent up with the coffee, which Mr. Holmes would serve in the drawing room. I heard the sound of a piano, then the famous tenor started singing. So the two vaudevillians had been invited to provide the entertainment! Then a female voice joined in—Mrs. McCormack, the former toast of Broadway! She had a lovely voice. We stood in the servants' hallway, listening.

Then Mrs. Brennan appeared. "They must have finished their coffee by now. You, Molly. Go up and see if the cups have been returned to the tray. If they have, you may bring them down. Make sure you are not obtrusive. Hug the walls and only move when you are not being observed."

"Couldn't Daisy—" I began. I didn't want to give the alderman another chance to notice me.

"Daisy has other duties. Get a move on."

I had no choice. I went up the stairs, through the swing door, and along the grand hallway. The Greek statues stared down at me with disapproving looks. The drawing room door was half open. A huge fire roared in the marble fireplace at the far end of the room. The heavy velvet drapes were closed. In spite of the room's enormous size it gave the impression of being overfull. Little tables of knickknacks, more potted palms, stuffed birds under glass domes were dotted between the heavy velvet sofas and armchairs. The alderman was sprawled in one of the armchairs. Daniel was perched on one end of a sofa, next to a pale young woman and the tenor. He had his back to me as he concentrated on the entertainment. In one corner stood a grand piano, at which Mrs. McCormack was seated. At the moment she wasn't in the spotlight, but playing light background chords for another performer. Billy Brady was standing at the piano. He had a rich, stirring voice and he was reciting the famous Irish ballad, "The Wearing of the Green." It was one that I knew and I stood in the shadows against the wall and listened, as enraptured as the rest of his audience.

"So pull the shamrock from your hat, and throw it on the
   sod.
But never fear, 'twill take root there, though underfoot 'tis
   trod.
When laws can stop the blades of grass from growin' as
   they grow
And when the leaves in summertime their color dare not
   show,
Then I will change the color, too, I wear in my caubeen;
But till that day, please God, I'll stick to the wearin' o'
   the green."

The ballad finished to hearty applause. I saw the coffee cups piled on a tray on a low table in the bay window. With any luck I could pick them up without being noticed by the alderman. I moved forward cautiously, hugging the wall as directed, dodging carefully around the many brackets full of ornaments that hung along the walls throughout the room.

"Splendid, Billy. You'll be reciting that again on the parade float, will you?" the alderman said, still clapping.

"I always do, Alderman. The public has come to expect it."

"They do love you, Billy. So what comes next?"

"For my final recitation tonight, I thought I'd do something a little different," Billy Brady was saying. "A little more risqué, shall we say?"

"Ooh, risqué!" The ladies giggled. "Please remember there are ladies present, Mr. Brady!" One of them fluttered her fan.

He had turned to the piano and was fumbling with an open box there. As I bent to pick up the tray Billy said, "Ah, ready to proceed, gentlemen!" He had put on some kind of military cap and had a large gun tucked under his arm. "Now for my impression of the man who is dear to the hearts of all New Yorkers, especially the New York Irish brigade. That inflictor of law and order on us, whether we want it or not—Mr. Teddy Roosevelt himself!"

There were cheers and jeers from the crowd. Billy took up position. "Welcome, my boys, to the time when men were men, and I was the manliest of them all!" (Chuckles from the audience.) "Let me tell you the tale of San Juan Hill," he boomed, "and the day that brought me to fame."

There was something about his voice that made me look up. I stared at him, seeing him for the first time. To act the part of Teddy Roosevelt he had put on bushy whiskers. And the big booming voice . . . I tried to stifle the gasp that escaped from my mouth. I backed away, and into one of the brackets that stuck out from the wall. An ornament on it wobbled and fell over with a loud crash.

Billy Brady looked up and his eyes focused on me. I put down the tray on the nearest table and fled. There was no mistaking that voice. It was the one that had bellowed at me on Ellis Island. And he had been wearing the same false whiskers that night, too.

They must have been part of the props case he had brought with him for the afternoon's performance. Of course, an actor would know how to play any part. It would not have been hard for him to slip into the guard's room unnoticed and borrow a uniform jacket for a while. The paunch was probably a pillow stolen from a dormitory bed. And with the paunch and the whiskers he looked completely unlike himself.

I ran back along the hall, expecting to be grabbed at any moment. Did the others in that room know? As long as Billy was performing I was safe. But after that—he could track me down anywhere in the city and kill me at his leisure.

I stood in the cool darkness of the servants' passage. Think! Think clearly. Then suddenly it came over me in a wave of relief. Daniel was in that room. It didn't matter how thick he was with Alderman McCormack, he wouldn't let me be killed by Billy Brady. All I had to do was to go back upstairs and get Daniel's attention. Better still, I could write him a note. I'd find an excuse, any excuse—yes, I'd go back to get the coffee tray, and I'd find a way to slip the note to Daniel. I rushed downstairs and into Mrs. Brennan's office and grabbed a sheet of paper. I tried to think clearly as I scribbled the words. Now all I had to do was force myself to go upstairs again and get the note to Daniel. Maybe he'd noticed what happened in the drawing room and he was already on his way to find me.

I took a deep breath, went back up the stairs, and out into the entrance hall. The tenor was singing, and the sweet notes of "I will take you home again, Kathleen" filled the house. I crept along the hall, closer and closer to the drawing room, willing myself to have the courage to go in. Suddenly a door beside me opened and Billy Brady came into the hall.

I bit my lips together to stifle the gasp of fear. Keep calm, I told myself. I was in the hallway of a house filled with servants. He could do nothing to me here. My hand closed tightly around the note as I lowered my eyes and forced myself to walk past him.

My heart nearly jumped out of my chest when a hand touched my shoulder.

"You were the young girl who ran out of the room just then." Billy's voice sounded smooth and relaxed. "Had something upset you? Are you feeling all right now?"

Suddenly it dawned on me—he doesn't recognize me. With the severe cap hiding my forehead and the starched uniform I must look quite different from the woman he saw on Ellis Island. A wave of relief swept over me.

"Thank you, sir. I—I thought I saw a mouse," I mumbled. "I'm fine now, thank you." The words came out as a whisper.

I went to walk past him. His large presence was blocking most of the passage.

"I've seen you before somewhere, haven't I?" He stepped out, making it hard for me to pass. "Your face—I never forget a face, you know."

"Maybe last time you were visiting here, sir," I mumbled, still looking at my boots. "Now if you'll excuse me, I really have to clear up the coffee tray."

He let me pass. I was free. The drawing room door was only a few feet ahead of me.

"Wait," I heard him say. "That hair. I recognize that hair." Suddenly I was grabbed from behind and my cap was wrenched off. My hair tumbled free and at the same moment a hand came around my mouth, dragging me backward. "Ellis Island," he muttered into my ear. "You were the woman on Ellis Island. You recognized me, didn't you?"

I tried to struggle. We were still in a public hallway. He couldn't kill me here. Any moment a door would open and someone would come. Billy was dragging me toward the door on his left, back to the room from which he had just come. I fought, I squirmed, but his big hand was firmly around my mouth and his other arm around my waist so that he was half carrying me. When I tried to kick out at him, he laughed. Daniel was only separated from me by one wall. If I could manage one kick against that wall, if I could reach out and topple one of those statues. My toe tipped one plinthe but it was heavy marble and didn't even wobble.

"It's no use struggling," Billy whispered in my ear. "I'm much stronger than you."

As he heaved me inside the room I opened my hand and let the note fall to the floor. Then he shut the door behind us and turned the key with one big hand.

I had a second to glance around the room. It was a small music room with a couple of elegant brocade chairs, a piano, and a harp. Billy had obviously used it as his changing room, makeup and props were scattered on top of the piano and a large theatrical trunk stood on its end, open, with clothes hanging in it.

Billy's strong fleshy fingers were crushing my mouth. His other hand was still holding my hair so tightly that tears were spurting out of my eyes. "Well, isn't this a stroke of luck for me. The one person who could identify me. Not that your identification would stand up in court, seeing as you only saw me in disguise—but it would start people asking questions and I really don't want them to do that."

One thing was sure—I was not going to make it easy for him anymore. I swung out my leg and brought it back hard on his shins at the same time as I sank my teeth into his finger. I tasted blood as he wrenched his hand away.

"You little vixen!" He struck me a savage blow across the face, knocking me across the room. I slammed into the open trunk. It wobbled. He rushed to right it and gave me a savage kick. "You'll be sorry you did that."

"You were going to kill me, anyway. Just like you killed O'Malley—and that poor old photographer!" I tried to sound defiant, but all that came out was a gasp. My head was still singing from the blow.

"I don't want to kill you, you stupid girl. I didn't even want to kill Donny—"

"Donny?"

"He calls himself O'Malley now, but I recognized him right

away. He wrote me a letter. He thought he was so smart, but it turned out that I was smarter. His bad luck that I happened to be visiting the island that day, just as it was your bad luck to see me." He was looking around the room. It was as if I could read his mind. He was looking for something to dispatch me with. He snatched up a white scarf hanging in his trunk, then shoved me back into the carpet, his large knee holding me down in the center of my back. He was going to strangle me. I tried to make a sound, but his knee was crushing me to the floor. He was a big man, and very powerful. A man who could cut a throat with one stroke. "I'd better not kill you here. Too risky. That blood-hound Sullivan's in the next room."

"That's right," I said, turning my face out of the carpet to sound as defiant as I could, "And he knows I'm working here as his spy. Any second now he'll come looking for me."

"Then I'll just have to get you away before he comes looking, won't I?" he said.

"And how do you think you'll get me out of the house? I won't go quietly. I'm not afraid of you."

"Elementary, my dear, as that Sherlock Holmes is always saying. I'll take you out in my trunk. We'll get a cab straight to the Hudson River. Up and over into the water. Nice and simple. They'll never know what happened to you." While he said this he yanked me up by the hair. I twisted and turned, kicked and flailed. Just as I got up enough wind to cry out he stuffed a wad of cotton into my mouth, then bound it tightly with the scarf.

"I'm sorry about this. I really am." The wad of cotton was choking me and the scarf was covering my nose so that it was hard to breathe. "You have to understand," he said as he dragged me toward the trunk. I caught a glimpse of his eyes. They were not triumphant as I expected them to be, but darting nervously around the room, the eyes of a trapped animal. "You have to understand that I can't go on living like this any longer—waking up every day and wondering if this will be the day they'll find out about me and Plumbridge. And living with all that guilt. I was just twenty-one, for God's sake. I was the one they caught and they started torturing me. I would have said anything to make them stop. And when they let me go, I thought I was free." He was tipping unnecessary items out of the trunk. He glanced at me. "You probably don't have a clue what I'm talking about, do you?"

He had made enough room in the trunk. He ripped off the whiskers and I saw that he was really quite young. A young, harmless face just as you'd see in any Irish village. A spasm of pain crossed his face. "When I saw Donny sitting there on the bench, I knew I had to take my one chance. So I stayed on the island and I followed him. And if you hadn't seen me . . ."

He lifted me to my feet by my neck. Then he was pressing on my throat. He was going to kill me here after all. The blood roared in my head. Feign death before he really kills you, a voice whispered through the roaring. I let myself go limp. He picked me up like a piece of baggage and stuffed me into his trunk among the clothing. The lid slammed shut. I knew I should try to do something but I kept floating in and out of consciousness. I was crammed in there so tightly that there wasn't room to move, anyway. To know that Daniel was so close and had not come to my aid was a final, frustrating blow. Even if he found the note now, it would be too late.

Suddenly the trunk was moved. I was being bumped and tumbled, then carried. I heard cheerful voices exchanging greetings. "Thank you, George, you've been most helpful."

"So sorry you have to leave early, Mr. Brady."

"Ah, well, that's show business, as we say. Shove that thing into the back of the cab, boys. Yes, I know it's heavy. These props weigh a ton. Anyone would think I'd got a body in here! Ha-ha-ha."

I landed with one final thump, lying upside down. I tried to turn my head so that I could breathe what little air remained. There was a keyhole. I just prayed enough air was coming in through it. Not that staying alive was going to help me. I'd only drown when I was thrown into the water, but I wasn't going to give up hope until the last second of my life.

I felt the trunk rattled and shaken as a carriage sped off. So Daniel hadn't suspected and now it was too late. What a stupid ending, I thought. So many dreams, so many hopes, and it was all going to end like this. If only I could have landed a good kick on Billy Brady, the way I had kicked Justin, I would have enjoyed seeing him lying dead beside my kitchen stove. It annoyed me that I hadn't been quick enough or smart enough or strong enough. It's stupid being a woman, was one of my final thoughts before I blacked out again.

I came to with a jolt. We were no longer moving. The trunk must have been taken from the cab. I heard it scraping on concrete as I was half carried, half dragged. This must be it, then. The dock with the ice-cold water waiting below. How long did it take to drown? Hadn't I heard that it was a pleasant death—except that I couldn't imagine any death being pleasant.

"Good-bye little lady," I heard Billy's voice above me. "I'm sorry it had to end like this. I really am."

I was hurtling downward. The blow when the trunk hit the water smashed my face against the wall of the trunk. Icy water rushed over me, so cold that it took my breath away. I tried to gasp and nearly swallowed the cotton jammed in my mouth. My heart almost stopped as I fought to breathe. The icy water was in my face now. I tried to move my foot and suddenly it kicked free. So did the other one. The trunk must have broken open as it hit the water. Unfortunately I was underneath it, but that was easily remedied. One thing I could do as well as any boy was swim. I'd had my training in the cold, rough Atlantic breakers and I could still beat my brothers in a race across the bay. How lucky that Brady hadn't thought to bind my arms.

I struck out and gave a mighty kick that propelled me to the surface. Above me reared the blackness of the dock and behind it lights were twinkling. All I had to do was swim ashore—except that the heavy woolen dress was weighing me down and I found it hard to breathe through that gag. It was so tantalizingly close. Surely I could make it. Then I realized something else—the current was taking me out. I was being swept along the shoreline

211

by an outgoing tide. I fought against it, but I was just about holding my own. The shore was no nearer and the cold was beginning to overcome me. It was getting harder and harder to move my arms.

There was a light ahead of me that appeared to be bobbing on the water. Suddenly I realized it was a rowing boat. Help was there, if only I could attract attention. I had to shout! I stopped swimming and fought with the knot behind my head. My hands were so cold I couldn't move my fingers anymore. *"Mmmmmm!"* I groaned through the cotton. It was a pathetic little sound that couldn't have traveled more than a yard. I tried waving my arms in the air, but the sleeves of my dress were black. Who would possibly see my frozen white hands in this vast black night?

I could hear the splash of oars and men's voices. I waved my hands violently and tried to swim toward them. But suddenly I knew I wasn't going to make it. I was too cold, too tired. I'd put up a valiant fight, but in the end the Hudson River was going to win. Sleep seemed almost inviting now. I closed my eyes and I wasn't in the river at all—I was lying in a warm bed, by a blazing fire, and Daniel Sullivan was saying, "Don't worry, Kathleen, you're safe now."

"Who's Kathleen?" was my last conscious thought.

❦ Twenty-three ❧

I opened my eyes to intense cold and discomfort. My aching body was being flung around as somebody dragged me away from the soft bed and the roaring fire.

"Don't take me away from the fire. I'm so cold. Leave me be," I managed to moan. "I want Daniel."

"It's Daniel you're wanting, is it?" said a voice that I recognized. I came back to full consciousness. There was an arm around my shoulder to stop me from being thrown around in a rapidly moving carriage. Even though it was dark in there, I worked out that the arm belonged to none other than Daniel Sullivan.

"Am I dead?" I asked.

"Not yet," Daniel's voice in the darkness said. "You'll be all right if we can get you out of those clothes and some hot liquid down your throat fast enough."

I was beginning to remember all the events of that evening— Daniel Sullivan sitting at the alderman's table, like old friends. "Where are you taking me?" I asked anxiously.

"Home," he said. "Back to Cherry Street. You have cousins there don't you? The ones who are minding the children. They'd take care of you."

I struggled to sit up. "No, don't take me there. I don't want to go there ever again. Please."

Daniel looked at me, then leaned forward to speak to the driver. "Take her to my place, Donovan. It's closer than HQ."

I fell against Daniel Sullivan as the carriage swung to the right. The arm around me tightened. My teeth were chattering violently and my feet and hands were burning as life returned to them. And I was beginning to notice the various aches and pains of my ordeal. I wanted to feel safe with Daniel, but how could I trust him now?

"How did you find me?" I asked.

"Find you?" he demanded. "Why else do you think I was dining with the alderman?"

"Oh," I said, wanting to believe it.

"Believe me, dinner with the alderman and his scatterbrained lady love is hardly the way I'd choose to pass the evening, but someone had to keep an eye on you. Not that I was very good at it, for which I apologize."

"How did you know I was there?" I asked.

"I've had one of my men following you since the night in the photographer's studio. When I heard that you had been stupid enough to worm your way into the alderman's house, I decided I had better get myself invited to dinner. He's always trying to keep in well with the police. I know the alderman. He plays rough."

"I know he does. He caught me snooping in his study. I was lucky to get away."

"You sure like living dangerously, don't you?" Daniel demanded.

"I know. I've been very stupid. But it was only when Billy Brady did his Roosevelt impersonation that I realized he was the man I saw on the island that night."

"So that's why you ran from the room. I wondered what Brady could have to do with it. I thought he must have been in the pay of the alderman."

"No, the alderman had nothing to do with this," I said. "He is involved in some pretty shady things, though."

"Which doesn't surprise me one jot." He chuckled. "So I suppose O'Malley must have been coming to blackmail Brady?"

"It was Billy Brady who betrayed the Plumbridge Nine," I said. "He was with them that night. He was the only one who got caught. They were going to torture him so he gave them names to save his skin."

"No wonder he had to silence O'Malley right away," Sullivan said. "If that got out, I don't think he'd be the darling of the Irish for much longer."

"You have to go and arrest him right away," I said. "Why didn't you arrest him right away? And why did you let me almost drown?"

"Let you? My dear girl, I can't forgive myself for being so inept. I stationed a constable outside the house to prevent anything from happening to you. I sensed something was wrong when you left the room and Billy followed not too much later, but I didn't want to cause a scene. I thought the alderman was involved, remember. And I knew my constable was outside the front door. I didn't realize he'd be stupid enough to help carry the trunk into Billy's carriage. If I hadn't come out and questioned him, we'd have been too late. We almost were too late, fishing around for you in the darkness like that. You must be some swimmer to have kept going in that current."

"I'm not bad," I said.

"You're full of surprises, Mrs. O'Connor," he said.

If you only knew, I thought. I was getting drowsy again. The pain in my limbs was dimming and it seemed comfortable to rest my head against Daniel's shoulder. Again I was awakened with a jerk.

"Come on, we're here," he said. He helped me from the carriage. We stood before an attractive brownstone on a tree-lined street. "Lucky that I live in Chelsea," he said. "I don't think you'd have made it to the Lower East Side. Let's get her inside, Constable."

I was half carried up a flight of stairs. A door was unlocked and I was taken into an austere and tidy room. It was so obviously a gentleman's room. Leather armchair by the fire. Ashtray containing a pipe on the side table. Desk on the far wall. Sporting print over the mantel. Daniel lit the gas lamps, then the gas fire in the fireplace. It hissed to life, sending out immediate heat.

"Thank you, Constable," he said as the policeman helped lower me into the armchair. "You can go back to HQ. I'll phone the chief and join you as soon as I can."

The policeman went, leaving us alone. Daniel crossed to the sideboard and poured from a decanter. "Here," he said. "Get this down you. It will warm you up."

I took a sip and made a face. "It's burning," I said.

"I can tell you're not a drinker. Go on, swallow it."

I swallowed, coughed, then swallowed again. He laughed. "From the face you're making, anyone would think I'm trying to poison you. It's the best brandy, I'll have you know."

"It tastes horrible," I said, shuddering.

"Now we have to get those wet things off you as quickly as possible," Daniel said. He disappeared into a back room, then returned with blankets, towels, and dry clothing. "I've nothing that will fit, but put those on. At least they're warm. Go ahead and change by the fire. Don't worry, I won't peek"—the same slightly wicked smile. "I have to make a phone call to headquarters and then I'll be in the kitchen, making you some hot tea while you're changing."

I struggled out of my wet clothes—why did they have to put all those buttons down the back? My numbed fingers struggled with them, but I could hardly call Daniel back to undress me, could I? The brandy was starting to work. I could feel the glow spreading out along my frozen limbs. I ripped open the remaining buttons hearing them strike the polished floor with a satisfying ping. I rubbed myself vigorously with the towel he had provided, then attempted to put on the clothes. Daniel had brought me a suit of long gentleman's undergarments, all in one. I put it on, then turned and caught a glimpse of myself in the mirror on the far wall. I looked so ridiculous that I burst out laughing.

Daniel came running through from the kitchen. "Is something wrong? I thought I heard you cry out."

"With laughter," I said. "Look at me!"

I held out my leg and my arm, completely engulfed. He started to laugh, too. "Woman being swallowed by octopus. You could be one of the living picture tableaux that are so popular in the theaters right now."

"Oh, Daniel," I said. "This whole thing is so ridiculous."

"You called me by my first name," he said. He came closer until I was conscious of the warmth of his presence and of the current running between us. I could almost feel myself drawn toward him.

"You called me Kathleen first," I said.

"So I did. So we have both made slips of the lip." He put his hands on my shoulders. "My brain is telling me to be sensible. Do you think I should be sensible at this moment, Mrs. O'Connor?" His eyes were challenging me—sparkling at me dangerously in the firelight glow.

"I think being sensible too often amounts to a boring life, Mr. Sullivan," I whispered.

"Then I fear I'm about to make another slip of the lip," he said, and bent to kiss me.

I had never felt like this in my entire life. Oh to be sure, I'd let enough boys kiss me, and some go beyond kissing too. But, to tell you the truth, I had wondered what all the fuss was about. Now I knew. My arms came around his neck and I pulled him closer to me. The blood was singing in my head again, but this time the feeling was very different. I understood now why men were sometimes mad with desire. I felt mad with desire myself, incapable of a rational thought. Then Daniel swept me up into his arms. As he carried me through to his bedroom I was brought back to reality with a jolt. Any moment now and he would discover that I was not the married woman with two children he thought me to be.

I struggled in his arms. "No, not in here. Take me back, please."

He looked perplexed. "I'm sorry, I misunderstood."

He placed me down gently on the floor.

"No, you didn't." I reached up and stroked his face tenderly. "Believe me, my feelings for you are genuine, but I have some explaining to do first. You should know the truth about me."

I went to kneel on the rug before the fire and held out my hands to the blaze. Daniel followed me silently and perched on the arm of the chair beside me. I didn't want to look at him so I stared into the flames.

"Daniel, I have a confession to make," I blurted out. "My name is not Kathleen O'Connor and I'm not a married woman."

"You're not Kathleen O'Connor?"

I looked away. "I've been living a lie and hating myself for doing it. I took her place to come here on the ship. The real Kathleen is dying in Ireland and this was the only way to get her children to their father."

"Holy Mother! You took her place! So that's why you moved out and deserted your babes in such a hurry. I thought it didn't ring true for you to walk out on your children so easily. Then who in God's name are you?"

"My name's Molly, Molly Murphy."

He stroked my wet hair from my face. "Molly. It suits you better than Kathleen. And tell me, Molly, are there any husbands or suitors I don't know about, waiting to beat me to a pulp for having designs on their beloved?"

"None, sir. I'm all alone in the world, and free and available."

"I'm glad to hear it," he said. "Then, being a gentleman, I shall not take advantage of a young lady half out of her mind with shock and restrain my passion until a more suitable occasion." He kissed me again, but tenderly this time. Then he got to his feet. "I'll go and make that tea now."

I watched him go with some regret.

❧ Twenty-four ❧

Now that Daniel Sullivan knew the truth about me, he behaved like a perfect gentleman and wouldn't let me spend the night in his bachelor apartment. I had a reputation to consider, he told me. Instead he got the Irish family on the ground floor to put me up for the night. They made me very welcome and in the morning their daughter lent me some of her own clothes. I wasn't going to wear that black maid's dress ever again. And I wasn't going to return it to Mrs. Brennan, either. I had learned my lesson. I was going to stay well away from the alderman and his household and leave the justice to police.

As I dressed and performed my toilet the next morning I was horrified to see myself in the mirror. My face was battered and bruised, black and blue like an overripe fruit.

"You can't go out, looking like that," Mrs. O'Shea said, shaking her head with concern. "Captain Sullivan says that a madman threw you into the Hudson River and left you to drown. I hope they catch him. The city's not a safe place for young girls alone, that's for sure. You need to find yourself a nice, reliable man to take care of you."

"Yes," I said. "That wouldn't be a bad idea." Actually I had a man in mind.

He showed up around midday and winced when he saw my battered face in the daylight. "Saints preserve us. Look at you!"

"I'd rather not," I said. "I tell you one thing, I don't think I'll be chosen queen of the St. Patrick's Day parade looking like this."

"The bastard," Daniel muttered, taking my chin cautiously in his hand. "I hope we nail him."

"Have you arrested him?"

"Oh yes, we brought him in last night, and he promptly posted bail and departed again. He's a cocky so and so and he's going to bluff it out. He doesn't think we'll be able to pin anything on him."

"But you have to," I said. "He's killed two people. He almost killed me. Can't I testify?"

"Of course, if we have enough evidence to get it to court, but he was a smart devil. He used disguises and gloves on both occasions he killed. No fingerprints, no witnesses."

"But I'm a witness," I insisted. "I saw him on Ellis Island."

Daniel shook his head. "Wearing a disguise. And then wrongly identified Boyle and the alderman. A good defense attorney would make mincemeat of your testimony, I'm afraid."

"But he can't be allowed to walk free. What about Ireland—won't they send you all the information on him and on what he did?"

"He was let off for naming his friends in Ireland. He's a free man as far as they're concerned."

"But he's killed two people to keep those facts hidden."

"The problem with that is that he came into this country under the name of Billy Brady. There is no document linking him to his real name. Once he's over here with a new name, it's almost impossible to link to his past."

The implications of what he was saying were just dawning on me. I had come to this country as Kathleen O'Connor. If my identity stayed a secret between Daniel and me, I was safe.

"So what are you going to do?" I demanded. "You can't let him get away with it."

"I'll do everything I can, I promise you," he said. "But you stay out of police business from now on."

"But the alderman," I insisted. "He's involved in shady dealings, too. Can't you do something about that?"

"Not if I want to keep my job," Daniel said. "Listen, Molly, you have to understand how New York works. Tammany Hall calls the shots. They make life easy for the police and we turn a blind eye on each other. It's not ideal, I agree, but that's how it is. Any policeman who went after a Tammany man would be digging his own grave. And if the alderman is involved in shady schemes, he's also much loved here in the city. He gives to all the charities. He arranges the most splendid St. Patrick's Days. And he's very, very careful. Anyone who tried to take him to court would find there were no witnesses and no proof."

"Then this is a corrupt city," I said.

"No more than any other city, I'd imagine. And it's a good city, too. My parents came over here, starving in the Great Famine. When Tammany came to power, my dad became a policeman. He rose through the ranks and earned enough to send me to Columbia University. That's the good thing about life over here. It doesn't matter what you start out as, you have the chance to rise above it."

"I'm hoping to make something of my life," I said. "I have to find a job—as soon as my face heals enough to go out in public again. I put my hand up to my swollen cheek.

"What sort of job are you looking for?"

"Not as a house servant. I don't have the temperament and I don't think, somehow, that I'd get a good reference, do you?"

Daniel came to sit on the arm of my chair, where I was wrapped in blankets beside a fire. "So what would you like to do?"

"You know," I said, "I've been thinking. I think I might have a flair for investigations."

"Holy Mother—what are you saying?"

"That I want to become the first woman detective in the New York City Police?" I asked, and laughed when I saw his face. "No, listen, Daniel. I've been thinking. When I left Liverpool there were so many people who were trying to trace their loved ones in the New World. Maybe I could establish myself as a people finder."

"Haven't you learned your lesson yet, woman? Private investigations, indeed, I've already had to fish you out of the harbor once."

"Oh, I don't mean criminal investigations. I'll leave that side of it to you. But there should be enough people in Europe who want to know whether a loved one is dead or alive, don't you think? And it certainly beats the only other job offers I've had so far."

"Which were?"

"Fish gutting or prostitution."

He laughed and slid his hand into mine. "There is another option," he said. "You could think of settling down."

I laughed. "Can you really see me settling down to lace curtains and afternoon tea? And do you have a suitable gentleman in mind?"

Daniel got to his feet and laughed, too. "No, I was just talking off the top of my head, as usual. I need to get back to work. I just came by to make sure you were doing okay."

After he left, I sat staring into the fire. I might be a newcomer at the game of love, but I had definitely sensed he was about to propose to me. Something had made him back off in a hurry. Was there something about Daniel Sullivan that he didn't want me to know?

By St. Patrick's Day I was on my feet and the bruises had faded enough for me to go out and face the world. The O'Sheas had been more than kind and allowed me to stay with them until I was back to health. I only discovered later that Daniel had been paying them for my keep. Reluctantly I decided that I couldn't impose on them any longer and told Daniel that I had to go back to the hostel.

"I think I've found something a little better than that," he said. "Not too far from where I live. One of our sergeants has an attic he's not using at the moment—lovely view across the river, quiet neighborhood, and no Bible reading."

"That would be wonderful," I said, "but I have no job and no money."

"It's sitting empty at the moment and I'm sure that Sergeant O'Hallaran won't be pounding on your door for rent straight-away," he said. "And as for that, I do have a little something to keep you going. Alderman McCormack was very distressed that you had to leave his employment in such circumstances. He had no idea that he had invited a dangerous criminal to his house, and he'd like to make amends to you and hope that you can find a suitable job that makes proper use of your talents." He handed me a leather purse. It felt heavy. I looked at him suspiciously.

"Daniel, is this a bribe?"

"It's a gift from a very philanthropic gentleman and if you're sensible you'll take it."

I was about to tell him that I had higher moral standards than that. I couldn't be bought. Then I realized that I was a fugitive criminal, had traveled under a false identity, and lied to the police. What would one more step down the road to crime matter? I took the purse from him. "You can thank the alderman for his kindness," I said. "And tell him that I'm turning my talent in another direction."

"So are you coming to watch the parade tomorrow?" he asked. " 'Tis a fine sight, and a great day for the Irish. I'd escort you myself but we're all on duty that day. But I'll guarantee it is a sight worth seeing."

I went with Daniel to see the attic on Twelfth Street. It was two rooms with a hallway between containing a sink. "I don't need this much space," I said. Then a wonderful thought hit me. "Do you think the sergeant would mind if more than one person occupied this attic?"

Daniel gave me a strange look. "What did you have in mind?"

I laughed, realizing what he must be thinking. "No, nothing like that. It's just that the little children I brought across to Amer-ica—they're living in a filthy, overcrowded place right now.

Their father is looking for a better situation, but works long hours and he has no time. They could have one room and I could have the other."

"You've a kind heart, Molly Murphy," Daniel said. "I like that in a woman—not as much as a neat little waist, of course, and a round little mouth, and long red hair and . . ." I had to remove his hands and remind him to behave himself properly or he'd ruin my reputation with the sergeant's family before I even got established there.

On the morning of the parade I went to the house on Cherry Street first.

"What's she doing, back here?" Nuala demanded as I stood at their front door. "Don't think we're going to take you back, whatever that softhearted cousin of my husband says."

"Oh, no thank you," I said. "I wouldn't dream of coming back here. I've a much better place. Hot water, nice view, good neighborhood. I came to talk to Seamus and to see if I could take young Seamus and Bridie to the parade today."

Seamus decided to come along, too. I took the two children by the hand and I told Seamus about the apartment as we walked to Broadway. He seemed to like the idea and was anxious to see the place for himself. I bought the children donuts and we sat on the curb, waiting for the parade to start. Fire trucks came first, their bells ringing loudly, their horses decorated with plums for the occasion. Then marching bands and green draped automobiles, one with the mayor in it, the next with Alderman Mc-Cormack.

"Lord love you, sir! God bless you, your worship!" The crowd shouted as he drove past. I think he noticed me among the crowd and smiled.

Battalions of men marched by, carrying banners. The NYPD, the firemen, and then rows of men with shamrocks in their caps—the Irish Builders Union. And there in the middle of them was Michael Larkin, head held high and striding out with the best of them.

"Michael!" Seamus, Bridie, and I yelled and waved. He looked around, saw us, and ran across to us.

"I've got a job like I said I would," he shouted. "On that new skyscraper on Union Square. Going to be the tallest in the world!"

He started to run to catch up with his mates then turned back again. "I get off for lunch between twelve and one!"

The floats were passing now—Irish dancers and giant shamrocks and harps. The children were entranced. So was I. Then I stiffened. Another float was approaching. It depicted an Irish cottage with mountains behind it and a big male voice was reciting "The wearing of the green"! The sign on it read Billy Brady, Ireland's Darlin' Boy.

I felt so angry and powerless. Why was he not in jail? Why was he free to stand there with that self-satisfied smile on his face?

Suddenly a man ran out of the crowd. "Traitor!" he yelled. "You betrayed those boys!" A shot rang out. Billy Brady crumpled and fell. Commotion followed. I saw policemen swarm toward the stricken man. Daniel arrived a few minutes later. An ambulance came galloping up and carried the body away. The parade started to move on again.

Daniel caught sight of me and came over.

"How could that man have found out?" I asked. "Do you think O'Malley managed to get word before . . ." I broke off, seeing something in his expression. "Wait," I said, "that wasn't one of your men with a gun, was it?"

"Of course it wasn't. We're here to uphold the law, not break it." He sounded genuinely shocked.

"Then how did they find out who Billy Brady really was?"

He stood watching the parade and said casually, "Of course, someone on the force might have slipped the information to local extremists—Irish freedom fighters, you know. They don't take kindly to traitors."

"So you're not going to go after the gunman?"

"Of course we are, although when the truth gets out, I don't think we'll find anyone in the crowd willing to testify."

"I don't understand the way New York works," I said.

"Then may I suggest that you stick around here until you do." He tipped his cap. "And that could take a long, long while." Then he strode off up Broadway, following the parade.

DEATH OF RILEY

New York, July 1901

"You want me to do what?" I demanded so loudly that a delicate young female walking ahead of us glanced back in horror and had to reach for her smelling salts. I burst out laughing. "For the love of Mike, Daniel—can you picture me as a companion?" Then I looked up at Captain Daniel Sullivan's face. He wasn't smiling.

He gave me an embarrassed half-smile, half-shrug. "I was only thinking of you, Molly. You do need a job, and you haven't exactly been successful in your search so far."

"So I haven't come up with the perfect job yet." I picked up my skirts to avoid the wet patches around a grand-looking fountain. It had a fine bronze statue of the Angel of the Waters on top, but at this moment the scene was anything but grand. A host of little boys, some of them naked as the day they were born, were scrambling in and out, standing under the curtain of spray before being evicted again, squealing and yelling as they avoided the nightstick wielded by an overzealous policeman. It was Sunday afternoon and we were doing what most New Yorkers did on hot summer Sundays—we were strolling through Central Park. For once Daniel's day off had actually fallen on a Sunday, and there had been no incidents to drag him away with an apologetic peck on the cheek.

It seemed as if pecks on the cheek were all I was getting these days from Captain Daniel Sullivan. Yes, I know that pecks on the cheek, properly chaperoned, are all that decent young ladies should expect before marriage, but propriety rather went out of the window when I was with Daniel. And I had hoped our romance might have blossomed into something more substantial by now, but as New York's youngest police captain, Daniel threw himself wholeheartedly into his job. I, on the other hand, had no job to keep me occupied.

It wasn't as if I hadn't tried. After my somewhat dramatic arrival in New York, I had looked for something suitable. The saints in heaven will attest that I really put my heart into it. I wouldn't have minded a governess position, in fact I'd have been good at it. But it didn't take me long to discover that an Irish girl, fresh off the boat, and with no references—or at least no references that could be verified (I had made some very convincing forgeries), would not be hired to teach the children of a good family. Nursemaid maybe, but I didn't think I'd last a week as a servant.

After that, I tried my hand at any job I could find, short of gutting fish at the Fulton Street fish market. I did draw the line at standing up to my elbows in fish entrails.

"You have to admit that there have been some rather spectacular disasters." Daniel voiced my thoughts for me, making me wonder whether he could actually read my mind.

"I wouldn't say disasters."

A breeze blew off the boating lake beyond the fountain, sending a fine curtain of spray in our direction. The cool tingles on my hot skin felt wonderful and I was tempted to stand there for a while until Daniel pulled me clear. "Molly—you'll get soaked to the skin."

"But it feels divine."

"It might feel divine," he said, looking down at me with those alarming blue eyes, "but that's a very fine muslin you're wearing, my dear. We wouldn't want other men ogling you, would we?" He led me firmly away from the fountain terrace, along the edge of the boating lake. I paused to look longingly at those rowboats. A couple came gliding by, the girl's face hidden by a deliciously decadent parasol—all frills and lace and froufrou—as she trailed a hand languidly through the water. Her beau, pulling manfully at the oars in rolled-up shirtsleeves, didn't look as if he were enjoying himself quite as much. Undignified rivulets of sweat streaked the beet-red face beneath his boater.

"You wouldn't say disasters?" Daniel repeated, chuckling as he led me away. "The shirtwaist factory?"

"So I got a needle through my thumb. It could have happened to anyone." I tossed my head, almost losing my straw boater into the water.

"And who sewed all those sleeves on inside out?" Those alarming blue eyes were twinkling.

"That wasn't why I was fired and you know it. It was because I stood up to that brute of a foreman and wasn't about to take any of his nonsense. All those unfair rules—docking their workers' pay every time they so much as sneezed. I knew right away that I'd never be able to hold my tongue for long."

"Then there was the café," Daniel reminded me.

I gave him a sheepish grin. "Yes, I suppose that counted as a spectacular disaster."

We had reached the dappled shade of spreading chestnut trees as the path left the lakeside. The effect was instant, like stepping into a pool of cool water. "Ah, that's better," Daniel said. "Look, there's a bench under that tree. Let's sit awhile."

I noticed that Daniel seemed to be feeling the heat more than I. His face was as red as the young man's in the rowboat and his wild black curls were plastered to his forehead under his boater. Of course, gentlemen are at a disadvantage on days like this, having to wear jackets whilst we women can keep cool in muslins. But he was a born New Yorker. I'd have thought he grew up used to this heat. I, on the other hand, had come from the wild west coast of Ireland, where a couple of sunny days in a row counted as a heat wave, and we had the chilly Atlantic at our feet whenever we needed to cool off.

Daniel took out his handkerchief and mopped at his brow. "That's better," he said. "I swear, every summer is hotter than the last. It's those new skyscrapers. They block the cooling breezes from the East River and the Hudson."

"It's certainly hot enough." I fanned myself with the penny fan I had bought from a street vendor last week. It was a pretty little thing from China, made of paper and decorated with a picture of a pagoda and wild mountain scenery. "Here, you look as if you could use this more than me." I turned and fanned Daniel too. He grabbed at my wrist, laughing. "Stop it. You'll be offering me your smelling salts next."

"I've never carried smelling salts in my life and never intend to," I said. "Fainting is for ninnies."

"That's what I like about you, Molly Murphy—" For a long minute Daniel gazed at me in a way that turned my insides to water, his fingers still firmly around my wrist—"Your spirit. That and your trim little waist, of course, and those big green eyes and that adorable little nose." He touched it playfully. Then the smile faded but the look of longing remained. "Oh, Molly. I just wish . . ." He let the rest of the sentence hang in the humid air, making me wonder what exactly he was wishing. He was young and healthy, with great career prospects—and a future that should have included a wife too. But I wasn't going to press him on this one. Who knew how men's minds worked? He could be waiting for a pay raise or saving enough to buy a house before he popped the question—if he did indeed intend to pop it. For once in my life I kept silent.

"I'm pretty content myself," I said gaily. "I have a fine big room of my own and a handsome fellow who comes to call from time to time, and I'm living in a big city, just like I always dreamed I would."

Daniel let his gaze fall and he sat there for a moment silent, his eyes focused on his hands in his lap.

"There's no rush for anything, Daniel," I said. "If I could just find a way to keep myself a respectable job where I wasn't abused or overworked . . ."

"Did I not mention the companion's position?"

I patted his hand. "Daniel—can you see me as a companion

to an old lady? Companions are pathetic, down-trodden creatures who cringe when spoken to and spend their days holding knitting wool and combing cats. I tried my hand at being a servant, remember. I wasn't born to be humble. And you know yourself that I can never learn when to hold my tongue."

"But a companion is not a servant, Molly. You'd be expected to read to Miss Van Woekem and take her for strolls around the park—that kind of thing. What could be easier?"

"She'd be crotchety and finickety. Old spinsters always are. I'd lose my patience with her and that would be that." I gave a gay little laugh, but still Daniel didn't smile.

"Molly, I'm sure I don't need to remind you that you do need to find some kind of job soon. I know the alderman gave you a small gift by way of apology for what happened at his house—"

"It was a bribe, Daniel, as you very well know."

"But it won't last forever," Daniel went on, ignoring my statement. It was funny the way the New York policemen seemed to become suddenly deaf at the mention of the word 'bribe.' "And you do have rent to pay, even though it's a modest amount."

"The O'Hallarans are being very kind," I agreed. "I'm sure they could rent out their attic for much more if they chose to." It was Daniel himself who had found me the pleasant top-floor flat owned by a fellow policeman. "And don't forget Seamus shares the rent, and pays for most of the food, too."

"I should think so, considering that you cook it and look after his children for him."

"I'm glad to do it," I said. "They're no trouble, and how would he manage without me, poor man, with his wife back home in Ireland just waiting to die?"

I had brought Seamus's young son and daughter to New York at their mother's request when she found that she had consumption and wasn't allowed to travel. And in case you think I'm some kind of saint, let me assure you that the arrangement suited my own purposes very well.

"You've a good heart, Molly," Daniel said, "but this arrangement can't go on forever. I'm not entirely comfortable with you living up there with a man whose wife is back in Ireland."

I laughed. "Not comfortable, Daniel? Seamus O'Connor is a perfectly harmless individual—you've seen him yourself. Hardly the greatest catch in New York. What's more, we have a kitchen and hallway between us to keep things proper, and Mrs. O'Hallaran downstairs too, keeping an eye on things."

"That's not the point," Daniel said. "People will talk. Do you want them saying you're a kept woman?"

"Certainly not."

"Then may I suggest you listen to me and find a suitable job for yourself that will not end in disaster."

His reminders of my dismal failures in the world of commerce were beginning to rile me. I didn't like to fail at anything. "If you really want to know, I'm still planning to follow my original idea and set myself up as a private investigator." I threw this out more to annoy him than anything.

Daniel rolled his eyes and gave a despairing chuckle. "Molly, women do not become investigators. I thought we'd been through all this before."

"I don't see why not. I thought I was pretty good at it."

"Apart from almost getting yourself killed."

"Right. Apart from that. But I told you. I don't plan to deal with criminal cases. Nothing dangerous. I still keep thinking about all those people when I was leaving Liverpool, Daniel. They were desperate for knowledge of their loved ones who had come to America. I'd be doing good work if I united families again, wouldn't I?"

"Did it ever occur to you that the loved ones might not want to be found?" he asked. "And anyway, how would you set about this—this detective business? You'd need an office to start with, and you'd have to advertise . . ."

"I know that too!"

"And if you discovered that the loved one you were seeking had gone to California, would you take the train to find him? Families of immigrants won't have money to pay."

"So I'd need some capital to get started." I paused to watch an elegant open carriage pass on the road beyond the trees. Lovely women in wide white hats and young men in blazers sat chatting and laughing as if they hadn't a care in the world— which they probably hadn't. "And I'd just have to take some cases that paid well."

Daniel turned to me and took my hands in his. "Molly, please put this foolish idea to rest. You don't need to set yourself up as anything. You need a pleasant, dignified job that pays the rent, for the time being, that's all."

"Maybe I won't be content with a pleasant little job. Maybe I want to make something of myself."

He laughed again, uneasily this time. "It's not as if you're a man and need to be thinking of a future career. Only something to bide your time until some fellow snaps you up."

His eyes were teasing again, all seriousness apparently forgotten.

"Snaps me up? But surely you know I'm a hopeless case? Already turned twenty-three and therefore officially on the shelf."

"You? You'll never find yourself on the shelf, Molly. You'll be just as fascinating at fifty."

"Hardly a comforting thought," I said. "Still a companion at fifty? Shall we go on walking?" I got to my feet. This conversation was definitely not leading where I wanted it to. Daniel had had several chances to state his intentions and failed miserably at all of them. It wasn't as if he were either hesitant or shy. Then he said something that made me realize how his brain might be working.

"I wish you'd give the companion's position a try, Molly. Miss Van Woekem is well respected in New York society. My parents really look up to her. Being with her would give you an introduction into society here."

Then it dawned on me. That was why he was hesitating— he didn't want to marry an Irish peasant girl fresh from the old sod. I'd left Ireland with its snobbery and class prejudice and crossed the Atlantic to find that same snobbery alive and flourishing in the New World. And he with parents who came over with nothing in the great famine! Well, if that was how Daniel Sullivan thought—I opened my mouth to tell him what he could do with his companion's job, and with Miss Van What's-it too. I stopped myself at the last second. He presumably thought he was doing this for my own good. He wanted me to fit in and become acceptable and accepted in society here. What's more, it certainly beat out fish gutting. What did I have to lose? "All right, if you think I should take it, I'm prepared to give it a try."

He stopped and put his hands on my shoulders. "That's my girl," he said, kissing me on the forehead.

"Should we try the Ramble today?" I motioned to the inviting woodland path that disappeared into the undergrowth to my left. The area of Central Park known as the Ramble was made up of a series of winding, intersecting paths through a thickly wooded copse. Only a few steps into the woods and it was hard to believe that you were in the middle of a big city. It was also one of the few places where it was possible to steal a kiss undisturbed.

But Daniel shook his head. "It's too hot for walking today. Why don't we head for that ice cream parlor?"

"Ice cream? That would be wonderful!" On a hot day like this, ice cream won out over kisses with me too. I had only just tasted my first ice cream and was still amazed at a place where such luxuries were available every day.

Daniel smiled at my excitement. "Don't ever change, will you?"

"I might well turn into a severe and snooty spinster when Miss Van Woekem starts to influence me," I retorted.

He laughed and slipped his arm around my waist. In spite of the heat and the fact that this was surely not proper behavior for a park on a Sunday, I wasn't about to stop him. We joined the stream of Sunday strollers on the wide East Drive. Half of New York had to be here. The upper crust passed by in their open carriages, oblivious to the stream of pedestrians beside them. On the sandy footpath it was ordinary people like ourselves, severe Italian mothers dressed all in black with a fleet of noisy bambinos, Jewish families with bearded patriarchs and solemn little boys with skullcaps on their heads, proud fathers pushing tall perambulators—every language under the sun being spoken around us. As we neared the gate the noise level rose—music from a carrousel competed with an Italian hurdy-gurdy man and the shouts of the ice cream seller. I knew that Daniel wouldn't buy ice cream in the park. You never knew what it was made from, he said, and typhoid fever was always a worry in the hot weather.

Suddenly a dapper little man in a dark brown suit and derby hat stepped out in front of us.

"Hold it right there!" he shouted.

"It's all right. He's only taking our photo," Daniel whispered as I started in alarm. "He's one of the park photographers."

I saw then that the man was pointing a little black box at us and we heard a click.

"There you are, sir. Lovely souvenir of the day," he said, nodding seriously. He had a strange accent that seemed to be a mixture of London Cockney and Bowery New York. He came up to Daniel. "Here's my card if you care to stop by the studio and purchase the photo for your lady friend."

As he handed Daniel his card he moved closer and I thought I saw his hand go to Daniel's pocket. It was over in a fraction of a second, so that I didn't know whether to believe my eyes. For a moment I was too startled to act, then, as I grabbed Daniel's arm to warn him, I saw the man's hand move away from Daniel again, and it was empty. I didn't want to make a scene, so I kept quiet until we had walked past the photographer.

"I think that man tried to pick your pocket," I whispered.

"Then he was out of luck," Daniel said, smiling. "I only keep my handkerchief in that pocket."

He slipped his hand into the pocket and I noticed the change in his expression. "Yes, the fellow was unlucky all right," he said, taking my arm. "Come on, let's get that ice cream."

* * *

A crisply starched maid showed me into the refined brick house with wrought-iron balconies on South Gramercy Park.

"Miss Murphy, ma'am," she said and dropped a curtsy before retiring. The old woman who sat in the high-backed chair by the window looked as if she had been chiseled from marble. Her face had shrunk to a living skull but the eyes that fastened on me were still very alive.

"Well, come in, girl. Don't just stand there," she said in a sharp, gravelly voice that sounded as if it had dried out like its owner. "What is your name?"

"Molly. Molly Murphy." Her look was so intense that I was startled.

She sniffed. "Molly—a nickname only suitable for peasants and servants. You were presumably baptized with a Christian name."

"I was baptized Mary Margaret."

"And that is a little too pretentious for someone in your station. Nobody below the middle class needs two names. I shall call you just plain Mary."

"You can call all you like, but I won't answer." I had recovered enough to challenge her stare. "My name's Molly. Always has been. If you don't like it, you can always call me Miss Murphy."

She opened her mouth, went to say something, then shut it again with a "hmmph."

"Let me take a look at you."

I could feel those dark boot-button eyes boring into me. "Are you not wearing a corset, girl?"

"I've never worn one," I said. "Back where I come from, we didn't go in for such things."

She made a disproving tut-tutting noise. "Daniel mentioned that you were newly arrived from Ireland, but he didn't say that you'd come straight from the bogs. When you leave here today I'll give you the money and you'll go to my costumier and have yourself fitted for a corset. And as for the rest of your clothing—I suppose I can't expect you to wear black in this summer heat. Do you possess a plain gray dress?"

"I don't possess much of anything," I said. "I had to leave most of my things behind in Ireland."

I didn't mention the reason I'd had to leave in a hurry. Nobody knew that but me. Nobody was going to know it.

"I'll have my housekeeper see if there is anything suitable for you in the servant's closet," she said.

"I understood that you wanted a companion, not a servant." Again I matched stares with her. With that hooked nose and those black little eyes she reminded me of some kind of bird. A bird of prey, definitely. "I don't get out much anymore," she said. "I like to be surrounded by things that are pleasing to the eye." My gaze followed hers around the room. It was indeed pleasing to the eye—not cluttered with too many knickknacks like other well-to-do rooms I had seen, it managed to be austere and elegant at the same time. The furniture was well-polished mahogany, with lots of silk cushions; a mahogany bookcase filled with rich leather tomes took up most of one wall. There was a lamp with a shade like a miniature stained-glass window and a couple of good, if somber, paintings hung on the walls. Not what one would call a woman's room, but a room of definite good taste.

"The lamp is from Mr. Tiffany," she said, noticing my eyes falling on it. "My one concession to the latest fads. And the painting over the fireplace—"

"Looks as if it's of the Flemish School," I said, studying the dark and rather too real-looking still life of a dead pheasant and some fruit. "Is it a copy of a Vermeer?"

She snorted. I couldn't tell if the sound was pleased or contemptuous. "It *is* a Vermeer," she said. "And how do you come to know about painting? Are they hanging Vermeers in Irish cottages these days?"

"I'm not uneducated, even though I may not be fashionably dressed. Our governess was a great devotee of art. She had visited all the fine galleries of Europe."

"You had a governess?" She looked at me incredulously.

"I was educated with the land-owner's daughters," I answered, hoping she wouldn't interrogate further on this topic.

She stared at me in a way that could be considered rude among equals, obviously deciding whether I was lying to her or too impudent to keep. "You have a nice enough face," she said at last, "and you carry yourself well, but that outfit has definitely seen better days. I'll have my dressmaker come in and measure you up. Maybe not gray. Doesn't do justice to the hair, which would be quite striking if properly arranged." In deference to my companion's position I had managed to twist my unruly red curls into a severe bun. Not too successfully, I might add. Trying to tame my hair was like trying to hold back the ocean.

"So if you know about art, and you were educated by a governess, you presumably know how to read more than penny dreadfuls."

"There's nothing I like better." I let my eyes wander to the bookcase on the back wall. "I love to read whenever I can."

"In which case maybe you'll turn out to be satisfactory after all, in spite of appearances. You can start by reading to me now. What do you like to read?"

"Oh, the novels of Charles Dickens—"

"Popular sentimental drivel, written for the masses," she said. "Why does one need to read about squalor when there is already too much on one's doorstep?"

"Jane Austen, then."

"Feminine frippery. You won't find many novels in this house, Miss Murphy. I believe that reading should be for two purposes only—to educate and to uplift. Now if you will pick up that slim volume lying on the sofa, you may read to me from it. It is a newly published account of last year's atrocities in China, written by the sister of a missionary who was beheaded. I am very much afraid there are some races that we shall never succeed in civilizing or Christianizing."

"The Chinese have a very old civilization and they might not have wanted to be Christianized," I pointed out.

"What rubbish you talk, girl. It is our duty to spread the Gospel. But then I suppose you are another of those Holy Romans. You've never learned the lessons of Martin Luther or John

Calvin, more's the pity. And now my goddaughter is thinking of marrying one. 'You'd better bring the boy in line before the wedding,' I told her, because I'll not attend any service where they swing incense and pray to idols."

I decided this was a time to keep my mouth shut and went to get the book.

"But Arabella is a headstrong girl and probably doesn't care a fig for anyone's opinion, even mine, though she knows she'll inherit everything from me," she added as I crossed the room.

I realized I was gritting my teeth with a forced smile on my face. I hoped Daniel realized what I was doing for him, because I wasn't sure who was going to break first, I or Miss Van Woekem. A white fur rug was lying behind the sofa. As I went to step on it, it leaped up, yowling, and clawed at me. So there were to be cats, after all.

"Watch what you're doing, clumsy girl," Miss Van Woekem snapped. "Now you've quite upset Princess Yasmin."

I forbore to say that Princess Yasmin had quite upset me as well. The large white Persian sat watching me with a look of utter disdain. I reached carefully past her to get the book. I need not have worried. She turned her back on me and started licking a paw as if I were of no consequence whatsoever.

At the end of an hour's reading the maid reappeared to announce luncheon.

"I will take mine here, on a tray," Miss Van Woekem announced. "Miss Murphy will eat at the dining table." She nodded for me to close the book. "You read surprisingly well for one of your station. The accent is uncouth, of course, but I am pleasingly surprised. Maybe you'll do after all."

"And maybe I won't," I thought as I followed the maid to the dining room. If Daniel thought this was easy work, he had never tried it.

I spent an uneasy meal sitting alone at a vast polished mahogany table, with the maid waiting attendance behind me. I won't say I didn't enjoy it, however. For one who has always had ideas above her station, according to my mother, this was the way I should have been eating all my life. And the food was delicious—some sort of cold fish mousse and salad, fresh fruit and tiny meringues for dessert and freshly made lemonade to drink. I began to think better of the job, especially when I discovered that Miss Van W. took an afternoon nap and I was free to browse in her library.

After tea taken at the little table in the sitting room, she instructed me to get her bath chair ready. The maid brought it into the front hall—an impressive wicker contraption on wheels—and helped Miss Van W. into it.

"You can wheel me around the gardens, girl. It is the most pleasant place to be at this time of day."

The central square of Gramercy Park was an iron-railed garden filled with trees, shrubs and flowers. I wheeled her across the street to the park's entrance, a wrought-iron gate facing the north side. As I approached, an elderly couple was leaving. The man, with impressive white mustaches, took off his boater, gave a sweeping bow, then held the gate open for us to pass through.

"Good evening, Miss Van Woekem. Seasonably warm again, wouldn't you say?"

Miss Van Woekem nodded to him. "Since it's July, that goes without saying. Good day to you."

As we passed into the gardens, she muttered to me, "Odious man. Just because he knew McKinley in Ohio, he thinks he can forget that his father was a grocer."

I pushed her around the park, enjoying the shade under the trees, the sweet-smelling shrubs and the banks of glorious flowers. I noticed a man in a brown suit and derby standing among those trees, blending into the shade as we passed. I wondered if he was a gardener, but he wasn't doing anything and there was no sign of tools. He just stood there, staring up at a house on the south side of the park, and didn't even notice us.

In the distance a clock struck six. "Time to go," Miss Van Woekem said. "I must change for dinner. My goddaughter may be joining me, if she doesn't get a better offer, that is. She is in town for a few days of shopping. You may push me home."

I wheeled her to the park gate and leaned on it. It remained firmly shut.

"Didn't you bring the key, girl?" she asked in annoyance.

"Key? I didn't know there was a key." I felt my face flushing.

"Of all the stupidity! Of course there's a key. We don't want to admit riffraff, do we?"

"You might have mentioned it before we set off," I said.

"You are most insolent and do not know your place."

"I thought you required a companion, which, by definition, is not a subordinate," I said. "If I don't suit you, then maybe you should look elsewhere."

We stared at each other like two dogs whose territories have overlapped.

"I think I'll manage to whip you into shape eventually," she said with a slight glint that could have been a twinkle in her eyes. "And you had better find a way to get us out of this park before nightfall."

I left the chair in the shade and walked around the gardens, hoping to attract the attention of a passerby outside the railings. But the square was deserted apart from two women servants who hurried along the far side and a carriage that passed me at a brisk trot, too quickly to be hailed. As I approached the southeast corner, which was the most wooded, I remembered the man in brown. I hadn't seen him leave the park, and he would have to have a key for us. But he was no longer standing under the trees. I looked around. No movement except for a squirrel that darted across the lawn.

Just then a large shrub close to the railing rustled. The movement was too big to have been caused by another squirrel. A cat, maybe. I moved closer, then froze when I saw the man in brown crouching down beside the shrub. He turned and looked around, nervously. I managed to shrink back behind a tree trunk just in time. Obviously satisfied that there was nobody to see him, he grasped one of the railings, removed it, slipped through the opening and then replaced the railing. It was all over in a second.

I watched him brush himself off and walk down the street whistling.

I was so impressed with what I had seen that it took me a moment to realize I had seen him before. He was the same man who had taken our photograph in Central Park.